W9-DET-270

DROWNED NIGHT

A Novel of the Abbadon Inn

WELCOME TO THE ABBADON INN.

It's on a quiet street in the charming Victorian town of Cape May, New Jersey. Built in the late 1850s as a rooming house by the enigmatic Nicholas Abbadon, the Inn has been used over the years as a brothel, a restaurant, a speakeasy . . . and more.

SETTLE IN.

It has withstood war, fire, and flood. It has survived the suspicions about the guests who died there and owners who disappeared, the rumors about what went on behind the closed doors of the third floor, and the whispers about Abbadon and his mysterious female companion.

Abandoned and vacant for years, it's ready for renovation. But as a new generation is about to discover, the Abbadon Inn has never really been empty at all . . .

ENJOY YOUR STAY.

DROWNED NIGHT

A Novel of the Abbadon Inn

Chris Blaine

BERKLEY BOOKS, NEW YORK

THE BERKLEY PUBLISHING GROUP
Published by the Penguin Group
Penguin Group (USA) Inc.
375 Hudson Street, New York, New York 10014, USA
Penguin Group (Canada), 90 Eglinton Avenue East, Suite 700, Toronto, Ontario M4P 2Y3, Canada
(a division of Pearson Penguin Canada Inc.)
Penguin Books Ltd., 80 Strand, London WC2R 0RL, England
Penguin Group Ireland, 25 St. Stephen's Green, Dublin 2, Ireland (a division of Penguin Books Ltd.)
Penguin Group (Australia), 250 Camberwell Road, Camberwell, Victoria 3124, Australia
(a division of Pearson Australia Group Pty. Ltd.)
Penguin Books India Pvt. Ltd., 11 Community Centre, Panchsheel Park, New Delhi—110 017, India
Penguin Group (NZ), Cnr. Airborne and Rosedale Roads, Albany, Auckland 1310, New Zealand
(a division of Pearson New Zealand Ltd.)
Penguin Books (South Africa) (Pty.) Ltd., 24 Sturdee Avenue, Rosebank, Johannesburg 2196,
South Africa

Penguin Books Ltd., Registered Offices: 80 Strand, London WC2R 0RL, England

This is a work of fiction. Names, characters, places, and incidents either are the product of the author's imagination or are used fictitiously, and any resemblance to actual persons, living or dead, business establishments, events, or locales is entirely coincidental. The publisher does not have any control over and does not assume any responsibility for author or third-party websites or their content.

DROWNED NIGHT

A Berkley Book / published by arrangement with the author

PRINTING HISTORY
Berkley mass-market edition / November 2005

Copyright © 2005 by The Berkley Publishing Group.
Cover design by Steven Ferlauto.
Interior art by Cortney Skinner.
Interior text design by Kristin del Rosario.

All rights reserved.
No part of this book may be reproduced, scanned, or distributed in any printed or electronic form without permission. Please do not participate in or encourage piracy of copyrighted materials in violation of the author's rights. Purchase only authorized editions.
For information address: The Berkley Publishing Group,
a division of Penguin Group (USA) Inc.,
375 Hudson Street, New York, New York 10014.

ISBN: 0-425-20676-9

BERKLEY® BOOKS
Berkley Books are published by The Berkley Publishing Group,
a division of Penguin Group (USA) Inc.,
375 Hudson Street, New York, New York 10014.
BERKLEY and the BERKLEY design are trademarks belonging to Penguin Group (USA) Inc.

PRINTED IN THE UNITED STATES OF AMERICA

10   9   8   7   6   5   4   3   2   1

If you purchased this book without a cover, you should be aware that this book is stolen property. It was reported as "unsold and destroyed" to the publisher, and neither the author nor the publisher has received any payment for this "stripped book."

To Matthew Costello, whose knowledge
of story, deep diving,
and fear—not to mention
the Jersey shore!—*all* proved
invaluable to the writing of this novel.

NOTICE TO THE PUBLIC

ABBADON INN

NOW OPEN

The Proprietor respectfully informs his friends and the public that
the above establishment has been newly built in the latest mode
from the continent including both spacious and intimate

Ladies' and Gentlemen's

Dining Rooms,

and an elegant yet reasonably priced

FIRST-CLASS RESTAURANT,

Private rooms, entertainment for discerning guests and every
accomodation and comfort are supplied by your host,
Cape May, October 2, 1856.
- Nicholas Abbadon

Mitchell & Wright, print.

ABBADON INN
203

CAPE MAY
BURNS

AWFUL CALAMITY

SIX HOTELS
DESTROYED

AFFRIGHTING
INCIDENTS

ABBADON INN
MYSTERIOUSLY
SURVIVES

ABBADON INN STANDS
UNSCATHED AMIDST ASHES

PROLOGUE

Cape May

August 31, 1929

ONE

Eileen turned and faced the two doors that led to the Ab-badon Inn dining room. He would be here soon, and now her heart beat so fast she thought it could explode.

The room behind her was filled, and most of the guests already felt the effects of the champagne. The piano player, a man who never smiled or said a word, kept playing though no one seemed to be listening.

She looked at the great clock that faced the fireplace from across the room.

He was late.

Then a thought: he might not come.

Or then—even worse—he *will* come.

The twin heavy wooden doors remained shut. Through the open windows Eileen could faintly hear the sound of the waves crashing on the beach.

She turned back to the happy crowd celebrating the end of the summer season. Though she knew some of them had to wonder: Should they be celebrating? Was this a season we should remember at all?

Jack, the glum-faced piano player, started playing a new Cole Porter tune, "You Do Something To Me." It seemed so out of place, so strange.

The doors gave out the groan of wood rubbing together, opening. She spun around.

And there he was.

Everyone in the room took note of his arrival. From those who knew him only by name, to those who had had actual encounters with him—people who had felt his power directly.

As usual, Jackson Bell wasn't alone.

Three people, all good local townspeople, surrounded him. Eileen watched how obsequious they acted toward him. Nodding, smiling. Did fear rule them or just greed and ambition? The fact that one of them was the mayor made the scene that much more sickening.

Eileen felt her stomach tighten.

Could she do this?

Could she *really* do this?

She was nineteen, but standing there she felt as if she were twelve. She clutched the same undrunk flute of champagne in her hand.

For a moment a hush fell over the crowd, then the sound slowly started again. The buzz, the chatter, the tinkling of the piano.

Slowly.

The chatter beginning again, but now with an anxious air in the room.

Then Bell saw Eileen. And though the room was filled with late-summer humidity, and despite the warm ocean breeze, she felt cold.

She forced herself to smile at him.

And then Jackson Bell left his friends behind and walked over to her.

"Eileen," he said.

His eyes—always so strong, a deep sparking blue, so unnatural in their brilliance as if lit from behind—seemed to drill into her.

She looked away. She had to. The intensity was too much for her.

He smiled. "Been waiting for me? Terribly neglectful to make you wait." He nodded at one of the men he had arrived with. "Of course there were things to attend to. Plans, you know. Things to be done."

Eileen nodded. "I—I didn't know . . . whether you would come."

He laughed. "Tonight? And to be with all these good people?"

He said the word *good* in such an odd way. As if the meaning of the word was anything but . . . good.

"Besides, this is my place, no? Like my home, this Abbadon Inn. I'd never miss a party here. And you, what did—"

But in that moment a wild-eyed woman erupted from the chattering crowd. She ran up to Bell and began hitting him with her balled-up fists.

"You! You're the reason he's gone. All Jimmy wanted was . . . was . . ."

The woman tried to continue flailing, beating her fists on Bell. But with each blow there was less power, less force.

Bell did nothing to restrain her. Like an engine sputtering out of gas, her sobs finally overwhelmed her anger. Until a man emerged from the crowd. Eileen knew him . . . the woman's husband. His eyes down turned, his fear of Bell so strong Eileen felt it could suck the air out of the room.

He put his arm around his wife.

"No," she moaned as he pulled her away. "No, no, no . . ."

Nothing she could do would bring her son back, or any of the others. Nothing. They were gone forever.

But it could be stopped.

A sick wave washed over Eileen.

It could be stopped.

If she could do what she knew she had to.

And now Eileen did something she used to do when she was a young girl in Philadelphia. Whenever really bad things happened, whenever her father didn't come home at night, and she saw that worried look on her mother's face.

Whenever there was any pain, or fear, or anything she just wanted over and past and done.

She would always try to imagine a future time when it had ended, when the bad thing was all over.

A time when all the bad stuff was gone.

But right now, she couldn't think a second into the future. There was only this terrifying *now.*

The clock struck ten P.M., the loud bongs interrupting the chatter and the smooth flow of the Cole Porter song.

There's no future for me now, Eileen thought.

But one way or the other, it would soon be over.

TWO

Bell kept his eyes on her. Every part of her wanted him to look away, to stop staring at her.

"You look amazingly beautiful tonight. But then, you always look beautiful."

The flattery rolled off his tongue so easily. And despite everything, she felt embarrassed. Though she knew that it should have made her skin crawl, made her stomach tighten into a knot.

She thought, *I should have to crawl into the corner and vomit from his words, his sweet, deceptive words.*

She felt a flicker of fear. Could he sense her reaction? Could that open the door to his seeing inside her?

Because if he saw, it could all unravel. All the plans, the meetings, the discussion. All the plans that now had Eileen at their very center.

Eileen, because she was the only one who could do this.

One of the men who made the plan, a lawyer who divided his time between Cape May and Philadelphia, a man who she often caught stealing looks at her, had said to her, "Eileen, you are the only one who can do this. And not just because you're beautiful."

Eileen had wished these past few weeks that she was anything but beautiful. *Give me ugly moles, a strange smile, anything to make me less attractive, less—*

Desirable. Because that's what was important to Bell.

Desire. In his deep sea-blue eyes. In the way he smiled, spoke to her. It was, in fact, the most important card she had to play in this desperate, deadly game.

Bell wants you, one of them had said. That is the only weapon we have. That, and the fact that—out of all of them—she could not be *seen.*

Seen . . .

My thoughts are not transparent, like the others.

A gift? More of a curse.

No matter, soon it would be over, one way or the other.

He leaned close.

"I see your flute is empty. Such a festive yet sad night, no? The last night of the summer season. Shall I refill it for you?"

Eileen looked down at her glass and couldn't remember drinking from it.

He looked around at the group of men that followed him. A short man with pimply spots on his face hobbled forward, something wrong with his twisted right leg.

The troll-like man took the glass from her while Bell downed his own.

"Two refills," Jackson Bell said.

Without a word, the dwarflike man took the glasses away. So chilling, how he took them away. Not a word, not a nod.

He just did it.

She reached out and touched Bell's hand. The man's skin was smooth, cool. Though the night was humid, thick with salty air, his skin was bone dry.

She spoke quietly. "And when our drinks come, I want to go away with you; I want to talk."

The man studied her. She knew Bell had to be incredibly wary. Despite his power. One didn't stay powerful without being so very careful.

He arched his eyebrows. "Away? From this," he looked around, "wonderful party?"

She nodded. So hard to remain in control. Hard, almost impossible. She looked around—no one who knew about what was to happen was in the room. That would be too risky. If they should bump into Bell and somehow reveal even the smallest bit of what was planned . . . that would be a disaster.

In this room, she was totally alone.

The two champagne flutes magically reappeared.

"Ah, additional refreshments. For our little adventure." He handed her one glass, then took the other. He clinked her glass. "To you." He took a sip. "To this night."

She tipped her flute back. A sudden strong breeze brought in another burst of wet, salty air from the Atlantic . . . a foreshadowing of the brutal winds and storms of the fall, and beyond that the icy grip of the coast in winter.

"To—tonight." She nearly stuttered saying the word.

"So," he said. "Where is it that you want to lead me?"

This time she reached out and took his hand.

"Follow me," she said.

And she led him out of the great dining room, to the lounge, to a passageway near the back of the Abbadon Inn.

THREE

Eileen walked to the passageway, narrow and ending in a door. She looked at Bell, smiled, and then opened the door to a stairway leading down to the basement of the inn. She grabbed a flashlight from a countertop.

"No lights downstairs?" Bell asked, smiling.

"They need to be rewired. The last storm did so much damage."

She flicked on the long flashlight. Despite having new batteries the flashlight shot a weak, yellowish beam onto the wooden step.

"I didn't know about these stairs."

She kept walking down.

"Not used much," she said. She caught herself speaking too fast, rushing. *Slow down,* she thought. Be careful. Don't make a mistake.

The stairs twisted at a small landing and now Eileen could smell the sea, the wet sand, the ages-old damp smell that never seemed to disappear from the close basement rooms.

Bell stopped at the landing.

"I'm intrigued—this leads to the rest of the basement, to storerooms?"

She nodded, lying. "Though my father has closed off sections."

Bell sniffed the air. "I can see why. Nasty down here. Thick. No place," he reached out and touched her shoulder, "for such a beautiful woman."

His hand touched the bare skin of her shoulder. His hand, so dry, fingers curling in just the slightest way. The touch made her feel dizzy, and her brain screamed . . .

You can't do this. You'll never be able to do this.

His fingers stroked her skin. "Must we come all the way down here? To talk? I love to hear your words. But this place? Certainly not very romantic."

She turned to Bell. She kept the flashlight down so her face was in the shadows. "Some day, this inn will be mine." She lied. Already her father planned on selling and leaving the inn. "And there are secrets I want to show you."

The light caught his slight smile.

"I like secrets. Just as long as we get back in time for more champagne."

"We will."

She quickly turned and continued walking down the splintery wooden steps that creaked and groaned. For a moment she thought she heard scurrying, the sound of living things scattering. Perhaps the Norwegian rats who claimed this as home, a dank base to launch expeditions to the upper rooms for the stray chunks of bread, the unguarded bag of flour.

The inn had always had a rat problem.

She reached the bottom. A wet sound, her foot in water. Eileen resisted the urge to aim the flashlight at the surroundings to get her bearings.

She had rehearsed this many times. Rehearsed it so she could do it with just this scant amount of light.

"Charming. And you are absolutely sure there are no lights down here? There must be some . . ."

She chewed her lip. "Y-you can try the switch—but nothing will happen. The bad wiring."

Was there a note of concern in Bell's voice? She was slim, defenseless—but was there now some concern in his voice?

"Maybe," he said, "we've gone far enough."

Her breath caught. "Just a bit farther. I need you to see this."

"A mystery?" He didn't move. "Mysteries can be dangerous." The tone in his voice shifted.

"Just ahead—" she started to move alone, deeper into the darkness of the bowels of the inn.

But Bell reached out and grabbed her wrist. He pulled her back to him.

"Only if I get a reward." And he pulled her tight and kissed her. At first there was just the hard pressure of his lips on hers. Cold and dry as his touch,

Then more, his lips opening. And she had to force herself not to recoil, not to pull away screaming.

She told herself to count to five. *At five I can break off this kiss—and it will be all right.*

One . . . two . . . three . . .

Lips moving against hers, hungry, probing.

Four . . . five . . .

She pulled away.

"Mmm," he said. "Even better than the champagne. Who needs champagne when I can have you?"

"Come," she said. And she reached down and grabbed his hand. She started pulling him down a narrow corridor lined by splintery two-by-fours. Then, on either side, the boards changed to stone walls. Not walls really, but giant stone boulders probably dropped here by glaciers where the land met the sea.

Sitting here, waiting patiently for the sea to grind them into sand.

They passed the stone corridor and reached an opening.

As the smell hit her, she knew it must have hit Bell, too.

The smell of the sea, open, waiting, there. In front of her, a massive sewer pipe that once fed the waste from the inn directly into the ocean.

Now just an open, unused vein that ran from the Abbadon Inn to the sea.

The rank smell was overwhelming.

She knew that would hit him first.

But then—in a moment.

"Wait a second," Bell said.

He reached out and yanked the flashlight from Eileen's hand. He whipped it away from her, and then scanned this room that connected directly to the ocean. The light caught a giant water cistern, filled with stagnant seawater that sat beside the pipe, a primitive flushing mechanism.

"What the hell? I . . ."

But he didn't need to say anything. Not when the flashlight scoured the room and finally caught the faces of the people waiting there. Faces he knew, even some faces that maybe he thought he controlled.

Eileen could only imagine the rush of thoughts that Bell gathered from these men. Harvesting their thoughts. The visions of violence, the plans, the horror—all hidden from him until this moment.

Now revealed.

"No," he said.

Other flashlights came on, all focused on Bell.

Maybe he believed that he could focus and stop them, one by one. And with time, he could certainly do that. They had seen that.

They had all seen the way everyone did what Bell wanted, how people crossed Main Street to avoid even passing him. How they locked their doors at night, and bolted their windows.

How they ended their summer early this year—those that could—and went away.

But now, down here, they had an advantage at last.

Eileen backed up.

Bell looked at her.

"Brave. But stupid. Beware of mysteries, I said. Remember—"

But before Bell could finish his sentence, one of the men who ran fishing boats from Cape May jammed a massive hook into Bell's spine, the type of hook Eileen imagined was used to catch the big fish—a marlin, or maybe a hammerhead. She'd seen those monster fish displayed on the dock, mammoth trophies dangling from a hook the size of a man's head.

Bell turned.

Her father, gray-haired, eyes looking so scared, acted next. He rammed a giant carving knife into Bell's midsection.

Red foam appeared around Bell's mouth. He mouthed a word, but the foamy red bubbles muffled the sound.

The lawyer, wearing a yellow slicker as if he was about to face a hurricane, swung a massive mallet at Bell's legs. The sharp crack reported the breaking of bones as Bell fell forward onto the wet floor.

She turned away.

They were only beginning.

She wanted to leave. But she couldn't move, couldn't do anything. The sounds, so terrible, filling the room.

Until—she recognized the voice—her father's voice.

"It's done."

For a few moments no one said a thing.

No one moved.

No one came up to say anything to Eileen. To touch her, to whisper words of comfort.

Not with so much blood on their hands.

And she knew that her part in this had been the most important. Without her, it would have been impossible.

She had led Jackson Bell into a trap, and it had been something only she could do.

Then she heard them working near the mouth of the giant sewer.

The fishing boat captain spoke. "Goddam sea can have him. Let the crabs finish the goddam job, chew the bastard into—"

"Jake. *Enough.*"

Her father again, aware that his daughter was still standing there.

Then Eileen turned. She turned because she had to see the end of this. Brown potato sacks, now stuffed full, were tossed into the opening of the sewer. The lawyer went to the water cistern.

"This will work?" he asked.

"Yes," her father said. "I've used it. It will work."

They had their lights pointed on the cistern filled with seawater.

But Eileen looked around the floor, and she saw the red splotches everywhere. *Will they just leave that,* she wondered? Or will that be another night's work, to remove those stains?

If the stains can be removed . . .

"Okay?" the lawyer asked.

Her father spoke for all of them.

"Okay, do it."

The lawyer turned a massive wheel, and water began flowing into the open pipe that led to the ocean. Now the smell from the stagnant seawater filled the room.

The men aimed their lights at the open pipe as water

carried the brown sacks away from the inn, away from the town, out to the impossible depths of the sea.

Jackson Bell was gone.

Eileen had that single thought.

Jackson Bell was gone.

And when she finally turned and started back to the stairs, back to the inn, back to what now seemed like another world, she didn't have the slightest idea how wrong she could be.

I

Welcome to the Inn!

August 1992

ONE

Ted turned back to the kids, the car's cassette player blaring some songs from *Sesame Street* while the kids argued over the music. Liz watched him, as she often did these days.

"Okay, that's it," he said.

Liz watched him as his eyes went from the turnpike to the rearview mirror. David—usually called Daver—at nine the big and bossy brother, and Megan, seven, looked at their father as if they didn't have a clue what they could have been doing.

"No more squealing, no more arguing. Bad enough with all this—" he caught himself—"traffic." He looked right at Liz. "Does *everyone* go to Jersey in the summer? Whatever happened to Long Island, the mountains . . .?"

He shook his head. Liz turned back to the kids and smiled.

The storm was over. Liz reached out and touched Ted on his forearm. He gave her a quick glance.

She thought, *The kids will survive. For now I have to get my husband through this. That's the real job.*

They were still a good couple of hours away from Cape May. More like a few bad hours. Daver and Megan were way beyond antsy. Escaping the city had been a nightmare. They should have tried to get away earlier—but the job at the Abbadon Inn had popped up in the last minute.

Ted didn't even want to consider it.

"We're okay," he said. "We don't need it."

But Liz finally convinced him, just as she had convinced him that it was a good idea to put her name on the Hotel and Inn Temp Registry.

"I have the background," she said. "We can get out of here, get a little extra money. It would be good in a lot of ways."

The money argument, she knew, stung.

Since he went on disability, Ted had lost all his overtime. And Liz wouldn't let him help his dive friends up in Jamestown.

"No way," she said, "are you leading amateurs down one hundred fifty feet to some dangerous wreck."

"One hundred thirty feet," Ted corrected.

But amazingly, he didn't fight her on it. For now, his sideline would go on hold.

And Liz could breathe.

Initially, she thought getting this replacement job managing an inn could be fun . . . free food and accommodations, the sandy beach.

She'd heard that Cape May was beautiful.

And the inn? From pictures, the Abbadon Inn looked regal, imposing—a grand old lady of an inn close to the water. Wraparound porch, wicker chairs, and—what did they call them?—gliders.

Yes, *gliders* . . .

Liz remembered that word from when she did *Our*

Town in high school. Those swinging love seats so perfect for lemonade and moonlit surf.

This might be good. This might help them all heal.

But there was no doubt that Ted was bringing the clouds with him. She had gotten the call on Monday. They had to make a snap judgment to take it or let it slide. The money was good, managing the inn and the staff after the owner suddenly had to leave.

So suddenly, Liz thought. And the agency had no information about what might be the problem. So strange for an owner to leave in the middle of the season . . .

The agency had no details about the owner's sudden departure. They just said that Liz needed to be there by Saturday night.

Made sense. Middle of the summer, probably a full house, restaurant booming, the ocean finally getting to swimming temperature.

"Mommy," Megan said quietly. Liz turned. She was glad to see that Daver, two years older, had the sense to turn down the mayhem with his sister.

"Yes, Megan?"

"Will we have to go to the beach . . . every day?"

Liz laughed. She turned to Ted and saw a small smile crease his lips.

"Not every day. But you want to be out there first thing and start on those sand castles, right?"

"It's going to be boring," Daver said.

"Think so?" Ted asked.

Daver looked out the window. Liz knew that Daver, unlike Megan, had some understanding of what had happened to his father. Not the whole deal to be sure—but enough to make him concerned, cautious.

"The beach every day? I bet they don't even have cable TV yet."

Cable TV with HBO had become the rage in Brooklyn.

Liz was already thinking they were better off without dozens of new channels.

Ted looked over at Liz.

"No TV might be good for you," Liz said quickly.

"Great. Like going to a desert island."

Megan turned to her brother. "Are we going to an island? Like Gulligan's Island?"

"Gilligan's," Daver said. "You can't remember anything, can you?"

"Daver . . ." Liz said.

"Worse comes to worst, kids," Ted said, "we'll rent some videos, okay?"

Nobody said anything, confirmation that *that* idea didn't have any great fans.

"Don't worry," Liz said. "There are arcades, a movie theater, mini-golf, a water park, cotton candy, even an amusement pier. We're all going to love it."

Even as she said those words, they immediately sounded hollow and insincere.

But for now, quiet, save for sound of "The Rainbow Connection" from Jim Henson and Kermit, returned to the van.

Even after moving off the Garden State Parkway, traffic still crawled. Liz started seeing the early signs of a beach resort. The kids started looking out the car windows, excitement building.

"Look, a Dairy Queen!" David yelled.

They moved down Lafayette, heading toward West Beach Drive, and the ocean. The day, brilliant and hot, sent a curtain of heat waves rising off the pavement.

"Here we go," Ted said. "Franklin. We turn here."

He made a left. "And . . . we should see the ocean any minute."

Liz looked around. Yes, finally everyone was excited. Maybe this would be okay.

She thought, *It couldn't get any worse.*

Ted reached West Beach, the road clogged with people ferrying their beach gear—chairs, umbrellas, boogie boards, and a bevy of inflatable toys.

It all looked like so much fun.

But Liz reminded herself that she would be working, running the inn, its staff, the restaurant.

And sure, she had a piece of paper that said she was qualified, and a few years experience in Provincetown before she got married, before the kids, before . . . *everything.*

She tried to ignore the anxiety that—so far—she had successfully pushed away.

"Okay, we made it, everyone." Ted turned to the kids and made a funny face. "The Joisey Shore."

Megan laughed, and Daver smiled.

This could be good, Liz thought.

Then, *Please let it be good.*

The van crawled down West Beach, blocked by the throngs going back and forth to and from the beach. But Ted didn't seem impatient now, just enjoying the sights, the ocean glinting not far away, the great old buildings that stood watch over the breaking waves.

"Beautiful, isn't it?" Liz asked.

Ted nodded. "Cape May. The grand old lady of seaside resorts. I once knew a—"

He stopped. She knew he probably was about to launch into a story about a diving friend, maybe some discovery made not too far from here.

It would be okay if he talked about diving. Could even be therapeutic.

But for now, it was still too hard.

The crowds thinned as they reached the far end of West Beach Drive, and an improbably named street—Broadway.

Then she saw it.

"There it is," she said quietly. "That's the Abbadon."

"Wow," Daver said. "It's way bigger than I thought."

Yes, Liz thought. *Maybe too big. Could be a lot to handle. Dealing with the locals, making everything run smoothly.*

"Could use a fresh coat of paint," Ted said.

He was right. Peeling paint dangled from the roof of the porch, and also from the side walls.

"Still, she's quite something."

Quite something, yes. Liz hoped she was something. *Something to help us heal, something to pull this family together. Because . . . I can't do it myself.*

Ted pulled the van in front of the inn. A few people were on the porch, sitting in Adirondack chairs. "Let's leave the bags for now. Until we see what's up, okay?"

Liz nodded.

Her husband opened his door.

"Okay gang—welcome to the Abbadon Inn."

And they all stepped out onto the hot, steamy street.

TWO

The girl behind the desk, Ariella—or Ari as her friends called her—could see the street directly in front of the hotel.

And she immediately knew just who the people were who tumbled out of the white Dodge Caravan. Ari felt herself begin to breathe a bit heavily, just like she did before a big test. She didn't know what she should say to them, what she would say to them. A few guests were still finishing lunch. Some of them would be leaving that day, others had a few more days at the inn.

Some even knew that something had happened to the owner. And people could sense when things were somehow *off*.

Not a normal summer.

She saw Mrs. Plano come down the stairs. Maybe she had seen the people outside, too. Mrs. Plano, queen witch of the Abbadon, dressed in a starched linen dress with pale blue pinstriping.

Mrs. Plano, in charge of the housekeeping, and now with a few girls gone, threatening to put Ari on that duty, too.

The woman looked at her, and her eyes spoke clearly: *Don't say anything. Welcome them.*

The woman hesitated a moment, then sailed into the dining room.

Ari turned to the twin doors with beveled glass windows, sun slicing through the glass and making the swirling carpet glow. All that sunlight made the garish rug look alive. A red sea of living things, filled with reddish and green snakes and strange plants, twirling, twisting.

The doors opened.

And the new hotel manager—and her family—arrived at the inn.

Liz paused on the porch and turned to Ted.

"Gorgeous, no?

"As I said—needs some work."

"Yes, but look at this porch, the view, the sun—it's great."

"The ocean's too close," Megan said.

Liz laughed. "It's way down there, sweetie," Liz said. "You have a whole beach between you and the ocean."

That ocean glinted, and even behind her sunglasses, Liz squinted.

She turned back to the door. "Shall we?"

Ted pulled the door open, and they entered the inn.

The door creaked closed behind them. She heard Daver sniffing at the air. Though Liz saw open windows everywhere, it did feel stuffy inside, the air dry. Daver's allergies were usually under control . . . that is unless he went someplace with a half dozen cats. And back in Brooklyn there were families who did go cat-crazy.

He sniffed again. Liz saw Ted put a hand on his shoulder.

"You okay?" he asked. Daver nodded.

Liz turned to the desk and saw the young girl there. Long dark hair pulled back, glasses, a serious but beautiful face.

"Hi," Liz said. "We're the McShanes."

The girl nodded.

So quiet, Liz thought.

"I'm the temp manager?" Liz continued.

Then the girl spoke, and Liz knew why she was so quiet.

"I-I kn-know." The girl said.

The stutter was slight, just a bit of a catch at the beginning of the words. She obviously worked hard to smooth out her speech. Liz's heart immediately went out to the stone-faced girl. She saw her name on a gold pin on her blouse.

She thought, *If I'm here for long, I want to make that girl smile.*

"I'm Liz, and this—"

Ted stuck out his hand and smiled. "Ted. The temp manager's husband."

Liz guided her two children to the front. "And these are Megan and David."

The girl looked at the children, and her face seemed to soften.

"So, Ari, guess we need a tour, meet the staff, and Mrs. Plano, she—"

"Hello?" Liz turned to see a woman walk up to them, the smallest of smiles on her round face.

"We've been expecting you," the woman said, extending her hand. "I'm Mrs. Plano. Long trip?"

Liz shook the woman's hand. "Oh . . . traffic was bad," Liz said.

"Worse than bad," Ted added.

"Saturdays are always bad. So many people trying to get out of the cities. That's where you're from, the city?"

Liz nodded. "New York. Brooklyn. The Garden State crawled."

"I imagine. Well, this has been quite a week for us here. Quite a week, with Mr. Tollard leaving so suddenly.

"Mommy, I'm hungry. Can't we eat something here?"

Liz turned to Daver, a boy ruled by his stomach.

"We'll get lunch, Daver, but for now, you—"

"We're still serving lunch," Mrs. Plano said. "The kids could get a sandwich now. If they're hungry."

"Me, too," Megan said. "I want a sandwich, too!"

Liz looked at Ted. A silent plea for help.

"Tell you what. I'll go get them some food. You get the lay of the land from Mrs. Plano. Be easier that way."

Mrs. Plano nodded agreement. "Most of the owners and managers I worked under didn't have children. This will be . . . very different."

It didn't sound as though the head housekeeper was thrilled by the prospect.

"Okay," Liz said. "We'll chat, and you guys sample the kitchen, okay?"

She smiled at the kids who—at this point—didn't seem like happy campers either.

Maybe this is all a mistake, Liz thought.

Ted started ushering the kids into the sunlit dining room.

"Okay then. I guess a tour, maybe meet the staff. The regular staff that is." The woman glanced at Ariella. "Then anything I can do to help you settle in, I will be glad to do."

Said, Liz thought, *with not much enthusiasm.*

"Great, thanks. Shall we?"

Megan looked at the menu.

Ted knew she could read some, but chances were a lot of the items on the menu meant nothing to her. The young waitress apologized that there wasn't a children's menu.

"I see, Megan," he said, "that they *do* have a cheese-burger. And grilled cheese. That's always good."

"Cheese, cheese, cheese. Does *everything* here have cheese?" Megan said.

"Can't we go to McDonald's?" Daver said, doing his bit to help.

Ted turned to him. "No. I just got off the road. I am not going anywhere near a car for a day at least. I don't even know if there is a McDonald's nearby."

"Oh, there is!" A man two tables away, joined their conversation. Someone else making things easier. The man wore long, striped pants held up by suspenders and a short-sleeved white shirt.

As though he just walked out of a postcard of the seashore from days long gone . . .

"Thanks, but—"

"Come on, Dad. We don't want to eat here."

Ted grinned at the man seeming to enjoy his family in revolt. Ted acted quickly to end the rebellion.

"Make your picks now, or you can go hungry." The words sounded harsh, biting, and he immediately felt guilty. Megan's eyes quickly registered her feelings. Ted continued quickly, "And then we can hit the beach, swim. The ocean looks great."

Every breeze threw open the curtains, and the shining sea appeared in the gap.

"Okay?" Ted asked.

"I don't like the ocean," Megan said.

But she went back to the menu that dwarfed her. "I want . . . a grilled cheese. And a Pepsi."

"You mean milk," Ted corrected. "And you, my friend."

Daver went back to the menu. "Guess the cheeseburger won't kill me."

Ted smiled. "Guess you're probably right."

Ted looked around for the waitress. Liz had vanished behind the desk with Mrs. Plano, while Ari seemed to look away under Ted's glance.

He had been a cop.

No, he thought, *I am a cop. I've still got those instincts.*

Instincts that told him that something was wrong here. And that he now wanted to know what exactly was wrong with this place, this new home for his family.

THREE

Mrs. Plano led Liz up the stairs from the second-floor corridor.

"Up there are small rooms, and many share a bath. Some work is being done on a few. Great views, but small. Even with their own air-conditioning, they stay mighty stuffy."

Liz started up the stairs, but Mrs. Plano put a hand on her arm.

"No need to trudge up there, Mrs. McShane—"

"Liz," she corrected. Mrs. Plano hesitated, and Liz felt that the name correction didn't take. "Might as well see everything."

"Only two guests there now. One's been here quite a while. Some writer from New Hampshire, or maybe it's Maine. Rented for July, and just stayed. He sleeps late. Another guest checks out today. We tend to fill the rooms down here first."

Liz hesitated. Seemed odd for an inn to have a guest for

the entire summer. But she suspected that there was a lot to
learn about Abbadon.

"And the other rooms up there?"

"Empty. Or being, as I said, worked on. Paint, plaster.
This is a very old inn. Always work to do."

Mrs. Plano didn't add anything, so Liz pressed.

"Empty? Is that unusual?"

"You could say that. But this entire season has been a
little odd. And now that you're here—"

Liz grinned. "It's even odder?"

And the woman laughed, a genuine warm laugh that
gave Liz hope that she might be able to win this woman
over. Because she knew if she didn't, then the weeks of August could become interminable. Despite their need for the
money, she wanted it to be fun for the family.

But then the woman's smile faded, as if holding a smile
wasn't something easy to do.

"Maybe I better show you the kitchen now."

She started to walk away from the stairs.

"Oh, there're also storerooms up there. And you can get
to the tower room, which needs a lot of work."

Liz looked up the stairs, imagining the sole, sleeping
guest. She guessed she'd see him at dinner. But why would
someone stay here for the whole summer? Sure it's a nice
inn and everything, but still . . .

She hurried to catch up with Mrs. Plano.

Ted walked with the kids down a hallway lined with pictures from the inn's past. The pictures showed assorted cel-
ebrations at the Abbadon: what looked like a masquerade,
then a big dinner party, a political fund-raiser with a big
elephant carved out of ice.

Then a few recent photos. One color picture showed a
short, barrel-chested man standing next to a tiger shark
twice his size. The picture caught the blood running from

the shark's jaw, probably the place where the crew had gaffed the animal to bring it aboard.

Big shark. Tigers couldn't be *that* common here. Not only was it a prize size-wise, the fish was a rarity.

Ted didn't like sharks. But then who did?

He knew the drill. Leave them alone, and they leave you alone.

Except, that wasn't true at all. Sharks had a stupid and dull sense of mission. And if for some reason they got the idea that you were somehow interesting . . .

That you needed to be *explored*.

That you might be food.

Then, an eight-foot shark could quickly turn into one's new best friend.

It wasn't just surfers that had problems with the "amazing predators," as the nature programs referred to them.

Most of the divers that Ted knew had at least one hair-raising shark tale.

Close calls. And sometimes a lot more than a close call.

"Oooh," Megan asked. "Is that blood?"

She had sidled up to Ted and now stared at the same picture.

"Cool!" Daver shouted.

The young girl at the desk looked at them.

Megan tugged at her dad, yanking his hand, "They don't have sharks like that here, do they, Daddy?"

Ted looked at her. In a flash he could see any chance of getting Megan into the water *this* summer evaporating. Her experiences at the beach had always been bad: she didn't like the waves, she ran from the foamy surf, always something . . .

After a while, Ted and Liz watched her turn her back on the ocean altogether.

Out of sight, out of mind.

And that was it, at least as far as Megan was concerned.

"No," Ted said. "They caught that fish far away."

"No, Dad," Daver said. "See that boat? Says 'Cape May.'"

Ted turned and tried to bore his eyes into his son as if they were lasers, as if he could burn away any ability Daver had to discuss things that could disturb Megan.

"The boat, yes, but it probably went really far out to sea to get . . . that."

"Pro'bly?" Megan asked.

Screwed this up, Ted thought. Totally. Should have just kept on going, moved right past the picture.

But then—was that really possible? They'd see everything here sooner or later. You can't hide anything from kids for too long.

For a moment the cloud was back. So easily summoned. A picture, a red stream of shark blood, a few words . . . and there it was.

Ted looked over his shoulder and saw the doors that led to the kitchen. Through an oval window, he saw Liz.

"Hey, there's the kitchen, and there's Mommy. Let's go see what's cooking."

He led Megan away. He turned to see Daver studying the picture, still fascinated by the photo, standing for a moment more, and then joining them.

Ted pushed open the kitchen doors.

"Well, you may get very confused," the black woman laughed. "Lord knows, we do!"

Liz looked at the woman, Estella, and her twin sister, Lucy. Or was the woman speaking Lucy, and the other Estella? They wore identical cook outfits—flowered dresses all but hidden by giant snow-white aprons. Both had gray hair that looked like a crown on top of their dark faces.

"Mama used to say, 'You two each dress differently now, help people *know* who you are.'"

"But we said, 'Mama, you can tell easily, 'cause we are different. And we want everyone else to learn we are different, too."

Liz nodded, smiling. "I may need a while."

One of the women touched Liz's arm. "Don't worry, Mrs. McSh—"

"Liz," she said.

"Don't you worry. We'll help you. We're just glad—" the cook looked at Mrs. Plano standing to the side— "someone's here. To run things. Wouldn't be right to have a whole summer, and no manager."

"I'll do my best. Got so much to—"

The doors to the hotel and dining room opened, and she turned to see Ted lead the troops in.

"Hey, guys." She turned back to Estella and Lucy. "This is my husband, Ted, and Megan, David . . ."

The women each shook Ted's hand but quickly came up to the two children.

"Well, aren't you two going to have some adventure this summer?"

Again, Liz caught the one not talking firing a quick look at Mrs. Plano.

Things weren't being said here. And before too long Liz would find out what they were.

"You can explore the hotel. And there's the beach, the arcade, the rides. Yes, this will be some adventure for you two." The cook stroked Megan's brown hair, pulled back in a ponytail.

"Smells great in here," Ted said.

One of the cooks looked at Ted. "You gotta get the sauces going early if you want them ready for dinner."

Mrs. Plano came into the circle. "Estella and Lucy cook their mother's recipes. This restaurant was once very famous for its food."

"Once? We think it still is!"

The women laughed, and Liz felt that these two—sooner or later—would be good allies, and maybe a place to get the answers to her questions.

Then Mrs. Plano turned to Liz.

"I could show you downstairs. Unlike a lot of places, the Abbadon has a basement. Mostly just the fuel tank down there, and some empty spaces we just don't use. So—maybe you'd like to see your rooms now instead? Get your bags? You have two nice rooms upstairs, at the back end of the hall."

Away from the staircase, and the third floor, Liz guessed.

"Yes, that would be nice. We could use a rest and—"

"And tomorrow you can get settled in. See the books. We haven't started using one of those new computers, you know. I make Ariella enter everything in the registry book anyway. Some things shouldn't change."

"Right," Liz agreed. She reached out and took Ted's hand, then turned to Estella and Lucy. "And we'll be very much looking forward to dinner."

The cooks stood side by side. They were more than twins, Liz guessed. Best friends, and probably with their own silent communication.

"Try our fried chicken tonight. You'll love it!"

Liz smiled, took Megan's hand, and then they left the kitchen, back to the main hallway of the inn.

The sun slid behind the town of Cape May, and the ocean turned a shimmering bluish-gray.

Ted and Liz sat on the porch, while the kids played nearby. Megan raced one of her favorite ponies with shocking purple hair, while Daver battled with his horrible monster figures that Liz guessed came from an equally horrible cartoon.

She'd like to control what he watched more, but Ted said every kid watched those cartoons these days.

"Not going to hurt him," Ted would say. And she guessed he was right.

She looked at him now, staring at the water.

She thought, *Maybe this isn't a good place for him. Maybe . . . this place is all wrong.*

If that was true, she'd better find out now.

"Want to take walk?" she asked.

"Along the beach?" She nodded. "Think these two will join us?" Ted asked.

"Not joining us won't be an option." She looked around. "Though they'd probably be perfectly safe here."

A few guests sat on wicker rockers and the glider. No other families with kids stayed at the inn, though Mrs. Plano said that they did sometimes get kids. But Liz guessed that the Abbadon wasn't exactly a beach resort that catered to families.

She stood up. "Okay, guys, we're going to take a little walk along the beach."

Daver and Megan both began to protest. There were monsters to be fought and ponies to be groomed.

But Liz took them both by the hand, cutting off any discussion.

Liz held Ted's hand as they strolled the walkway that ran beside the tall reeds and dunes of the beach.

The kids now discovered the fun of a beach at night, as they rolled in the sand with their toys, then leapt up into the sky before crashing down into the cool cushiony sand.

They were fine. And that meant that now Liz could talk to Ted.

"Ted, is this all going to be okay?"

He turned to her, his blue eyes catching what little light was left in the sky. The first thing that had attracted her was those eyes. Killer eyes. Brilliant. Illegally blue, she used to say to him. They were irresistible.

And she didn't resist.

"What do you mean? This is gorgeous. It's perfect. The beach, the inn. Why . . . you think it's going to be too much for you? I mean, I'll help. I told you—"

She gave his hand a squeeze. "No. I know I can handle the inn. Once I learn where everything is, and who everyone is. That will all be fine."

"Then what are you talking about?"

Another hand squeeze.

"*You.* Is this place going to be okay for you?"

He looked away. He didn't expect that question. No, he had let her know that he didn't want to talk about it, that he wanted it forgotten.

Though she knew that there was no way it would ever be forgotten.

He made a hollow laugh. "Okay for *me*? You make it sound as though someone like me could go a little bit *off* here."

"No. Ted, that's not fair. It's just when I took the job, for us, to get away—"

"Let's not forget we needed it. Once I kissed my overtime good-bye. A cop's base salary, even on disability, just doesn't cut it."

She could hear the bite in his voice, and now she wished that she hadn't brought up the whole thing.

But there was no backing out now. "It's just that looking out there," she glanced at the ocean, "I'm thinking maybe this is stupid. This is wrong. Maybe—"

He turned back to her and grabbed her around the waist, gave a squeeze, and then slowly pulled her close. "Look, you. This is fine. It's perfect. The kids will love it. And we'll be okay as soon as you stop worrying about me. What you *should* be worrying about is getting some younger people into the inn. God, did you see those dinosaurs on the porch."

Liz laughed. The clouds momentarily broke.

"Bet they're regulars, Ted. Probably been coming here since they were kids."

He laughed—such a great sound. Another thing she loved, along with those eyes. His great, infectious laugh. Joyful, positive. Something she didn't hear too often these days.

"Well, they're not kids anymore. We should recruit some of that crazy crowd that plays in Wildwood."

"You mean *destroys* Wildwood. I like the Abbadon just the way it is, nice and quiet."

"We should turn back. Getting dark."

"Yeah, the kids will be excited. New beds, a hotel room. It will take them a while to go to sleep."

"I'll leave that to you. Maybe I'll check out the bar."

"And maybe I'll join you after the kids are down . . ."

She looked up. The Abbadon Inn was ahead, back from the beach, but so tall and with the upper rooms showing a necklace of lights that encircled the inn. She could see only a few room lights on, most of the others were dark.

They walked back to the Abaddon in silence—but it was okay.

FOUR

Ted left the room with the kids still testing their twin beds as trampolines. Liz had already given them a five-minute warning, and it was time for him to vacate the premises and let the mom work her sleepy-time magic.

He walked down to the Abbadon's bar, the Ten Bells Pub. Just off the dining room, the bar was a dark wood square that surrounded an island of bottles and a row of beer taps. A few people sat at the bar, a middle-aged couple dressed up, probably fresh from dinner, and an older man who looked at the TV hanging from a wall. The sound was muted, but Ted saw that it was first inning of what would surely be another of the Mets' debacles as they faced the Dodgers.

The bartender, a stumpy man with a craggy face and a feeble attempt at a comb-over, looked up. He didn't give any indication that he knew that Ted was the husband of the new manager.

"What'll I getcha?" The man asked.

Ted stuck out his hand. "I'm Ted McShane. My wife is the new temp manager."

The man nodded. The information didn't seem to have any impact on him.

"And your name?"

"Billy."

Billy. Old Billy certainly wasn't the most talkative bartender Ted had ever bumped into.

"What's on tap?"

"Got Miller, Bud, and Beck's."

"Beck's sounds good." Billy nodded and grabbed a pilsner glass, tilted it, and then filled it to the top with just a margin of a foamy head. He put in front of Ted, the foamy head dribbling over the side. Then Ted took a deep sip. After this long day, it tasted great.

He noticed the couple nearby look at him. He nodded, smiled. He guessed that privacy would be at a premium while they were here.

Lot of people to say hi to, a lot of people watching what you did.

Maybe that's okay, Ted thought. Because he knew, and Liz knew, that being alone certainly wasn't working for him.

Ted took his beer and walked out the separate entrance of the bar, to the porch.

No one sat outside now. There was a bit of chill in the air, the breeze off the cool ocean.

He took another big slug of the beer. Icy cold, clean, clear. That was another thing he had to watch.

How much he drank.

He had watched it creep up. More and more drinks, until finally Liz confronted him. He promised to ease up, and he did. Then Liz started talking about plans, an idea she had . . .

Plans that all led here.

He took another slug.

He looked at the ocean.

Plans that all led here.

And where did that path really begin? Where did that yellow brick road start that took them from their Brooklyn apartment in Park Slope, saving to buy a little two-family house . . .

Took them from that world, that life . . . to this place.

He knew all too well where it began.

He walked closer to the railing. The sea . . . so close. Just out there. He could smell it. Feel its chill on his arms.

No, he told himself. *I don't want to think about it. Christ, not tonight. I don't need to remember it. I don't want to replay that movie again.*

But by now he knew better than that.

Like slipping into the front car of the roller coaster and then some burly guy pulls the big lever, and there's no getting off. The coaster climbed to the very top, racing to the frightening plunges that lay ahead.

The yellow brick road.

A mere five months ago.

Beginning with a ship called the *Andrea Doria,* sleeping, buried at a depth of over two hundred feet. A ship that—though totally dead itself—continued to kill.

Ted sat down on one of the wicker rockers.

And despite everything, once again he remembered.

There comes a point for most divers when they start to consider diving the *Andrea Doria.*

Unlike the *Titanic,* which plummeted two miles down, the *Andrea Doria* sunk in 1956 when the much smaller *Stockholm* rammed it, lay—temptingly—in just over 225 feet of water.

Two hundred and twenty-five feet!

So *close.* How could the great liner not tempt the many recreational divers that lived in the Northeast, frustrated by the meager opportunities offered by dives in the cold gray waters of the North Atlantic?

Two hundred and twenty-five feet!

And not only that, the wreck was so close to the shore. Any dive operator could get out there and back in a long afternoon. Divers would pay top dollar for the privilege, the adventure of diving a genuine ocean liner, a queen of the sea lying on her side, at such a shallow depth.

But not quite shallow enough . . .

Recreational divers, all those open-water certified guys in their dry suits, were supposedly restricted to a maximum of 130 feet. And that should have kept the *Andrea Doria* out of their reach. But it didn't—and each year divers attempted a quick run, dodging nitrogen narcosis, and usually making their way back up.

Usually . . .

The dead ship claimed divers' lives on a fairly regular basis.

But then there was a breakthrough, something that opened up the ship to even more divers. That invention was nitrox, a breathable mixed gas that kept the nitrogen levels low so a diver could stay down longer, and some thought mistakenly . . . go deeper.

Deep enough to really dive the *Andrea Doria,* to swim outside its enormous hull, to peer into its openings and see the gloomy darkness inside. The ship became a major destination for the newly empowered nitrox-breathing divers.

"I dived the big liner," they could say, and live to boast about it at the shoreline bars and clam joints.

But a few had another goal. A few wanted to go inside, to explore the confusing maze that is a great liner sitting on its side, the hallways twisting and turning. Even after studying the deck plans, the interior of the ship could quickly turn into a debris-filled labyrinth.

A death maze, as some found out—easy to enter, a bitch to get out of.

A bit of confusion here, a wrong turn at a juncture, and panic would spread like air escaping from a leaking tank. And once panic arrived there was usually no way out. One bad decision piled onto another bad decision, until death wrapped its firm hand around the diver.

The dream of the mother of all wreck dives had—somehow—turned into a nightmare.

The *Andrea Doria* still killed.

And maybe, Ted thought, *that was part of its allure.*

Ted looked at his beer. All gone. Funny, how they seem to simply vanish.

He got up from the chair and walked back into the bar. Billy Plano, now alone, watched the Mets getting hammered.

"Could I have another?" Ted asked.

Billy seemed reluctant to yank his eyes from the screen and take Ted's glass.

"Not a good year for the Mets," Ted said, as Billy filled the pilsner glass.

Billy looked up. A faint crease of a smile, then he nodded.

And for a moment, Ted's cop instincts kicked in, thinking, *What's he know that I don't? Or what's he hiding?*

Billy put the beer on the counter, and Ted put two more dollars down.

"Thanks," he said, and he walked back out to the chilly porch. Somehow it was better sitting out here, where he could look at the sea barely visible in the moonless sky.

He sat down again on one of the wicker chairs. Another sip. And like a diver exploring those twisting hallways and corridors, he let his memory continue to re-create how it happened . . .

How—as they say—it all went down, and went so wrong.

* * *

He got the call at the Red Hook police station, which had become the base of operations for his group of NYPD divers. When they weren't doing search-and-recovery dives connected to accidents, they pretty much had a routine like any other cop.

When things got slow, they'd go out on patrol.

But this day, the captain called him and his dive partner, Larry Bergman, into the cramped office of the Red Hook precinct.

"You guys up for a little R and R?"

Ted looked at Bergman. Sometimes the dives could be dangerous, sometimes just gross. It all sounded glamorous, but more often they were the garbagemen of the deep, hunting for body parts.

Then the captain explained what he meant by R and R.

Some recreational divers—experienced guys—had gone into the *Andrea Doria,* and never come out.

"Shit," Bergman said.

Ted spoke up. "But what does that have to do with us? That's not a police deal. Bad news and all, but—"

The captain held up his hand. "Except one of the divers happens to be the son of an upstate congressman. So now, guess what? Suddenly it *is* a police matter. He asked the commissioner's help in recovering the bodies. So that's exactly what we will be doing." The captain shook his head. "Or at least you will."

"When?"

It was October. The Atlantic, was cold and turned choppy this time of year, with the ebbs and swells of the end of hurricane season knocking at the door.

"How about tomorrow? Weather permitting, of course."

"Weather permitting," Bergman said. "Great. Thanks for the gig, Captain."

Their captain, an old-time veteran only a year away from retirement, laughed. "My pleasure, guys."

The yellow brick road.

It began there . . .

And then they followed it to Mill Basin and the police launch that took them over the *Andrea Doria*. On the next day—a gorgeous blue sky, October when life and the whole world seemed at its best.

But of course, that was on the surface.

They didn't know what waited down below.

Liz peeked open the door to the kids' room—what looked like a small study that had been converted into a small bedroom. All was quiet, the slice of light from her room cutting across two sleeping bodies.

She shut the door quietly.

Sometimes Megan would wake up in the middle of the night, needing to pee but also really just needing to cuddle, a bit of reassurance. Liz hoped that she remembered to come into this room to get to the bathroom—or to claim her late-night hug.

Then Liz sat down on the small easy chair, complete with vintage antimacassars.

She thought of Ted downstairs. Probably sitting at the bar. She didn't worry about him having too many drinks. Not the way she used to, not after they had talked.

Not after she let him know that, after Liz's own family history, she wouldn't let that happen to her family. No way.

And he had heard her clearly.

Despite the pain, despite the nightmares that she knew still haunted him, he cut down immediately. The hard liquor vanished, and he nursed his beers.

Though she could still feel his craving for something to bring that blessed fog.

Something to make it all go away.

He was down there. Probably sitting alone, thinking, remembering . . .

She could go down. Maybe she should go down.

But what if one of the kids woke up, came here, and looked for her?

No, she had better stay and wait.

Leaving Ted—for now—on his own.

FIVE

The police launch bobbed on the choppy water. Though the skies were a brilliant blue, the off-coast waters were clearly flecked with foamy white chop.

There were five people aboard. The boat captain and his mate, both cops, but neither of them divers. Then Ted and Bergman, the dive team. And Charlie Hodge, a trained diver, aboard for backup.

Ted had reviewed with Bergman the dive plan of the congressman's son. He and his buddy had indeed dived on nitrox and that should have given them more down time. Their plan was to enter an opening near the bow of the ship, used by so many teams it was called the "main entrance."

Once they entered there, they could have easily explored a few of the forward rooms and then made a quick dash to the surface with bragging rights about having gone inside the ship.

That was their plan.

But dive plans were just that. Something happened, and they didn't come up.

Ted and Bergman had suited up quietly, checking each other's suits that would keep them dry and even relatively warm once they hit the wreck. The dry suits were bulky and awkward, but they made up in comfort what they lost in sleekness.

Ted remembered how glad they were to drop over the side, to leave the crazily bobbing ship for the relative steadiness of the fall to the wreck.

In minutes they were there.

Close to the opening at the bow, with no sign of the divers.

It had been agreed that Bergman would go in first, then Ted. Taking turns, the way a search and recovery was done . . .

After checking that they were "okay," both floating, neutrally buoyant beside the opening, Larry gave a thumbs-up and entered the hole, the gash made when the *Andrea Doria* was hit by the *Stockholm* nearly forty years earlier.

Bergman disappeared, and then Ted followed. His headlamp caught the bright orange color of his partner's dry suit, even though visibility in the murky water couldn't have been more then ten feet. He could barely see the walls of the ship's corridor, just a dull, sick green that matched the debris-laden sea.

Larry moved deeper into the corridor, and Ted followed.

So far, they didn't see any signs that anyone had been down there in a long time.

Had the divers changed their plan? Had they dived somewhere else and neglected to tell anyone? It was a possibility; divers did it all the time. In which case he and Bergman were wasting their time there.

Deeper into the ship, Ted kept a mental record of the turns they took. If he had been breathing air, narcosis would render such mental mapping a joke.

But nitrox kept the mind clear.

Still, keeping a record was no piece of cake. But, with both of them doing it, they should be okay.

Then—and Ted remembered this so clearly—he checked his gauges and their downtime. They had been coasting along the sunken ship's corridors, finding nothing. If he had been in the lead, he would have called the expedition over then and there, and headed back to the surface.

They still had decompression stops to do on the way, and every minute cut their margin of safety.

But Bergman moved farther into the wreck, his orange suit fading, swallowed by the murk.

What the hell was he doing?

Had he seen something?

Ted kicked—a bit too hard—and tried to catch up to him.

But the corridor was empty.

Where the hell was Bergman?

Ted knew he was breathing too hard. Not a good thing. He looked at his gauges again, but now his dive computer was beeping, telling him what he already knew.

Time to get the hell out . . . and up.

Where the hell was Bergman?

Ted turned to his right. Some kind of room there; maybe a storeroom with the door hanging off. He didn't know where they were in terms of the deck plans.

Then he saw Bergman.

Hovering over two divers.

The dead divers. Ted could see the story . . . the divers had probably been hunting for souvenirs. The position of their bodies, pinned, wedged under shelving, told the tale. One of them had maybe grabbed something from the shelves and—apparently—got caught.

The scenario was so clear.

One got caught. The other came to help. The first one panicked, grabbed at his friend, clutching, holding on for dear life.

Actually—holding on for death.

Disorientation, fear, then—inevitably—death for the two of them.

The scene made Ted's own breathing quicken. No way they were getting those bodies out now. No way.

They had to leave.

He moved closer to Larry.

And then saw that his partner had a different idea.

Shit—he was trying to free the body. Bergman always liked to have a successful mission. Ted was the one who could walk away.

Bergman tried to unhook one of the divers; the dead diver's rig had snagged on the struts of the exposed wire shelving. The pinned diver's hands were still locked on his buddy's suit, holding him tight.

A nasty embrace.

Larry pulled, tugged. He was strong. Moved free weights in the gym every day.

Ted knew—

No way he was leaving the bodies there.

And then Ted, bobbing just a bit back, with a different perspective, saw the twisted wire shelving *move*. The first divers had yanked it, but now it was ready to shift again, to slide.

Ted watched it move onto his partner.

First, a prong pierced the dry suit. Gas began escaping. Larry moved to examine the leak without realizing that he might be pinned, trapped like the other diver.

Then, his eye on Ted, Bergman looked at the shelving across his bulky muscled frame.

Larry started pushing.

The shelving moved a centimeter or so, then fell down.

Larry had stepped into a wreck-diver's trap.

As if someone had planned it just to capture him, baited with the two corpses.

Ted's computer started beeping more frequently.

And windows all over the fucking place were slamming shut. Windows to the surface, windows to not getting bent, windows to maybe seeing the goddam blue sky again.

Now it was Ted's turn.

To do something.

To act.

To save his friend.

And Ted really had only one question in his mind about that.

How . . . ?

How the hell do I do that?

SIX

Liz closed the book. The last three or four pages had been a blur. Some novel where people talked, and Liz couldn't care less.

But maybe it wasn't the fault of the book.

Her mind was elsewhere. Down below.

Below, she thought.

Funny how she would think of it like that. Her husband, her rock, her family's rock, downstairs, maybe alone, maybe striking up a conversation with the bartender.

She didn't really worry about him drinking. She knew him too well, and that corner had been turned. She believed he would be okay now.

But the demons? They would always be there, only now he wouldn't completely anesthetize himself with his friends Jack Daniel's or Old Grand-Dad. He watched his limit, a few beers.

Tonight, he may be alone with those demons, so close to the water.

What was I thinking, she had to wonder? *I thought that with the beach and sun, and being busy with a rambling inn, this might be good.* Yes, and taking the kids to the boardwalk, the rides, the arcade.

New memories to make the others go away.

Except . . .

Now it was so clear, so obvious, just like the ocean sitting out there. No warm images of boogie boards and inflatable dragons could hide the fact that the ocean was so big, so deep, so eternally eager to claim those who came into it.

The emotionless sea, armed with a dull grayness, totally indifferent to the deaths it caused.

She knew: Ted was down there, looking at it, thinking, remembering.

Liz got up and put the book on the small table by the high-backed easy chair. She walked quietly over to the door that led to the small room where the kids slept.

Opening the door slowly . . .

Reminding her of that story, "The Tell-Tale Heart." And the crazy loon who lets a crack of light fall onto the bed of an old man, his victim for some crazy reason that only Edgar Allan Poe knew.

Except I'm not crazy. Least not yet, she thought.

She opened the door a crack and looked at Daver and Megan. Both curled up, sound asleep. Their window was open an inch, and the sheer curtains blew in gently.

Safe and sound, she thought. Sleeping like logs, as the saying goes. *So maybe I can go downstairs and try to scare some of those demons away from my husband.*

Ted cradled the beer in his hand.

He wondered if there was any way to stop this fucking ride, stop this flood of memories, this replaying of each horrible moment?

He knew the answer.

Impossible. Not when there existed the possibility that he could have done things differently, that somehow he could have had that one clear, saving thought that could have changed everything.

The short answer?

There was no way to stop this ride.

Windows slamming all over the place.

Ted knew that a diver's worst enemy was dealing with too many variables at the same time. The great wreck divers had taught him that, the ones who pushed the envelope for the sheer excitement of gathering loot that the ocean didn't want to give up.

Allow two, three, maybe four things into your head, and you won't deal with one of them, not with any clear thought, not with any kind of plan.

He saw Larry pinned. Probably the congressman's son had weakened the shelving. Maybe he had even stupidly used some tools to get behind it.

Then they died down there. But not before they left a trap, a lobster trap for a human.

Ted could see Larry's eyes burning with the effort, as Ted pulled on the structure but still tried to stay clear, focused, single-minded. Ted came closer. He knew that his well-trained partner would have already pushed aside that first bad thought to appear.

The thought that screamed *panic*. The thought that made divers grab for their buddy and clutch them tight, hold them fast, drowning, killing both of them.

Larry was too good to let that one sneak up on him.

So it was safe for Ted to swim closer and, through the murky water, look at his partner's situation.

The situation sucked.

The shelving structure had cartwheeled forward, and

Larry's upper torso now appeared firmly pinned. Ted considered his options, even as he knew his bottom time had to be fucking over, that the decompression stops were already in danger of being shortened to a deadly length, or cut altogether.

He swatted away those thoughts like flies, only the flies would grow bigger, more insistent, to hummingbird-size, then bat-size, becoming raptors hovering around him, all while he tried to see what he could do.

Job one . . . *what can he do to get Larry out?*

Larry's eyes didn't say much. There was nothing for his partner to do but watch Ted act.

His torso was pinned. The shelving structure dug into Larry's dry suit. Cold water now probably filled it, and hypothermia wouldn't help the situation.

Ted looked for a place where, with the right force, with the right leverage, he might move the shelving without having any of the ragged metalwork dig any deeper into his partner.

He saw the spot. It looked good.

Ted reached down. He planted his feet against he floor. He took a breath, knowing that his breaths were limited. Each breath was another marble out of the jar, another stolen jelly bean until the jar would be empty.

Wedged in position, hands locked on the metal, he tugged upward.

At first the shelving moved. A half inch, a full inch; he was making headway.

But then there was a sound.

Larry screamed through his mouthpiece. Where the metal had punctured Larry's dry suit on the side, it now twisted a bit, and—when Ted looked—he could see that it had dug in deeper.

Through the suit, deeper now, into the skin.

The murky water, filled with floating debris, now became tinged with color.

A deep smoky color that bloomed from Larry's body.

Fuck, Ted thought. *Fuck, I cut him. I cut the poor, trapped bastard.*

And now the raptorlike thoughts swooped low and close, thoughts looking to perch on his brain, to distract him, to destroy him.

Nitrox so low, flying away like the puffy tendrils of a dandelion. The time for the decompression stops expanding. And then a last insidious thought: could he find his way out, fight his way out of the sunken liner, to even have a shot at reaching the surface safely?

Focus, Ted told himself. On one thing, *one* fucking thing only. Free Larry. Get him out.

Through the now red-tinged murkiness, he looked for another place to grasp. He saw a place that—while it didn't look that promising—at least might not cut into his friend.

He locked his hands on the metal.

And then, a moment that Ted knew he would never forget.

An intimate moment that he saw nearly every day—he felt Larry put his gloved hands on Ted's.

Ted looked up.

And Larry shook his head.

Shook his head . . .

And then pointed with his forefinger up. Jerked the finger up.

As in, *Time to go, buddy.*

Ted shook his head. His hands were locked, ready for another try.

Larry shook his head, widening his eyes, and even spoke through his mouthpiece.

Ted thought he made the words out, garbled, distorted.

Get the hell out of here.

Get the hell out of here now.

Larry did another finger jerk.

And then he did something that, even with the terror that Ted was dealing with, made his eyes water behind his mask.

He took Ted's hand and shook it. Shook it, as in, *Goodbye, buddy. You tried, but there's no reason for both of us to die. You know that, and I know that.*

So—

Get the hell out of here.

Larry released his partner's hand.

With both hands he made a waving motion, *Be gone. Get going.*

Ted hesitated.

But true to the manual of surviving depth, Ted focused on that one thought. No way to save Larry and get him out of here. No way. And if Ted left now he might survive.

Might.

Another few minutes, and Ted would be dead or bent.

Ted reached out and grabbed his partner's hands and squeezed them.

And then, fist kicking back a bit, his nitrox so slow he couldn't bear to look at his gauge, he turned.

He made his way out of the ship, leaving his partner, alive, trapped, behind.

SEVEN

A hand fell on his shoulder.

Ted had been quietly sobbing.

At least he's not sitting in the dark living room at three A.M., Liz thought.

"Hey," she said.

Ted turned around, and in the yellow half-light of the porch, she could see him blinking back the tears.

"You didn't come up," she said.

He nodded. "Yeah. I sat down for a bit." A small smile. "Checked out the ocean."

"Still there, I see."

He nodded. Liz pulled up a wicker chair. The air had turned cool, and she wished she had brought down a sweatshirt. She looked at his empty beer glass.

"How about another?"

Ted shook his head and smiled. "No, had my quota for the night." He looked at her. "But go ahead . . . if you want."

"No. I'm ready for bed." She looked back toward the porch door that led to the bar. "How's the bartender at the Ten Bells?"

"You know nice Mrs. Plano? Turns out he's her husband. Or maybe ex. And not exactly the most talkative bartender I ever met. The guy wouldn't cut it in Brooklyn."

She nodded. "Ted?"

He hesitated. "Yeah?"

"You okay. Here. With this?"

"Okay? Am I . . . okay? About as okay as I can be, Miss Elizabeth. Okay as I can be. I'd like to still be working, I'd like—"

She reached out and squeezed his hand. "I know. But your leave isn't forever. You'll get back to it."

He made a hollow laugh. "Just as soon as I can sit in the dark and not cry? I'm working on it, babe. Doing my goddam best."

His hand didn't squeeze back.

"And you know, Liz, it wouldn't be so bad if it didn't hurt us in the pocketbook. I get my base pay. But show me a cop who doesn't live or die with overtime. We all just pretend that it isn't a factor."

Another squeeze. "You'll get it back. This is only for now. Temporary. Right?"

Another look at her.

"Right."

Megan woke up. She didn't have to pee, like she sometimes did. She just . . . woke up.

And for a moment she didn't know where she was. She pulled the covers tight, right up to her nose so she could see, but with the fluffy cover protecting her.

Where am I? she wondered. *This isn't my room. I don't see my ponies on the shelf, or the glow-in-the-dark stars that Daddy put on the ceiling.*

Then Megan saw the other bed, the outline of it catching the glow of the light from the window. She saw the shape of someone in the bed.

Then she remembered.

We're at the inn!

And that's Daver, sleeping right next to me.

She let the covers slip down a bit. Daver's right there. Everything's okay. Daver, who was so much bigger than she was, sleeping right there.

Then she saw the light at the door, the door that led to her mom and dad's room. They were close, too.

Megan pushed the covers off a bit.

Maybe she did need to pee. Maybe she did want a drink of water.

Maybe she'd just get up and see her mommy and daddy before she went back to sleep.

Megan sat up and slid off the bed. The rug wasn't the soft rug from home, but something ropey and rough. It didn't feel good on her feet at all.

She walked to the door, the doorknob shining in the light.

She opened the door.

"Mom . . . Mommy, I—"

But when she opened the door, the room was empty.

"Maybe," Liz said, "you should talk to someone while we're here. Keep up the counseling. It wouldn't hurt."

"And it wouldn't help. I know what I have to do."

"You do?" Liz's words came out more skeptical than she wanted, with more of a bite.

"Yes, I do. I simply have to stop reliving everything that happened. Stop playing 'what if' and fucking 'maybe.' Once I do that, everything will be fine."

She nodded. "So that's all?"

She was tempted to add something like, *You haven't been too successful at that so far.*

But Ted didn't deserve that.

"Ted, if this isn't a good place, if this isn't the place to be—for us, for you—we can go somewhere else. We don't have to stay here."

Now his hand squeezed hers. "Look, this place is fine. It's beautiful. I'll find tons to do. The money will help. The kids will keep me busy."

"You sure?"

"I'm sure, and—"

The porch door opened.

"Last call," Billy said.

The bartender barked out the words then retreated to the safety of the barroom.

"Maybe I *could* do with a beer," Liz said.

"Coming right up," Ted said, and he got up and followed the bartender inside.

Megan stood there. The funny lamp that looked like a plant, with metal vines curling around, lit up the room, leaving only small pockets of shadow and dark.

"Mom," Megan said more quietly.

Where was she? the girl wondered. *She should be here, and Daddy, too. It was night; they should be in bed, getting ready to sleep.*

She looked back at her room, with Daver sleeping. So dark now. It would be hard to walk back into it. She thought about waking Daver. Maybe he'd know where Mom was.

But to do that now, she'd have to walk back into that dark room.

She heard a sound.

A voice. Muffled, the words unclear. The sound coming from out *there*. From out in the hallway, the long hallway with the dark green rug that ran from end to end.

Maybe Mom was talking to someone? She was going to

run this inn. There had to be a lot of important things to do.

Megan walked toward the door, stepping from the rug onto the shiny wood floor, grabbing the doorknob, and then opening it.

The hallway was empty.

But she still heard the sound coming from down there, down at the end of the hallway. A voice. Someone talking. And Megan kept walking, one foot in front of the other, moving toward the sound, knowing that it had to be her mommy.

They clinked their glasses and took deep sips of the beer.

"Cold beer. That's one good thing about this place," Liz said.

"There are a lot of good things. The ocean, so close, the food will be great, and just about the best wraparound porch I've ever had the pleasure to sit on."

"Yeah, the Abbadon isn't half bad. Think the kids will like it?"

"Summer at the shore? What's not to like?"

Then the words became clearer. Megan heard the word "no," then a laugh. Followed by, "I see."

But not her mother's voice.

She could turn and hurry back to the room. Maybe her parents were there now.

But no—they would have seen her in the hallway. They would have come down here and whisked her back to bed.

Tucked her in and made her feel so safe and sound.

She was at the end of the hallway. The only sound was the voice at the door. Someone talking. She could see if her mom and dad were in there. All she had to do was turn the doorknob and open the door.

Megan grabbed the doorknob and slowly turned it.

The door clicked open. She gave it a small pull.

Stairs. Leading up. To the top of the inn.

Megan shook her head. This was wrong, this wasn't the place where her parents were. She started to feel as if she might start crying.

She turned and looked down the still-empty hallway, chewing at her lower lip, fighting to hold back the tears.

And when she turned back to the open door . . . someone was there.

EIGHT

"Maybe tomorrow we can—" Liz began.

But the scream cut her off in midsentence. She knew the sound immediately.

"Megan!" Ted said.

They both jumped up and ran into the inn. Ted ran ahead of her, taking the carpeted steps two at a time, scrambling. Liz was just behind. Their little girl's scream had cut through the night, over the sound of the waves hitting the shore.

And when they got to the upstairs hallway, they saw Megan backed against a wall and man facing her. Ted let Liz go to the front.

"Honey, what's wrong?"

The man—with thinning gray hair, glasses, a few days' growth of beard—started to speak.

"I'm sorry. I didn't know she was there, I came down—"

Megan was shaking, her eyes wide.

"I was looking for you, Mommy. You weren't in the room."

Liz looked up at Ted, feeling the pang of guilt. She saw that Ted had his eyes locked on the man.

Liz stroked Megan's hair. "What did you do, honey?"

"I—I woke up. And you were both gone. I heard something . . ." She looked up at the man. Liz guessed, from his bloodshot eyes and the slight slur to his speech, that the man had been drinking.

He licked his lips. "I may have made some noise. Didn't know I disturbed anyone. The place—especially upstairs— has been so empty lately."

Megan turned to Liz. "I thought it might be you. I thought you might be *here*."

Ted came closer now.

"Okay, honey. It's alright now." He turned to look at the man. "This is one of the guests. That's all. He just startled you."

Liz stood up. "Sorry. Guess Megan must have startled you, too."

The man smiled. "Nearly jumped out of my skin." He said it as if it was supposed to be funny. But she noted there was no humor in his voice.

"Martin Bridger. I live upstairs. Or have been for a while."

The writer, Liz thought. She didn't know his books, but he did scary stuff, supernatural. Had a best-seller a few years back.

And odd choice of word . . . *live* . . .

But what was he doing here as a long-term resident of the Abbadon?

"We're Liz and Ted McShane—we'll be managing the place while Mr. Tollard is away."

Megan tugged at her hand. "Mommy, I want to go back to bed."

Ted reached down and picked her up. "And that's exactly where I'm going to take you, pumpkin."

Liz watched her daughter cradle her head into Ted's shoulder, safe and sound.

"You go on, Ted. I'll be right there."

Ted carried Megan away.

"We had been just downstairs. Thought the kids were down for the night. Sorry if she spooked you."

The man smiled, stepping out to the hall and shutting the door behind him.

"If I scare that easily, I'm probably in the wrong line of work." He took a breath. "No harm done."

And then, for a moment, she watched Bridger's eyes narrow as if he was about to say something, tell her something important.

But . . . nothing.

"Just stepping out for some air."

Or maybe a seaside bar, Liz guessed to herself.

"I'll see you in the morning," she said. "And sorry again."

Bridger walked beside her as she headed toward her room.

"Not a problem. Don't give it another thought."

Martin Bridger walked along the cement walkway until he came to stairs that led down to the beach. He could see the outline of huddled shapes dotting the empty beach, lovers curled up, finding privacy and seclusion on this windswept beach.

Some might look up, check Bridger out as he trudged past them in his poplin pants and white linen shirt that was surely overdue to be washed.

They might—or they might simply continue caressing, fondling, kissing each other.

Such a clear and clean world they live in.

Where their passion is the only concern they have. A flickering romance, or maybe just the lust that comes to life at night on an empty beach.

Bridger heard the crash of the water as the calm, sleepy, night ocean continued to pound out waves with what seemed like a lack of enthusiasm.

Making waves—even though no one was there to run into them, to jump over the breaking surf, to squeal, to scream out in pleasure.

He stopped and looked back at the Abbadon.

The owner of the Abbadon Inn, Peter Tollard, was gone. Something must have happened to make him leave so abruptly, to abandon the inn.

The way kids used to say its name . . . *Abandon* Inn.

He left so suddenly.

And whatever had happened, whatever he had seen, must have scared Tollard. Scared him enough to make him leave . . . *immediately.*

Running away.

Bridger had to wonder. Can you run away from everything? Or did you bring it with you, no matter how far away you ran?

Like the ancient story, "Appointment in Samarra." You try to run from your fate, and yet run to it,

Bridger looked up at the night sky. Dark clouds dotted the sky, like outcroppings of rock in a sea of sand. Then down to the couples on the beach, some of them probably passing a cheap bottle of red wine back and forth, mingling the kisses with warm swills of wine.

Bridger would have his own reward at walk's end, a few blocks into the streets of Cape May, to the little hole-in-the-wall that was a Sargasso Sea for the local alcoholic crowd. The place seemed always open, and the bats and balls kept on coming inexpensively; an affordable place to mix the bullshit with Seagram's and a foamy beer chaser.

After a few of those, Bridger could just let his thoughts go. He'd even enjoy the barroom debates about the forever-hapless Mets or the eternally conquering Yankees.

A place like that was his salvation. A place of sanity.

He heard some laughter. A woman's voice. Maybe just a young girl. Squealing at what? The first attempt to undo a top, to untie the knot that held a tiny top in place? That first delicious step to a deeper, more serious lust . . .

The giggle, the first ripple of pleasure, or nervousness.

Bridger navigated well away from them. Close to the sleepy surf.

He looked to his right, already close. Had he just casually drifted closer to the lazy rolling water? The water looked black as oil in this dark, overcast night.

Just wandered closer . . .

Or had something been subconsciously pulling him, drawing him near, while he thought about the shapes on the beach and their awkward trysts.

Reeling him in, closer to the sea.

Just paranoia, Bridger thought. *Have I gone that crazy that I imagine the sea pulling at me, trying to secretly lure me?*

My thoughts are so twisted these days . . .

It wasn't always that way.

When Bridger had come to the Abbadon he had been look-ing for . . . what? Salvation? A bit pompous maybe, but there was no doubt he was hoping to get saved. He couldn't really talk to anyone about the problems with his writing.

All of a sudden, the stories, the ideas—they all evapo-rated. Like waking up on your birthday, and finding out that the pile of gifts sitting in the corner was only the prod-uct of a too-good-to-be-true dream,

All imaginary, and worse, now all gone.

Where had those ideas come from, those characters who

walked with such confidence, or with such fear, across the landscapes of his stories?

Christ, how did they all disappear?

Was it the result of some Faustian deal? Here's some success. But, oh, by the way, I will have to remove it all. Just take it away someday.

I will, though, leave you a steady hand to hoist a shot glass or four.

How about *that?*

And then he came here. Following the trails of legend, or myth. He came to Cape May, to the old Abbadon Inn, with its checkered past, its stories of death and destruction, of re-birth and secrets. He came here for that.

But that's not what he found.

That same demon now proposed another deal; it had something else in mind. Something he couldn't tell anyone.

Not now. Not yet.

Because how do you tell them . . . the people who ask, the ones who seem so interested to meet, gosh, a "real writer," to meet someone who conjures nightmares . . .

How do you tell them that now it's become so hard to write the scary things, the horror, the stories that make their skin crawl? How do you tell them that maybe you can't write those stories once they become real?

How do you tell them *that*?

You can't.

You can't tell them that what was once the product of a fertile imagination now haunts you, in the night at first, then all the time.

And it didn't matter that Bridger walked in the darkness now.

The sun could be blazing, and he could still feel the swirling eddies of fear that whipped around this town like a hurricane that would never leave.

And at its center, the eye.

Bridger looked left, spying the stone steps and metal

railing leading up to the road, the streets, to good old Flanagan's . . .

And in that eye?

Why, that would be me, Bridger thought.

And he turned and left the beach and the heaving young couples all behind.

NINE

The first days seemed to overwhelm them all. Liz tried to get a handle on all the workers' schedules, from Arielle, who split the days and evenings she worked the desk with two other girls, to Mrs. Plano, who seemed to be at the inn nearly 24/7.

And then there were workers supposedly struggling with repairs in the tower room, now off-limits to guests. The workers, barrel-chested, beer-gutted guys whose work pace seemed agonizingly slow, were bold enough to let their gaze last a second too long on Liz when introduced.

They know my husband's here. And yet they feel they can gawk. She knew Ted could easily explode if he caught them.

Maybe she should warn them.

You do not *fuck with my husband, unless you'd like a hammer planted squarely in your skull.*

And despite Ted's dumping plenty of sunblock on

Megan and Daver, they both had picked up reddish blotches where Ted had missed spots.

Nothing too dramatic, and now Ted could see just how careful he'd have to be.

Megan still resisted having anything to do with the water, while Daver could spend the whole day jumping in and out of the rolling waves.

And when the kids finally went to sleep, she and Ted talked each night, sitting on the porch, watching the dining room staff clean up, listening to the baseball game echoing from the bar.

This isn't bad, Liz thought. *This is going to be okay. I'm doing the work, and my family's okay.*

Later Liz would think, *God, how things can surprise you.*

Like a sucker punch she didn't see. She had been looking at the bookings—which were down—and checking food orders from the Goudge sisters. They told her what needed to be ordered from the supplier, but they told her that they always, *always,* went to the farmers' market to get their own vegetables.

All seemed well.

Then Liz interviewed a girl to replace a waitress who had just quit after a fight with the cooks.

And in the quiet of the afternoon, standing in the dining room, poised between lunch and dinner, Liz would learn that sometimes people don't tell you things.

The young girl's name was Julie Kaye.

Her handshake was slight and tentative. She looked older than Liz would have expected, more like someone who had been in college and was maybe having trouble getting her life going.

As they talked, Julie brushed her hair off her forehead.

Mrs. Plano had already interviewed her, but it was up to Liz to say if she was hired.

"So, you've done this before?" Liz asked.

The girl nodded. "Lots. I mean I used to work at the old Creighton House before it burned down."

"That—that's a restaurant? No inns like this?"

"Oh, and I worked at the Chalfonte. When I was in college I worked at different places . . . I gave Mrs. Plano a list."

Liz saw the girl look over to the front desk. Maybe she knew Ari, maybe that's how she knew about the opening.

"Then, when you graduated you came . . . ?"

Julie shook her head. "No, I . . . I didn't graduate. Things didn't go well." A small smile. "I guess college wasn't for me."

"So then—you'll be able to stay here, when the season is over? Apparently the Abbadon gets quite busy in October."

A warmer smile "The water's perfect then. As warm as it can be . . . just before it starts turning cold. It's beautiful here."

"I bet. Well, if you continue with us, that would be good. Most of the waitstaff leaves."

The girl seemed to think about that for a moment.

"I can stay. I mean—I think I can stay."

Technically, they were done. The girl had waited tables before, and the Goudge sisters and Mrs. Plano could get her trained and ready for that night's dinner.

But something about the Julie's eyes made Liz think that—somehow—she had something more to say.

"You glad to be back in Cape May?" Liz asked.

Those eyes narrowed.

"I—I didn't have much choice. I needed to work. To come back."

She looked around the room. The afternoon sunlight revealed dust motes dancing in the air, a stream of glistening fairy dust that poured into the room and fell on the polished hardwood floor.

She smiled. "My options . . . were kind of limited. I didn't know about what happened though until I came back. Maybe I would have—"

"Happened? Something happened . . . with your parents?"

The girl fixed on Liz with her eyes, confusion playing there.

"Nobody told you? You didn't see the papers?"

Though the room was warm, Liz felt a slight chill. She didn't like secrets. Secrets hurt people, secrets were never good. She had brought her family here—and there was a secret.

"Nobody told me—told *us*—anything."

The girl looked away, and now she glanced at Ari over at the desk.

If there was a secret here, she'd find it out—now.

"What is it, Julie? What happened? When you came back?"

Slowly the girl's eyes came back to Liz. She took a breath.

And she started telling secrets.

"Is it time now?" Daver asked.

He stood between Ted and the ocean, this young strapping boy that Ted guessed would end up taller than he was. Taller, smarter, luckier . . . all the things parents wish for their kids.

"In a bit," he said.

The days at the beach, his days playing beach dad, had developed a certain routine. There was time to sit on the beach, with Megan digging in the sand, her back to the ocean, and Daver performing endless crazy jumps into the breaking surf, or catching rides on his boogie board until Ted knew the gritty sand must have invaded every crack and crevice of his lean body.

Then, there would be a trip to Extreme Ice Cream.

Enough flavors so that they wouldn't hit the bottom of the list even by summer's end.

Ted had noticed some of the mothers checking him out, probably wondering, *What's his story?*

A few giving him looks that maybe showed a different kind of interest.

Or maybe, Ted thought, *I'm just imaging that.*

Child care does leave a lot of room for idle thoughts.

"I wanna go for ice cream now," Daver pleaded.

"Oh, you do, do you? I'd be careful because maybe we won't go at all."

Megan looked up from the bowl-shaped indentation she had made for her ponies. She still totally avoided the water, and Ted was beginning to think that there was nothing he could do to change that.

"Daddy, we *aren't* having ice cream today?"

"Yes, we are. I mean, we are when it's time to pack up. Your brother is just growing a tad impatient."

Ted looked up at Daver. "Chill, Daver, okay? Go catch a few more perfect waves."

"Okay, Dad." Daver turned and, with a spray of sand kicked up by his heels, ran back to the water.

One won't go in. One won't stay out.

Maybe I should do what my brother did to me, Ted thought. Scoop Megan up and carry her into the water kicking and screaming.

At least she'd learn that no sea monsters would eat her.

Ted let that image play in his mind for a second. Nope, that definitely wouldn't fly. In 1992 we know better than to do that to our kids.

Ted remembered how he cried, all of five years old, held tight by his big Marine brother. Big, tough, amazingly strong, holding Ted up as he swam so far out, holding him long enough, until little Ted finally stopped crying.

Until he could finally see *it's okay.*

Ted shook his head. It started there, his fascination with the water; a fascination with the beauty and the power, but also the darkness and threat of the ocean.

There had been times, when diving a deep recovery, that Ted could feel that five-year-old boy just beneath his skin.

At least I don't cry anymore.

Megan made her pony jump out of its sandy paddock. *She's having fun, so maybe I shouldn't worry about her fear of the water.*

Looking at her, he knew what it would take to make him cry now.

If something should happen to her, or Daver, or Liz.

Yeah, that would do it.

He looked up at Daver emerging from his last wave, grinning.

A few more minutes, and they could haul anchor and walk to Extreme Ice Cream.

Ted grinned.

The other moms awaited.

Julie had walked to the window, closer to the shafts of sunlight.

"I thought everyone knew, the locals all do. Though I guess they're trying to keep it quiet. It is a tourist town, after all."

Liz nodded. Was it just luck that this girl had come here, bringing her some secret that nobody, not the agency, not Mrs. Plano, not the cooks, would ever have told her?

Or was the girl a little crazy? Left college. Or maybe kicked out of college?

Liz just nodded, urging her to continue.

"I had been back a few days, and everyone started talking about these teenagers who disappeared. A boy and a girl. Just vanished."

"They went on a road trip?"

Julie shook her head. She looked at Liz, as if gauging her interest. "No. Their friends say no—they were young, only fifteen each. The state police came. The whole town just sort of stopped. But I guess resort towns can't afford to scare people. So the story vanished from the papers."

"Did you know them?"

She shook her head. "No. They—" she looked around the dining room. "But when Mr. Tollard's son disappeared—"

Liz reached out and touched the girl. "Wait a second. You mean Mr. Tollard, the owner of the inn?"

"Yes. His son stayed here. He didn't get along with his father. Supposedly he always made trouble, real trouble, and—"

She stopped, and Liz wondered if Julie knew him.

"What was his name?"

"Peter. Peter Josiah Tollard. His father liked biblical names, a big Bible freak. They said that when his wife died, he got even crazier."

"You say that his son vanished with a girl? What do you mean?"

"One morning, the bed was empty, his stuff still there, but Peter was gone, his girlfriend, too." She took another breath. "Police were all over this place."

"God. And Tollard . . . ?"

Julie nodded. "Then Mr. Tollard left. But you know that. That's why you're here. He left."

Well, that explains a few things, Liz thought. Maybe even why the inn isn't exactly doing gangbuster business, and why Mrs. Plano acted as if she had to bite her tongue to keep from saying things.

Still, what did it mean, a pair of teenagers vanishing?

Not the first time that's happened. A badass son takes off and leaves his stuff behind.

But looking at the girl Liz guessed that there might be more secrets there, secrets that a longtime resident of the town would know . . . but maybe wouldn't share right away.

At least not yet.

A breeze fluttered the white curtains of the dining room, bringing a gust of fresh salty air. A punctuation point, a good place to end the conversation.

"So alright . . . thanks for telling me this. And you can start tonight?"

"Yes. I can. It will be good to do some work."

Liz reached out and took Julie's hand.

"Great, see you back here then."

The girl smiled and left the dining room, leaving Liz all alone.

Ted folded the blanket and stuffed it into the big canvas bag with an embroidered palm tree on it. He lowered the umbrella and then separated it into two pieces. If they took a detour, he could drop all this junk at the back of the inn before heading to the ice cream shop.

"C'mon, Daver. Give me a hand here. Or help your sister gather up her ponies—"

"They're *her* stupid ponies."

"They are not stupid," Megan protested. "They're smarter than you!"

Ted thought, *I am just not good at this.*

"Easy on the pony criticism, Daver, okay?" The boy gave Ted a look as though he didn't understand. "I mean zip it, got it?"

In a few moments, Ted's beach party was ready to move on. Megan had trouble slipping her pink jellies on, which necessitated Ted putting everything down again to help her. But soon they were ready to go.

"Onward troops," he said.

He marched his forces to the left, cutting in front one of the lifeguard chairs.

Ted looked at the lifeguards. *What do they think about all day?* Ted wondered. *Sitting up there, squinting at the glistening water. I'd begin to hallucinate that I was seeing bobbing heads and flailing arms.*

But as he got closer, he saw one of the tanned guards drop down to the sand, and run to the shore.

Not a bolt, but a good jog down to one of the red flag poles that marked the safe area to swim.

Ted stopped, turned, and watched him.

The guard moved the pole three or four meters closer to the center.

"Come on, Dad. The sand is hot."

Ted looked down at Daver. "I did tell you to put on your flip-flops, right kemosabe?"

"Kemo—?"

"Go on, put them on now."

While Daver slipped on his flip-flops, Ted watched the guard go to the other flag and move that one three or four meters toward the center.

Something was up.

He turned and looked up at the second lifeguard sitting in his chair.

"Problem out there?"

The young bronze kid nodded, then pointed.

"Getting these weird riptides all along here. We've been told to narrow the safe-swim area."

A whistle sounded: the guard down by the shore herding people into the new, narrower zone. Ted scanned the water. Hard to read tides. So much hidden below the surface. But riptides could be nasty, knock someone right down and drag them out and away before they knew what was happening.

He had a thought. *Daver was out in that water just a little while ago.*

Ted made a note to pay more attention. The lifeguards could be good, but he wasn't going to depend on them.

"Thanks," Ted said to the lifeguard.

Megan tugged at his hand.

"Come on, Daddy!"

And with Megan's hand wrapped around his forefinger, he continued on to the afternoon's big attraction.

TEN

Ted came up behind Liz, who stood in the kitchen with a piece of paper in her hand.

"I brought the troops back safe and sound."

She nodded. "Just a minute—" She looked up at the Goudge sisters, hurrying about the kitchen, while another woman worked a dishwasher. "This looks fine Estella, Lucy—" She couldn't tell which one was which. In fact, she doubted she ever would. "Sounds perfectly yummy!"

The evening's menu did sound good. If nothing else, they were eating some great food here.

"Thank you, Mrs. McShane," one Goudge said. They continued to ignore Liz's requests to call her by her first name.

Liz pinned the evening's menu back on the bulletin board and grabbed Ted's hand.

"They should only know what passes for cooking in my kitchen."

"What? We *love* your Rice-A-Roni."

Liz laughed. "The San Francisco treat, and always a hit at the McShane household."

"Gotta tell you, though, between the ice cream trip and meals here, you're going to have a much fatter husband by the time this gig is over."

She turned to him in the hallway, smiled, and gave him a quick peck on the cheek. "You could do with a few extra pounds." As she leaned forward, she saw Ariella at the desk, watching her. The girl seemed to be all eyes. Have to have a little chat with her. Tell her to get a magazine, try a book, *something* to stop looking around as though her eyes needed to take in everything going on.

She felt Ted's hand slip down her back, to gently pat the curve of her bottom.

"Easy, cowboy."

"Mmm . . . I could use a nap. How about . . ."

Liz laughed. "Got a zillion things to do. Kids okay?"

"In the rec room watching *Electric Company*. Daver lost the argument for what to watch. Though they did chase an old couple out of there who were watching a soap."

"Have to watch that. Paying customers, you know."

"I hear you." He stopped for a second, and his light manner shifted. *Funny how he can do that,* she thought. Like making a small adjustment to his emotional thermometer. Cop training? Or was it just Ted?

"And you, you doing okay?"

Liz smiled. "Fine. Everything's going well. Getting a handle on things. Slowly."

"You know, I could help."

She nodded. "I know. But right now, it's great you're with the kids. Give them some stability. Down the road, we can get a baby-sitter. I know there's a lot you could do."

"If Mrs. Plano allows. Sometimes, she gives me this weird look like . . ."

Liz was tempted to tell him about her conversation with Julie, about Tollard's son, the lost teenage kids. But maybe it's just the types of things that happen in a seashore town in summer. Maybe it was just that.

Or maybe not.

She'd tell him. But not now. Later. When the kids were asleep.

She heard someone behind her clear her throat, and turned to see Mrs. Plano there.

"Mrs. McShane, I'm afraid we have a problem for this evening."

Could they have lost another server? Why is it so dammed hard to keep a waitstaff? And training someone new took time, so the newbie didn't really help much at all the first few days.

"Julie not show up or something?"

"No. She's here. And I'll tell you this, that girl's been in a dining room before. That's the good thing. It's that Billy—"

The way she said "that Billy" told Liz that whatever she was about to hear would not be the first bit of difficulty created by Mrs. P's grim-faced husband.

"What's wrong with Billy?"

"He says he's under the weather." The woman shook her head. "He gets 'under the weather' when the season ends. He's usually more dependable." She took a breath. "I'm sorry."

"Okay, um . . . so no bartender?"

"Yes, there might be a few men I could call. But it's late, and a Friday, so it might be hard."

Ted took a step closer.

"I could do it. Nothing too tricky about it."

Liz saw Mrs. Plano fix Ted with her eyes. "You know your way around a bar?"

Ted laughed. "I think I have the pouring, mixing, ice thing pretty well covered."

"I guess it would be okay."

Mrs. Plano didn't seem too thrilled nevertheless.

"And the kids?" Liz asked.

"As long as they're in the TV room, they'll be fine. We can check on them."

"I guess so. Should be fine. Decided then. Ted, you're on the bar. You better get on it now . . . I see that couple from New York sitting there as though they've been marooned."

Ted grinned. "Yeah—saw them last night. Big Manhattan drinkers. Good thing I know what goes into a Manhattan."

Then he turned and walked through the main lobby, and into the Ten Bells Pub.

Mrs. Plano stood there. Liz thought, *Does this woman ever smile?*

"Anything else, Mrs. Plano?"

"No. Not really. Just that—the men doing the work—on the tower and cupola—you should be looking it over soon. So that they know you're watching them."

"I will. They work tomorrow?"

"Every day but Sunday. Though I doubt that it's much of a Lord's Day for those two."

"I'll look in on them and have a nice chat with them, then."

The older woman nodded, then, "I best see to the dining room,"

And Liz thought, *Who am I kidding? She's really running this place.*

"No. No way we are watching that purple thing!"

Daver had his hand wrapped around the remote. The TV's colors seemed washed out, the picture fuzzy. But that wouldn't be so bad if his sister didn't want to watch that new show about a stupid purple dinosaur.

But she had it on, and the dinosaur was bouncing around, clapping its dumb stuffed hands.

"I can't stand it when he sings!"

Then there was another little green dinosaur that was

even *more* stupid. Daver had to wonder what this stupid show was about anyway.

Megan seemed to love it though, sitting on the floor with her ponies that, Daver could see, matched the dinosaurs' bright colors.

One TV for this whole place!

He had watched a man walk in before as if he expected this room that also had books, board games, and smelly couches and chairs, to be empty. The man with silver-gray hair looked at Daver and his sister and quickly turned around.

It's our room, Daver thought, *all to ourselves!* But his stupid, stupid, stupid sister had the remote.

The dinosaur began to sing.

"Oh, no way."

Daver knew if he actually ripped the remote from Megan's hand, she'd scream, Dad or Mom would come, and he'd get the lecture about how he wasn't helping.

And then there was this . . .

Unlike his sister, Daver knew that something had happened. Something to his dad.

Daver had only heard a few words here and there about it. But something happened on one of his Dad's dives . . . and now they were here.

So he didn't want to do anything to make his dad feel angry, not if he already felt bad. Not if things were already not right.

Daver stood up. "I am not listening to this. No way!"

He glanced at the lobby. It looked as though a few people had arrived for the weekend. The young girl at the desk was talking to them, finding their rooms; suddenly the inn looked busy. All Daver wanted to do was get out of this room and away from the dinosaur—

And those kids on the show? Grinning and singing as if there was nothing better than whoever was inside the big smelly purple costume.

He saw a side door. *Must lead to the back of the inn,* he guessed.

He hadn't explored there.

Eventually he'd explore the whole inn. So, if he hadn't been back there yet, maybe now was a good time.

He walked to the screen door and opened it. The door made a tiny squeak, but Megan didn't look up.

No . . . the show was that good.

Daver walked out the door.

Martin Bridger had quickly walked away from the TV room.

A few nights back he had scared that little girl. And though he made his living scaring people, he didn't want to startle her again. The inn didn't usually have a lot of children, but now these two were here all the time.

Bridger had to wonder . . . could that mean anything? The owner gone, now these two here. And not just for a few days, but for—maybe—the rest of the summer.

There was so much he wanted to figure out. He'd talk to the parents soon, the people running the inn. Maybe tell them what he'd found out about the place. They should know.

Yes, and perhaps warn them.

Nobody else would warn them.

Nobody else would know everything he had found out, and what it all could mean.

Bridger rubbed his lips. He looked over at the bar, the blinds drawn so that the dark mahogany bar looked like a dark island of sanctuary from the sunlight.

He checked his watch.

Not too early, he thought. A little cocktail before dinner. Something to take the edge off.

Bridger walked into the Ten Bells.

* * *

Liz walked past the new guests. The inn would be near ca-
pacity for the weekend, at least for the rooms that were
ready. That was good; she was beginning to think that she
might have jinxed the place with her arrival. Perfectly good
summer, great weather, and only half full.

What gives?

Then, as she looked into the dining room now starting
to fill, she recalled Julie's story, her tale of things gone bad
in Cape May. Local tales, stuff that Liz knew she should
probably just ignore.

Yes, it was good the place would be near full. Even a
few more kids had arrived, though too old to be any company for Megan and Daver.

That prompted her to go by the musty lounge. She saw
Megan sitting on the floor watching that new show, *Barney.*
Daver was probably curled up on the couch being a good
sport.

She knew that Daver was trying to help, trying to be the
good kid.

Liz didn't enter. *Let sleeping dogs lie,* she thought, turning quickly so neither of the kids saw her.

Everything's good, she thought.

And she really believed it.

ELEVEN

Daver let the screen door shut behind him, making a loud *whack*. Megan would be lost to her stupid *Barney* show and not even notice that he had left.

He looked around. The back area behind the inn looked so messy. Some large metal drums, one on its side, and patches of tall grass that somehow sprouted through the sand.

You can't grow anything in sand, can you? Daver wondered.

He saw a shed, the wood gray and splintery, with one small window that looked as if it was painted black.

Tools, Daver thought. *Bet they keep tools in there. And paint.*

He looked up. Were there any guest rooms that overlooked this messy place?

But no. It didn't seem that way. Though he did see some small windows on the inn, he saw none of the windows with the nice white curtains that seemed to be everywhere else. So no rooms faced back here. Everything faced the ocean, and the sides.

He went down the few steps to the sandy path.

Good place to hide here, he thought. Good place to get away. He didn't like being in a place with so many people, old people who smiled at him. The hallways might be fun to run down—but so far he hadn't done that. What if someone came out of a room and Daver barreled into him?

That wouldn't be good. Mom would get mad. And she'd tell Dad. And Daver didn't want to do anything to make Dad angry. Though he didn't know what happened—not exactly—he knew something bad had happened to his father. And he loved his father more than anything.

That's why they were here, why Mom was working at the inn.

And why he had to find secret places, like this.

He walked closer to the shed, and now he could see that the windows weren't really black, just grimy, so dirty that they only looked painted.

He went closer to the windows. Daver had to stand on his toes to get a good look, but he still couldn't really see anything.

He did make out some cans and a machine of some kind, maybe a big lawn mower—or something else. Everything else was in the shadows, just too dark to be seen.

Daver looked to his left, at the door. A silver padlock over a latch kept it shut.

So, no way could he open the door.

Though the wood looked so splintery . . . He ran his fingers over the wood, and it frayed like that nasty cereal his mom ate. Shredded Wheat. Just like that, and—

A spike of the wood slipped into his finger.

"Ouch," he said.

He looked at the sliver. It had slid deep, then broken off. Now the wood hid, buried under his skin.

"Shit," he said.

It wasn't a word he used often, certainly not around his parents.

But here, he was all alone. He looked at his finger and tried to suck at the splinter. Then he picked at the skin, scratching now. He could feel the splinter causing pain. He had to get it out, he just *had* to.

He scratched some more. The place where the splinter had slipped in grew red, inflamed, and then Daver saw a tiny drop of red.

It was bleeding now.

He sucked at his finger again.

When he looked again, the red was gone for moment, and then another tiny drop appeared. With his other hand he pressed from the bottom, just as though his finger were a tube of toothpaste. Pressed and squeezed, until—

Another suck, and he could see the wood sticking out. The blood came out a bit faster now. And while he squeezed again, a drop fell to the yellow-white sand. He could see it there, standing out against the sand.

Just the tiniest tip of the wood splinter sticking out. Maybe he could grab it, close his fingers on it, and oh-so-carefully slide it out. He wished he didn't chew his fingernails—his mom was always yelling at him.

Don't chew your fingernails. Stop chewing your fingernails.

He could really use some long fingernails now, little pincers to remove the wood. He'd have to hope that his grip was tight enough—and his fingers were small enough—to close tightly on the wood.

Taking so much care not to push the wood back in, he used his index finger and his thumb, closing slowly on the wood sliver.

He thought he had it, though some fresh blood made it hard to see.

He pulled up his finger tweezers. No wood, and a little

squeeze on his wounded finger told him that the splinter was still there.

Okay, then . . . another toothpaste squeeze, and then another grab.

So slowly . . . like he was one of those safecrackers he saw in a movie. Turning the tumblers so carefully to open the vault to the gold.

He pulled back.

He could see it. A long, thin spear of wood that had been buried in his finger.

"Gotcha!" he said. "Got—"

He heard a noise.

Something close. A sound he couldn't recognize. Not another person. But sounds, movement, around the side of the shed.

Had it been going on for a few minutes and he simply had not heard it?

He tossed away the splinter, waving his hand like a wet rag in the air. He wouldn't touch the wooden shed again (though it would be fun to explore what was inside).

Now he wanted to see what was making that sound, so close, just around the corner of the rickety wooden shed.

Ted took a rag and wiped the shiny wooden counter. The bar was beautiful, not unlike a ship, a square bar, surrounded by wood and chrome places to put down a frothy beer as he dribbled off the excess foam.

So far, business had been slow. Of course it was only seven o'clock. Could be some of the guests would drift in after dinner.

For now, Ted didn't have much to do.

At least he was glad he had *something* to do. How long could he have let Liz work the place before he did something besides just escort the kids to the beach, to the arcade, to Extreme Ice Cream?

He thought, *How long before doing only that put me around the bend?*

And though he didn't tell Liz, he knew doing only that would, if anything, eventually drive him crazy.

He didn't tell Liz about sitting by the ocean, little Megan with her back to the water, while he stared at the sea.

Haunted, that was the word, wasn't it?

And Ted thought, *I don't like being haunted.*

No fucking way.

Someone walked into the bar.

The writer, Martin Bridger.

"Bar closed?" he asked.

"Nope, open for business. Just filling in."

Bridger nodded. He looked at the stools surrounding the bar and took his time selecting one, as if it was the most important decision of the day. While Ted wasn't a detective, he had taken enough courses in the academy to think that he had the necessary observational skills to eventually make detective.

Maybe not now. Not for a while.

But it was a dream.

And looking at this Bridger character, this writer who had scared his little girl the night before—unintentionally, to be sure, but still scared her—

He had the thought. *This guy is even more haunted than I am. Why is he here for almost the entire summer? What the hell is that all about?*

Running from something? Looking for something? Ted guessed that a writer had to be a little eccentric. Sitting in a room, making up stuff. Events, conversations. Had to be real weird. Day in, day out. Certainly stranger than patrolling streets, breaking up family fights, grabbing some shoplifter, rolling some drunk into jail.

All day, in a room somewhere, making up shit.

Weird.

"What will it be?"

Bridger had finally settled on a stool. His back to the sea. Strange. Most people would probably sit on one of the sides of the square to get a look at the darkening sea.

Bridger cleared his throat. "Um, gin . . . and tonic."

"Right," Ted said. Nothing too complicated there. "Bit of lime?"

Bridger nodded.

"Any special gin?"

Bridger shook his head. The man might be a writer, but he didn't speak too much.

Or maybe he just needed something to get his evening going.

Ted threw some rocks and a slice of lime into a tumbler, followed by a generous hit of gin. Then he picked up the soft-drink dispenser and hit the button and filled the tumbler with tonic.

He put it down in front of Bridger.

"Put it on my room bill, please," Bridger said.

Ted nodded and turned away—but not before seeing Bridger grab the glass with two hands, and drain half the drink.

A two-fisted drinker, Ted thought. He'd be at home in the seedy gin mills of Red Hook, the places where you can cut the stale stench of beer with a knife, where the yellow stains of cigarette smoke color everything a permanent sepia.

Ted moved away from Bridger. Probably other guests would come in, now that the supper hour was ending. The sea outside had lost all its blue and turned gray. And from there, it would darken to indigo black, a night sea full of secrets.

He looked to his left.

Bridger had finished his drink.

"Another, please."

And Ted fixed his lone customer another gin and tonic.

TWELVE

Daver listened to the noise. He looked up at a sky filled with gray and milky white clouds, and for the first time he wondered if it was bad idea to be back here. Nobody knew he was here, nobody at all—not even Megan, who was glued to her dopey show.

He heard a scratching noise, then a squeak.

Daver thought, *Maybe it's a kitten!* He could see the back door of the kitchen, a big exhaust pipe shooting out smoky clouds. Sure, this might be a perfect place for a kitten to come.

He took a step around the side, slowly now, not wanting to startle what might be there. One step in the sand, then another, so slowly, until he reached the corner of the building, and—taking care *not* to grab the corner of the splintery shack—he peered around the corner of the shed.

For a moment he couldn't tell what he saw.

Bits of white, and spiky things, then something dark, something completely unfamiliar. Until he recognized a fish fin, then another, and the dots of dark color turned out to be eyes, and the spiky things bone, and—

Then two things moving amongst the pile of cleaned fish, with quick jabbing movements, darting here, darting there, until one popped up in the pile.

Daver had never seen one before.

Not a real one. In cartoons, yes, and comics, but not real one, not even in Brooklyn. But the nose and tail were so recognizable as the fat gray rat burrowed and scurried amidst the giant pile of dead fish. Another rat surfaced, and its tail made a slithery noise as it glided over the wet slimy fish flesh. They both made squeaking sounds, as if they were talking, excited maybe they had found something that they could actually eat, something that wasn't bone, that wasn't only a rubbery fin.

And Daver noticed this:

The rats, both of them, took no notice of him. They were only five, maybe six feet away. Surely they could tell he was there, they could smell him, see him?

Yet they kept up their digging, scurrying.

Daver backed up, thinking, *Maybe this isn't a good place to come. Maybe I shouldn't ever come back here again.*

Another step, eyes locked on the rats. He didn't want to turn, to make noise and somehow let the bold rats—that's what they were, *bold*—see him.

Do rats bite? Do they attack?

Another sliding step in the sand, and he was almost back to the edge of the building, leaving the nasty rats to their feast.

Another—

When someone grabbed both his arms.

Then Daver made a noise, some kind of strange cry, and the rats looked up.

* * *

A middle-aged couple, the man in a striped seersucker jacket and pants, the wife a bit too fleshy in her sleeveless dress, sipped wine at one corner of the bar.

The writer still sat at his spot. Every now and then, he'd pull out a small pad and make notes.

Though on his third gin and tonic, Ted was glad to see him finally taking his time with the latest installment of alcohol.

Tending bar was one thing, dealing with drunks was quite another.

A waitress, Julie, the new one, came to the side of the bar. She was older than the others and looked more at ease.

"Two red wines and a Coke," she said.

"Coming up," Ted said. He pulled down two red wine glasses—at least he knew what color wine went in what shaped glass—and uncorked the liter of cabernet.

As he poured he felt the girl's eyes on him. One glass, then the other. Still, she stared.

"You the regular bartender?" she asked.

"Does it show that badly? Thought I was doing a good job of pouring."

As if to prove him a liar, a drop of red wine hit the outside of one glass and dribbled down the side. He grabbed a bar towel and wiped it.

"Just filling in."

She smiled again.

And Ted thought, *I could be crazy, but is she flirting with me? What's with the stares?*

In which case he'd better disabuse her of any ideas.

"I'm married to Liz. The woman who hired you."

Julie nodded, but she held her stare. Then, "Nice to meet you."

It didn't seem like his information had changed anything.

He smiled back and didn't do anything for a second.

Then Julie said, "And the Coke?"

"Oh, right. Sorry."

Good one, Ted thought, *get a little lost in some kind of fantasy with the new attractive waitress, and forget part of the drink order.*

He placed the drinks on her tray.

"There you go."

"Thanks," she said as she turned away.

And for a moment Ted felt as though he had lost some kind of competition.

Score one for the waitress.

"And what do you think you're doing back here?"

The man held Daver's arms tightly, almost pinching him. His face was close enough that Daver smelled the strong stench of something bad.

The rats had scurried away at the man's voice, and now flies hovered over the fish carcasses.

Daver turned back to see the man.

"I just came back here, I just wanted to see—"

"I just, I just . . . This is no place for the guests. This is for the workers, and for garbage, and—" the man laughed. "For the rats. You don't want to play with the rats, do you?"

Daver shook his head, feeling scared.

The man released Daver's arms. "Well, if you don't want to play with the rats, there's nothing else back here."

Daver wanted to tell the strange smelly man that he wasn't a guest, that his mother ran the inn, that he lived here.

But instead he just stood there, shaking, trying hard not to cry.

"Rats, my tools—" the man banged the shed door. "Nothing to play with here." He laughed. "So get out of here."

Daver nodded but didn't move.

"Go on," the man said.

Then Daver turned and ran back to the screen door.

* * *

Ted poured himself a club soda, still rattled from his encounter with Julie. *Funny,* he thought, *how even the things we think can make us feel guilty, and how that guilt makes us do stupid things.*

He drank down the soda.

The writer took out his pad again and wrote something.

"Why not just leave it on the bar?" Ted asked. "Not like we're jammed for space."

Bridger looked up.

He nodded. "Wouldn't want to unsettle some of the"—he lifted his tumbler and made a little salute with it—"good Abbadon Inn guests."

Ted walked a bit closer.

"Your next novel? Something scary?"

Ted was no reader. The *Daily News* and some books for his police courses, that was about it. Oh yeah, and a Dirk Pitt novel on their last summer vacation in Old Forge. Books weren't really part of his life.

"Novel?" Bridger shook his head. "I wish. But definitely scary, my friend."

Now the writer killed his drink.

"Another?" Ted asked without a great deal of enthusiasm.

Bridger made a broad smile. "No, think I had enough for now. How about a Coke?"

Had Bridger witnessed the little exchange with the waitress? And was the order of a Coke a little jab, a little playful. *I saw what happened, I know what you were thinking.*

"Coke, sure."

Ted filled a glass. Then to cover his faint tinge of embarrassment, he said, "So, something scary . . . but not a novel. What is it then?"

Bridger watched Ted carefully, and any evidence of a smile evaporated from the writer's face.

"Well, if it's not a novel," he said as if delivering a

lecture to a schoolboy, "if it's not something I made up, then what would it have to be?"

Ted looked at the man. He wasn't sure what to make of the writer. Combative, weird, a little crazy. Maybe all three?

"Not made up. Then, I guess it's something real."

Now Bridger smiled.

"Exactly. Something real. Something we call the 'truth.'"

"So you're writing the truth about something. So what, if I might ask, are you writing the truth about?"

Bridger took a sip of the Coke. *This bastard's enjoying the suspense,* Ted thought, beginning to decide he didn't much like this long-term resident of the Abbadon.

"Why, it's something you'd be very interested in. Or should be."

"Yeah? What's that?"

"The truth about this place." Bridger looked around. "The truth about the Abbadon Inn."

"Truth? It's an inn. What truth?"

Has it gotten colder? Ted wondered. His arms had a bit of gooseflesh, as if a sea breeze had blown into the bar.

Bridger looked at his watch.

"You asked the right question." He stood up. "And my guess is that back in—where are you from, Brooklyn?"

"Yes. How—"

"That back in Brooklyn you aren't a bartender. That would be my guess. As for the truth, there's so much of it I'm afraid I have no time now. Got an appointment. Someone to see. Way the hell over on the other side of this sleepy town."

Damn good storyteller, Ted thought. *Has* me *wanting more.*

"But don't worry. I'm not going anywhere for a while. We'll talk again."

Ted nodded. *A strange guy with strange secrets.*

And based on the two games Ted had just played, one

with Julie, the other with Bridger, he'd have to say that now he was oh for two.

"Excuse me, could we have refills?"

Ted turned back to the dapper couple sitting close, with their now-empty wineglasses.

THIRTEEN

Daver ran into Liz at full speed, and the force of his crash sent her banging into a wall.

"Daver!"

He stood there, eyes wide, looking up. Liz saw a few guests in the dining room looking down the hallway at her.

"Why did you do that?"

For a second, Daver said nothing, just stood there, eyes blinking, until Liz recognized that her son was struggling not to cry. She put a hand on his shoulder.

The kitchen door opened, and Julie came out with an expertly balanced tray held high. Liz nodded and smiled.

Then she leaned close to Daver.

"What happened, Daver? Did something happen to you?"

His eyes darted left and right, and for a moment Liz's imagination was filled with the horrible fantasies of all those bad things that could happen to your children, fantasies vague but loaded with the power to destroy, to terrify.

Finally, as if enduring torture, Daver looked up.

"I went out back."

Out back. Liz knew that there was the Dumpster for garbage, a shed for tools and paint, a place used by the men working on the tower rooms. Nobody ever went back there.

"Why did you go back there?"

Liz heard the disapproval in her voice and immediately regretted it.

"I—I was bored. Megan had that stupid *Barney* show on. There's a door. I just went out there."

Did he do something back there? Is that what this is about? Did Daver touch something he shouldn't have? Break something? Is that it? Did he get in the shed?

"There's the little house . . ."

"The toolshed."

He nodded.

"And, and—I got a splinter. The wood is all splintery." As evidence, he held up his finger. And as he went on with his tale, Liz started relaxing. After all, nothing *really* bad could have happened, could it?

I would have heard that first. That's the first thing he would have said.

"I tried to get it out."

"You should have come to me."

He nodded again, barreling on with his story. "I squeezed my finger hard, really hard. I got it out. Even without any fingernails."

She smiled. Her bright-eyed son without fingernails. How many times did she think about the small anxieties that made him chew at his fingernails? What conversations between her and Ted had he heard?

So hard, Liz thought, *being a parent, being a wife.*

Just *being.*

So damn hard.

"I got it out, and then I heard sounds."

"Sounds? What kind of sounds?"

"I didn't know, but I walked around the shed. And there was some old stuff from the garbage, chunks of fish, bones, and rats—" He had said the word *rats* loudly. A couple was standing in the lobby talking to Ari, and they turned to look at Liz and Daver.

She leaned closer and gently said, "I wouldn't say that word too loudly." She looked at the lobby. "Know what I mean?"

Daver's eyes shot over to the reception desk. "Oh, right."

Liz gave him another gentle squeeze. "I'm glad you saw them. They could be a problem, a big problem. But I will talk to men who do the work on the grounds, and—"

Daver shook his head.

"No. That's not it. I saw the rats and just stood there. I was frightened, and this man came up behind me."

Immediately, Liz was back into fear mode. The next words could take her almost anywhere, and she knew only one thing: they wouldn't take her anyplace good.

"What happened then, Daver?"

"I backed up into this man. He held me there and asked what I was doing. He was scary, Mom, really scary."

Again, her son teetered close to the edge, right up to the point of tears.

"It's okay, Daver. You understand, it's okay."

Another look toward the reception desk, and the couple still seemed engrossed in their little scene transpiring in the hallway.

Hardly any privacy in this damn inn, she thought. *My family and my life constantly exposed.*

"He held my arms and asked me what I was doing back here. I told him—I told him that you ran the place, that, that—" Daver stopped. "But he didn't care, Mom, he didn't care!"

Liz looked her son right in his crystal blue eyes. She didn't want him to leave a single detail out. Nothing.

"And then—?"

"He finally let go, and I ran in here. Ran to tell you."

Liz took a deep breath, so grateful to be at the event's end. "Okay, there are a couple of things to tell you, alright?"

"Yes."

"First, I don't want you going back there, ever. It's for the garbage and the tools and the workmen. Just don't go back there, okay?"

"Alright. I won't."

"And here's the most important thing. Ready?"

"Okay."

"Don't tell your father what happened."

Liz knew Ted. She knew exactly how he would react. People become cops for a reason. And some of those reasons might not be too good. Ted used to tell her that some of the guys he worked with could easily work for the other side. They could work either side, as long as they got to push people around and play with guns.

Then there were the others.

Cops like Ted. Cops who viewed the job as a way of keeping the universe from chaos.

A way to make things right.

That was Ted.

He was hardwired for doing the right thing. But he didn't get it from his parents, both of whom were too busy just getting by to spend much time molding their son's world view.

And should anything threaten to send his world closer to chaos? Whether it was the back streets of Red Hook, or a choppy sea in winter, Ted would do whatever had to be done. No questions asked.

If Daver told his father about the man who scared him, it wouldn't be pretty. And right now Liz didn't need any more stress.

"Do we have a deal?" she asked.

"Yes. But Mom—"

"Uh-huh?"

"Does that man work here? Will I seem him again?"

"He probably does, Daver. And trust me, I will talk to him. Just a stupid man who does some work around the building, you understand?"

"Yes."

"So now, why don't you go back into the kitchen and ask the Goudge sisters to fix you and your sister some nice plates of ice cream, okay? Tell them that it's a special order from the boss."

And there—just a flicker—a smile. The clouds parted. The moment passed. They had a deal.

She had to hope that Daver could keep a secret. Then she could give the worker a piece of her mind. Maybe even fire him—though that could present problems. The locals were probably a close-knit group. Until she understood the politics of the inn and Cape May, she was better off treading lightly.

Daver went though the swinging doors for some ice cream, and Liz had to think, *God, do all mothers love their children this much?*

Bridger walked away from the sound of the surf, the sky and ocean both now darkening to equal shades of indigo.

Every day here he felt more a part of this beautiful seaside town.

And he thought, *Every day I know more and more of its secrets. Eventually, I'll know more about this town than anyone.*

But it wasn't really the town he was interested in.

Not that the town didn't have an interesting history. Fascinating, from the mid-nineteenth century when it became a place to escape the hellish heat of Philadelphia and Washington, and even New York. The queen of the ocean resorts, the grande dame. A place for the wealthy, who'd only look at the sea, let the breeze wash over them as they swirled their bourbon in glasses filled to the top with ice hauled from the great icehouses of the Adirondacks.

That is until Prohibition, when more sordid characters entered the picture. The gamblers, the rumrunners, those who used the genteel seaside town as a cover for an operation that supplied booze up and down the coast.

Yes, all very interesting, and each of the old inns with a part to play, each with its cast of characters.

He was learning a lot.

But Martin Bridger had started specializing. Not all of Cape May, not even all the storied inns and their tales.

Just one.

The Abbadon.

It was a natural fit. An inn with tales of murder behind its walls, murder and debauchery. Home to the finest bordello in a town that was soon renowned for its bordellos. But with a difference.

An inn where people vanished, while someone used the inn as base for—what?

Ah, that he didn't know.

Not yet. There was a hole in the tales of the inn, a hole firmly centered in the 1920s. Dark years, where the history of the people who lived there, worked there, had vanished.

He had some names, a few events. The strange puzzle was slowly coming together.

But long ago, Bridger realized that his staying at the Abbadon wasn't about writing fiction anymore.

No, fiction was an idea that had long since passed.

He turned down a street where the pavement was cracked. Probably on some neglected list to get repaired after the summer season ended, or maybe after the next season.

Or perhaps these cracked sidewalks were far enough off the beaten path that they'd never ever be repaired.

Bridger looked around. Quite desolate here. Funny, nerve-wracking, especially for a horror writer.

You write scary things, and then it's so easy to imagine scary things.

His steps were the only sound.

Then, a bit of movement to the side, and twin cat eyes glowed from atop a metal garbage can. The cat watched him.

It's okay, kitty. I'm not about to disturb your prowl.

He looked at the house number as he passed a building.

Looking for number twenty-seven.

He passed a few clapboard houses that all looked ripe for a paint job or the convincing sales pitch of a siding salesman.

But then, you need money to put siding up. And none of the residents of these places were likely to have any money for either paint *or* siding.

What we have here is skid row, Bridger thought. Shanty-town. A place way off the map and in none of the travel brochures.

Then—

Number twenty-seven.

The worst house on a block filled with ramshackle joints.

Bridger stopped for a moment. He felt as excited as a kid. Who'd think that inside that house there were so many secrets revealed, with so many more to come.

Each night, a few more, bit by bit, as Bridger's note-books filled, as the pieces came together.

He pushed open a crooked gate and walked up the cracked walkway to the door, cracks yielding overgrown tufts of grass.

Bridger walked up to the screen door and knocked.

"Come to bed."

Ted stood at the window.

"Dunno. Kinda wired tonight. The bar got a little busy. Did you see that?"

"Yes. Too crazy for you?"

He turned to her. "You mean, like maybe I'll start hitting the bats and balls again?"

"I hate that expression, 'bats and balls.' Makes hard drinking sound like some kind of kid's game."

"Every rummy in every sad smelly gin mill in Brooklyn uses it."

"Exactly."

"Anyway, I think I'm well over my alcoholic phase, okay? Had a few beers after I closed up. You know, I actually liked it, doing the bar I mean . . ."

For a second she saw him hesitate. As if he had something to say, but held back. Too late to press him.

And Liz thought, *I hope he can't read me as easily.*

"So come to bed."

"Yeah, I thought—"

She kicked the covers off, revealing her short purple teddy.

"No *nothing*. Come to bed, and let's unwind you *and* me a bit."

"If you insist. I guess we're a bit overdue, hmm?"

"Way overdue." She looked around the room. "I wonder how many people have played in this room?"

"Tons." He walked over and sat on the bed. "You can almost feel all those decades of horny guests." His hand started a slow caress at her knee, then up, until it hit the short teddy. He kept on pushing, sliding the material up. "Can't you?"

"Now I can." She laughed. "Absolutely."

It was late when Bridger finally reached Ocean Drive.

In the east, over the ocean, he saw the first pale shade of purple, as the night got ready to yield to the sun.

No way he could go back to his room on the third floor and sleep. He'd walk by the ocean and think.

At one point a police car passed him and slowed, studying him. Bridger nodded, waved.

No, I'm not drunk, he thought. *Just so incredibly excited, officers. Yes, and I know it's a tad late. Or early. But if you knew what I knew, you couldn't sleep either.*

He stopped and turned to the ocean.

That's part of the story, too, isn't it? The town, the Abbadon, and the sea.

All connected. The picture slowly becoming clear.

That is, if you believed it all.

And did he? Did he believe something that would make even his faithful readers blink? Readers who could buy into almost anything? Aliens buried under icy mountains. Undead things that could assume any shape. People cursed with powers that twisted their minds in terrible directions, sending them spiraling into some private hell of death.

His readers bought it *all*.

But . . . could they buy this?

He laughed then, aloud, as even more light crept though the opening of the black curtain of the sky.

Would they buy it even when it might all be true?

God, and if it was all true, there would be only one person gathering all the pieces.

Me.

The ocean picked up the first hint of light from the east. The tiny spits of white on the choppy sea now visible.

Alive, moving, churning.

Bridger shivered, then moved on.

II

And the Sea
Shall Claim Them . . .

FOURTEEN

The boat, a powerful charter fishing boat fitted with deep-range sonar and outrigger fishing wings, kicked into high speed as soon as it left the docks of the Cape May harbor.

The morning sun shined like a massive searchlight, blinding, a brilliant white light that made the choppy surf glisten as though the surface had been sprinkled with diamonds.

Jack Tyler, CPA and private financial advisor, and his business friend, Ken Spoletta, sat in the front of the boat.

They both smiled, the anticipation on their faces making them look like kids.

For Captain Andy Berg, he'd seen it many times. Eager, successful guys who could easily afford the $1,000 fee for the boat, his services, and that of his mate, Carlos—all for the chance to bring home a trophy.

Captain Berg himself knew well the world they came from, the world of high-pressure meetings and world-spanning trips in pursuit of clients and financial deals.

Heart-attack land.

So a decade ago, after a big pre-bubble-burst score, Andy bailed from the street to the sea and never looked back.

Funny thing, he actually made money doing this. The *Wanton Lady* was his second boat, state of the art, fast as hell, and perfect for bringing home anything from a giant marlin to a rogue hammerhead.

Though he didn't tell his clients today, it was much more likely that it would be a hammerhead they'd bring home. Still, a nice ten-foot hammerhead made a nifty trophy. Though explaining to the wife why you had to have the monster stuffed and mounted, at the cost of another thousand, could add stress to what for many of them had to be already rocky marriages.

The wives didn't love a big stuffed fish hanging over the fireplace, with dull glass eyes and jagged teeth.

The perfect accent for the holidays.

And though the aquatic taxidermists who waited for the charters back at the dock never told the clients, there wasn't a hell of a lot of their big fish that was used for the trophy.

The teeth, some of the head. The rest, just a generic plastic foam cast, which the customers thought was made from the actual fish.

Which, Cap'n Andy knew, was bullshit.

Carlos came beside him. The young Puerto Rican worked his butt off, wanted his own ship someday. You could have ambition, even here in the deep waters off Cape May.

"Captain, they'd like to come up. It's okay?"

Andy nodded. "They're paying for the ride, Carlos. Send 'em up."

In a moment, the businessmen, dressed in khaki shorts, sparking white sneakers, and tasteful IZOD polo shirts, were standing by the helm.

"This baby moves, hmm?" the shorter one said.

Captain Andy turned and gave them both a big grin. "Want to see how fast?"

More gleeful little-kid smiles.

"You bet," Ken said.

Andy pulled the throttle back nearly all the way, and the two customers rocked back on their feet before grabbing a railing to steady themselves.

"Holy shit!" Jack said.

"Great to have when the storm clouds roll in, you know?" Andy said. Another smile. Entertainment was part of the business, and he didn't really mind. Not if it got him out on the sparkling water all summer long, and then let him travel and hibernate during the icy cold winters.

He eased up on the throttle.

"Burns up a lot of gas though, but good to know its there."

"Nice boat," Ken said.

"Yeah—wanted this one for a few years before I took the plunge. Has everything. See here?"

Captain Andy tapped a round screen.

"Same sonar you find on the pro boats. Hell, better than the sonar on some of the navy's ships. Goes deep, and gives a great picture of the bottom. Shows any movement."

Jack leaned close. The sonar just showed the bottom, a squiggly line that bumped up and down as the boat skimmed the choppy surface. He looked up at the captain.

"Sweet! Guess you're gonna get us some big ones, hmm?"

"You can bet on it, guys."

Though there had been days where the *Wanton Lady* came home empty. Most of the clients took Cap'n Andy's offer of a free trip in the future as a pretty decent consolation prize.

Word of mouth was also important. They'd go back to the pricey expense-account lounges and restaurants of

New York and talk about their trip, the big fish, the great captain.

Ken leaned close for a look at the sonar, then up at the horizon to the east.

"How far *are* we going?"

Captain Andy turned to them, one hand on the wheel—though with an empty sea he could have let it just sail straight on its own.

"We're gonna move off this shallow part of the shelf, and then we'll hit some currents that start to come up from Miami right about now. Nice warm water, bringing *muy* fish. Which means that the fish you want will be waiting right there."

"Marlin? Groupers?"

Time to play the old sage.

"Never can tell, guys. Always a surprise, know what I mean?" The men nodded, in on the cosmic fishing mystery. "And you just gotta love surprises, right?"

Yes, there was a little bit of a performance in this, and that wasn't so bad. Captain Andy found the fish, they did the work hauling them in, and everyone went home happy.

Not a bad deal at all.

Captain Andy watched Carlos toss out buckets of chum in the water, the red quickly gobbled up by the churning foam of the *Wanton Lady*'s twin propellers.

He had already brought the lines in and rebaited them, including the twin metal gauge lines that went down deep.

Right down to hammerhead country.

If nothing decent showed up, Andy hoped he could at least deliver a fat hammerhead that would keep his two clients busy for a few hours. Busy, and aching for days after.

Nothing biting so far, though. And while that did happen on occasion, it was still strange. Andy's right hand rested on the throttle, his left locked on the wheel guiding the *Lady* straight to the east, toward ever-deeper waters.

Come on, Andy thought. *Something's gotta bite.*

He saw Ken and Jack, sucking on their Coronas, having already raided their supply of sandwiches.

Bottom line: boredom was close, then Andy would start to get looks, and then the ole fisherman's attempts at explanation would have to begin. Bad weather to the south, or the current changed, and isn't it a great day for a trip on the sea even if we didn't get any fucking fish?

All of it bullshit.

Complete and total bullshit.

And then, offering them a free ride for another trip someday which would mean a complete and total loss in the future. Build up enough of those guaranteed fish freebies, and it could kill you. *Cut right into my winter snow-bird fund,* Andy thought. Fewer crisp twenties for the dancers at the Pink Flamingo in Fort Lauderdale.

He saw Carlos look up. His mate knew that if they didn't get anything, his chance of a big fat tip from the gringos from the city would vanish.

Andy looked at the mezuzah he had screwed to the side, near the wheel. Not that he was religious. His father hit the temple only when one of his golf buddies croaked. His mother tried a bit of shul with Andy.

But Andy didn't take too well to that.

Still, if there was any place to have a little respect for God, this was it. The sea with its unpredictability and its dangers—man, that had to be God's realm.

"Cap'n, think maybe we should toss a few Coronas in along with chum?" Jack turned to his friend, and they grinned. Still happy campers. But not for long. Andy smiled, cap pulled down low, eyes squinting as he steered into due east. Sonar picked up what looked to be schools of fish; but nothing of size, nothing big sniffing around the outriggers' baited hooks.

Carlos tossed another shovelful of the greasy, bloody chum into the water.

A lone gull enjoying the free lunch swooped down and snatched up a piece of the garbage fish used to entice the real fish to come check out the boat.

"Shit," Andy said to himself.

Another look at the sonar.

Then—he saw something. A moving blip appeared on the screen, vanished, then back, clearly within the net of lines that trailed down from just below the surface to the deep water below.

Come on, Andy thought. *Whatever the hell you are. Come on. Bite!*

Off the sonar again. Fuck.

There. It appeared again.

Definitely interested.

That's right, baby, if you liked the chum, you'll love the good stuff we have on the big lines. And each one wrapped around a nasty little surprise.

A big fat gleaming hook designed to dig into your maw and hold on until you come right up beside the Lady, *and I can put a bullet in your primordial brain.*

Now Andy's eyes were locked on the sonar, waiting, waiting, waiting . . . and then—

The high-pitched scream of one of the lines running out.

Carlos moved faster than the line.

Jack and Ken scrambled to the twin fighting chairs, ready to do battle. The energy level went from zero to a hundred in the bat of an eye.

The line kept running out. Carlos would wait until he had the pole in the first chair before throwing the latch to stop the animal's attempt to flee with the hook it now had embedded in its jaw.

That "line," screaming through the oversized reel, was actually steel-gauge wire.

And chances were what they had here was a shark, most likely a hammerhead.

Not the most glamorous catch.

But hell, thought Captain Andy, *I'll take it.*

I'll fucking take it.

FIFTEEN

Liz moved through the sun-drenched dining room, the carpet bleached by the brilliant sun.

A few tables clattered with the quiet noises of breakfast.
Sugar poured into coffee, a knife cutting a breakfast sausage,
butter spread on perfectly browned toast.

Ted was already down at the beach with the kids. Weather
called for a few days of rain coming up. Bad for business,
but Liz could use the break.

We handled this, she thought. Came into the inn, got
everything humming, answered all the questions.

She was feeling good about her decision.

In fact, could be it was a great idea to come here, she
thought.

But there was one thing she worried about.

Daver's encounter with the workman.

Liz had hesitated in going up to the tower and the third
floor where they worked on the rooms there, doing things
that would probably go on for the whole summer.

An easy job to milk, she guessed.

She hesitated, because she didn't like confrontation.

But the alternative was worse. Tell Ted? Her husband would definitely not underreact. No, Ted would find the guy, and when it came to his kids, he could be scary. He took the job of "dad" very seriously.

Maybe too seriously.

No, best she handle this herself.

Which meant, now that she had gone over the day's menu with the Goudge sisters and checked with Ariella about who was checking out, it was time to go upstairs.

"Whoa, what the hell we got, Captain?"

Carlos manned the wheel, while Andy came down to inspect the rod and line. The rod was embedded in a deep sheath that went between Jack's crotch, about as phallic a symbol as you could get.

In between gasps of air, Jack gave the giant reel a few turns. Then, in answer, the beast on the other end would tug, and the release would play out more of the steel line.

A long, fucking tiring game.

"Wanna give your friend some time fighting our new friend?"

Jack nodded. Andy knew that the businessman's arms had to be aching, no matter how many times he went to the executive heath club. Aching, and it would get worse. They'd return home with a tale and a trophy, and muscle burn that would last for a week.

But also with a lifetime of stories to regale other masters of the universe within the New York City waterholes.

Jack undid his harness, and with Andy guiding him, stepped out of the chair. Tricky moment this; if the creature on the end of the line did anything unexpected, they could be screwed. The fish could start running *big time,* and if they didn't put a stop to it, the line would be all played out.

Basically, game over.

Back to square one, with unhappy fishermen.

Ken took over from his friend, the harness tight over his bulging stomach. He looked eager, but Andy could see that he'd obviously have a tougher time doing the hard work.

Andy glanced at Carlos. At some point, they would probably welcome the mate doing some of the fighting . . . once the novelty wore off and the pain set in. Carlos nodded, getting Andy's wordless message.

The big fish pulled out a few more yards of line.

"Reel, Ken," Andy said. "Every time he takes some, you take some back, too. You gotta *fight* the fish."

Ken looked up, his face beet-red, the veins in his arms bulging.

God, I hope the guy doesn't have a coronary.

Ken reeled in a few feet, then a few feet more.

That's it, Andy thought. *Get tired, fish. Then come up here to the surface. Come see who caught you. And then, you know what? I'll make all of your pain go away with a shell to the head.*

But the line ran out some more. Clearly, the fish wasn't ready to give up just yet.

And that's okay, Andy thought. *It's a beautiful day to be out on the water.*

Liz took the back stairs to the third floor, the old servant's stairs just past the kitchen area that zigzagged up the back of the building. She hadn't spent much time on the third floor. Only a few of the rooms were in good condition, and besides Martin Bridger, there was no one else staying up there.

Liz imagined that when Tollard, the owner, returned, he'd accelerate the room improvements; the painting, the new bathrooms, whatever was on the long list that Mrs. Plano showed her.

The back stairs ended at the far end of the corridor. The three rooms down at this end were closed, as was the entire tower floor. A makeshift barrier closed off this section, an attempt to keep the noise and dust away.

Except there was no noise, no dust.

It was all perfectly quiet.

"Hello?" she inquired.

She moved past one open door. The floor of the room was covered by a fine coating of white powder, a sign that sheetrock had been cut. A light glowed from the bathroom. Liz walked into the room, past the bed, the rich wood frame also covered with dust.

No one here, she thought.

The two workers should have been up here, cutting, sawing, installing, painting, and—

Into the bathroom.

A new toilet lay on the floor on its side, gleaming white. A hole in the floor exposed the pipe for the toilet.

Could it be that they're waiting on a plumber?

Tools surrounded the toilet, an electric drill, a Phillips screwdriver, a scattering of screws. Waiting for something to happen.

Liz turned round. The room, a washed-out sea green, was small. The ceiling angled in a foot or so, giving the room a strange perspective.

Even when the room was all fixed up, it still wouldn't be a place she'd ever want to stay. Over the empty bed frame, Liz saw a painting. A triple-masted schooner churning through an enraged sea. That, too, wore a mask of dust.

Idiots, she thought.

Why didn't they take the picture down? Someone will have to clean it, get the damn dust off. Or maybe the owner was going to toss that bit of maritime kitsch.

Over the bed might be the perfect spot for a velvet Elvis.

She turned and walked out to the corridor.

And then on into the other rooms, all open, all in various degrees of having work done. Or rather, undone. It all looked as if someone had rung a permanent lunch bell, and the workers had disappeared weeks ago. But it was mid-morning. Liz had seen their schedule, the list of jobs they were doing—they should be *here*.

She left a third room, painted a rose red. The floor bore the waffle imprints of the men's shoes who had walked back and forth. She came out to the hallway, past the curtainlike barrier that closed off this end, to the rooms open for business. Bridger's room and a few others, empty now. She walked past the main stairs to the narrow staircase that lead to the tower room.

Maybe they're up there.

Liz had been in that room only once, towering high above the inn, with a stunning view of the sea and the town.

She walked down the hallway. Bridger was most likely still asleep. She rarely saw the writer surface till about noon, always with a gentle smile, his seersucker jacket pocket bulging with a notebook.

Liz had to wonder how people imagined the people who wrote their favorite books. Did they see the little—or not so little—idiosyncrasies that made them writers, made them people who created fantasies out of their head?

People who probably spend a dangerous amount of time living in their fantasy world, lost to their dreams.

Liz reached the separate stairs to the small tower room. She opened the door, and it creaked. Could use a shot of WD-40 there. She started up the stairs. A lightbulb on a wire hung from a rafter. Maybe they were doing some rewiring here, getting some lights.

Up the steps, until she came to the tower room. The air close, humid, thick—she coughed as soon as she entered.

The room's windows were shut tight, and though they were in need of a cleaning, Liz could still see out of them, to the blue-gray ocean, sunlight shimmering off its surface.

But the room . . .

Bits of wood lay on the floor, and a sawhorse next to a ratty chair with a cracked seat exposing tufts of yellow stuffing.

Deserted. Nobody doing anything up here, nobody cutting wood to replace worn planks in the floor, nobody plastering the wall. Again, the room was empty.

Another breath, and Liz felt as if she could taste the veil of dust hanging in the air.

She went to the main window that faced the ocean. Reached down and grabbed the old-fashioned metal handles.

She tugged.

The window didn't budge, perhaps painted into its locked position. Years of reapplying paint sealing the room tighter than—

A coffin.

Her hands froze.

Why did she have that thought?

Coffin.

Why would she think that, here, high above the inn, the sea just there? So far removed from a coffin, removed from the idea of anything buried, but—

Another tug. Useless.

The window was sealed.

Nobody here or in the other rooms. The small tower room felt so close, stifling, as if the walls themselves could be slowly tightening around her, imperceptibly tightening.

She let go of the metal handles and backed up. Her foot kicked a piece of wood, a jagged foot-long section of splintery wood. She looked down and saw that one end had a tinge of red paint.

She took a breath of the claustrophobic air, then she reached down and picked up the piece.

She looked at the jagged end, at the red paint, the deep maroon, the nearly blackish red color.

Paint, she thought.

Paint.

Then, *Not paint.*

She let it fall to the floor, and turned and walked down the stairs, away from the strange, airless room.

"Dad, I'm going in."

"Okay. Just watch how you drift, kiddo. Watch the flags. I don't want the lifeguard to blow his whistle at you. Got that, Daver?"

Ted saw his son smile. "Right, Dad. No whistles. Gotcha."

Then Daver grabbed the boogie board and raced into the surf as though it might all evaporate if his feet didn't hit the water fast enough.

God, how he loved that boy.

The life, the energy, the unblinking bravery that was a nine-year-old boy.

It wasn't until later that fear and doubt and confusion would come, he imagined. All the adult stuff to cloud over that shining light.

He looked down at Megan, marching her horses around her sandy paddock, her back still to the water.

Maybe, Ted thought, *I should just scoop her up and carry her into the water. Maybe that would shake her out of—what is it?—her fear?*

Ted knelt down close to her.

"How's your herd this morning, Megan?"

She looked up at him with her dark eyes, so serious.

"Missy is sick, and now all the other horses are sad."

Ted nodded and made an O with his mouth. "And Missy is . . . ?"

Megan gently stroked the rainbow mane of a pure white horse.

"Maybe something she ate?" As soon as Ted made the

joke, he regretted it. Fortunately, Megan took the question seriously.

"No. It's something else. And the other horses are worried. See, Daddy?"

Ted leaned closer, giving the herd a close inspection.

"Um, yes. I see. Worried horses. Well, I'm sure Missy will feel better in a while. Maybe she'd like to play in the water?"

Immediately, Megan shook her head. "No. No, Missy doesn't like the water. None of the horses like the water. None of them!"

I hear you, Ted thought.

Ted reached out and stroked his daughter's hair. "Maybe some shade then—oh, and speaking of which—"

Ted produced a tube of sunblock, "Time to give you another coat." He opened the top and squirted a big glob onto the tips of his fingers. He coated her shoulders, taking care to let no spot go uncovered.

He heard a whistle.

His head shot up.

One of the lifeguards waved at someone to get between the red flags. But after a quick scan, Ted picked out Daver, nicely between the flags, in the middle of a boogie board ride that sent him shooting up to the shore, wearing a grin that couldn't be larger.

Ted went back to applying a second coat of sunblock to Megan.

SIXTEEN

Liz walked over to Estella Goudge, chopping onions with quick, practiced moves that looked lethal.

The cook looked up and smiled.

"I always cry when I do this," Estella said, wiping her eyes, smiling.

Liz smiled back. "Estella, I went upstairs looking for the workmen. You haven't seen them, have you? They're supposed to be working, and Mrs. Plano is out, so—"

The woman looked away. *Some conspiracy here,* Liz wondered?

"I don't know, Mrs. McShane. But I *did* see one of them out back before. Maybe they're there. Getting tools. Or something."

The cook looked Liz right in the eye, a look that clearly said that there might be more to the tale.

"Okay. Thanks. I'll go check."

Estella nodded and went back to her chopping.

* * *

Ted positioned the umbrella so that Megan and her pony parade were now fully shaded.

He didn't have faith that he had covered all of Megan's exposed spots. One miss, and she'd have a fiery red blotch that would have her in tears.

Just trying not to screw up, he thought.

He reached into a backpack and pulled out the local paper, the *Cape May Star and Wave.*

Some news on the presidential race. Bush versus Clinton. Did any of it matter?

Not in my world, Ted thought.

Then, turning the paper over to scan the bottom half, another piece.

TEENAGERS STILL MISSING.

He started reading. The state troopers were involved now, searching the desolate area inland, dragging the bay, checking with their friends.

Then the name of the boy.

Peter Tollard. Same name as the owner of the Abbadon. Strange. Coincidence?

Easy, Ted thought, *I'm not a cop here.*

Of course the teenagers could have run away. But then Ted knew that when that happened, somebody knew. A friend, a relative, someone who knew the plan and would come forward.

In this case, there seemed to be nothing.

Big story for quiet Cape May.

The type of story that rattled the locals and didn't go down with the tourists too well. He continued reading the paper.

The paper rattled in the wind . . .

Then he heard the lifeguard's shrill whistle.

He looked up, and the lifeguard was running down to the surf, running toward Daver.

* * *

"Jesus Christ, my arms hurt," Ken Spoletta said.

Captain Andy saw the man grimace as he fought the monster on the other end of the line. Not easy work reeling in a killer fish. They don't call the thing Ken sat in the "fighting chair" for nothing.

Andy turned to Jack. "Jack, I think you better spell him. Unless you want Carlos to do some work on it."

There was a bit of challenge in the comment, as if they might be too flabby to bring the fish in themselves.

Jack answered quickly. "No. No, that's okay. I'm ready to go."

Andy helped Ken lock the reel into position so that he could step away from it.

"Easy now," he said, unbuckling the harness. Ken started to hurry to step out. Andy put a hand on his shoulder. "Steady, Ken. You just wanna step out nice and easy, and—"

The line started running again, as if the fish knew this was a good opportunity to gain some line. Andy still made sure that the man stepped out smoothly. Then he guided Jack into position, buckling him in.

"Don't start reeling until you're all locked in," Andy said.

Jack nodded, buckling the large straps across his waist and chest. Then he looked up at the captain.

"Okay?"

"Okay. Give that fish some fight."

Jack started turning the reel, reeling in a few feet at a time.

"Man, you know, I can feel it getting tired," Jack said. "I can feel the bastard giving up."

Bastard? Is that what he is? Andy thought.

"You're heading down the homestretch, gentlemen. In a few minutes we'll see what you guys got. Tell you one thing—it's big, whatever it is."

* * *

Liz went out the back door by the kitchen. She saw the shed, the Dumpster, the scruffy tufts of grass dotting the sand back there. *This whole area could use some major work,* she thought. It's hidden from the guests, but even at that it looked overly neglected.

Neglected, just like the upper floors.

She saw the shed and walked over to it. The door was open a crack, and she grabbed a metal latch and yanked it open.

A man sat inside, squatting on a crate, an open bottle on his shelf, a magazine in his hands and—in the shadows— she saw him quickly try to zip up his baggy jeans.

Liz felt sick.

"What the hell are you doing?"

The man looked up.

His eyes darted to the bottle, then to the magazine that had just fallen to the floor.

"I—I was on a break."

Liz began to think that maybe she should have had Ted handle this.

"You scared my son."

The man shook his head. "Your son? I didn't scare *nobody.*"

Christ, his words were slurred, not even ten-thirty and the guy was totally in the bag.

"My son came out here, and you grabbed him, scaring him."

The man kept shaking his head, and then his eyes looked up.

Liz spun around. Another man stood there now, blocking her exit from the toolshed that smelled of sweat and booze and God knows what else.

"Gotta problem here, Ed?"

The other worker. Their names came to Liz, quickly

rattled off by Mrs. Plano. Ed and Ralph, brothers or cousins, the guys working on the rooms. The handymen.

Handymen who didn't do shit.

"Are you the one that scared my son?"

The man grinned, chuckled. "The one?" Another laugh, rougher. "The *one*. If you mean if I told that boy that he didn't belong back here, then I guess . . ." He took a step closer to her now, only inches away. Ralph didn't seem to be as drunk—and that scared Liz even more.

"Yeah—I guess then that's me."

The man behind her stood up. Liz looked around the room. This was crazy. She wasn't in Appalachia, this was no backwoods community in fucking Tennessee.

She looked back to Ralph. "You two are supposed to be working upstairs. It doesn't look like you've done any work in days, maybe weeks."

"We, we—" Ed stammered.

But Ralph put up his hand. "We were waiting for supplies, right? Can't do shit without supplies."

"Really? Somehow I doubt that."

Another step closer. "Oh, it's true, lady. Can't do anything without the right supplies."

Liz shook her head. "I'll ask Mrs. Plano about that. But for now, I want you two off the property."

Ralph's eyes narrowed. "What? You're firing us? You're fucking firing us."

"Shit," Ed echoed from behind.

"Until I see what you've done so far, what you're supposed to do. And I don't want you around here scaring my son."

"You can't fire us, lady. You didn't hire us, so you can't fire us."

The shed door flew open, and Liz saw Estella Goudge.

"What are you two doing here? Drinking again? 'Bout all you two do, far as I can see."

And Estella reached in and grabbed Liz, pulling her out into the brilliant sun.

Liz stood by the cook, realizing that maybe she had just been rescued.

"I want you two off the property now. Or I'll call the police."

Ralph kicked at the shed door. Then he turned to his partner.

"Get the fuck up, lame ass." The he turned to Liz, still standing, watching, shoulder to shoulder with Estella. "This ain't over, lady. No fucking way."

"And take your smelly booze bottles, too," the cook said.

Ed staggered out of the shed, and then Ralph turned away, but not before giving Liz a final glance.

Estella patted Liz's arm. "Yup, 'bout time someone fired them. Best thing you've done since coming here, Mrs. McShane."

Liz turned to her. "Thanks for after saving me—"

"Why, I didn't save you, I just—"

Liz squeezed Estella's hand, "And after saving me, you call me Liz, okay?"

The woman smiled, patted Liz's arm, and together they walked back into the Abbadon Inn.

"That fish is giving up. You boys got it?"

Captain Andy signaled to Carlos. "Ken, you want to go hold the rudder steady? I'd like Carlos down here to haul the prize aboard."

Ken nodded like any good loyal seaman and scrambled up the ladder to the pilot's deck. Andy knew that Carlos would put the engine into neutral and all Ken would have to do was keep the rudder straight.

In a moment Carlos stood beside Jack.

Andy leaned close to Jack.

"Okay, this is the beauty part, Jack. Just keep turning that reel, nice and even, nice and steady. And in a few minutes we should get a good look at what you have."

Jack struggled for every inch of metal wire on the spool. But now the clicking turns of the giant reel weren't answered with the singing whine of line being pulled out by the fish.

This fight was just about over.

Just about, Andy thought as he reached over and picked up what looked like a long hollow pole.

"Nice and—"

The fish broke the surface, and for a moment everyone aboard had a fantastic view of the hammerlike head rearing out of the water, teeth gleaming, so visible.

"Shit," said Jack.

Andy stayed close to him.

"Ten feet . . . God, maybe twelve, Jack. Twelve fucking feet of hammerhead."

From above he heard a "woo-hoo." Captain Andy turned and gave Ken a grin. He had the best view from up there. He could easily see the length of the fish from tail to head.

"It's a monster!" Ken yelled down.

Andy grinned. *We got happy customers today.*

"Okay, almost here, Jack. Keep reeling."

Another click, then another, and now the shark stayed on the surface. An hour and half of fighting had left it exhausted, especially with that massive hook buried in its maw, digging deeper.

Andy didn't like the endings of these things. All the mystery gone, the fight gone, the sheer power and terror of the creature vanished.

"Okay, that-a-boy," Captain Andy said.

Andy grabbed the gun and held it close.

"Almost there. Shit, maybe it's even bigger than twelve feet."

In truth, it was a bigger hammerhead than he had seen in years. Maybe the biggest. A true prize. He guessed that one of the men would definitely want to take this baby home, pay the one thousand-plus for a lifetime of bragging rights.

The shark's giant tail splashed the water, which Andy noticed had turned choppier. There was bad weather predicted a few days out—some storm cruising up from the south. And now, despite the sunny skies dotted with puffy clouds, the ocean had turned bumpy.

Let's finish this, Andy thought. *Get the poor bastard aboard.*

Another *click.*

The shark was only a yard or so away from the ship. The three men close to it could now see its dark, empty eyes; no sign of its death terror there. And its mouth opening and shutting, teeth grinding up and down, eager to bite anything.

"Jesus," Jack said.

Andy moved quickly. So many things could go wrong now. A twist of the head to a strange angle, and the hook could work itself out and the prize would swim away. And a hammerhead this big could stress any line, no matter how thick the metal gauge.

It was quite simply one hell of giant fish to bring aboard.

"Okay . . . hold on."

Andy leaned over. He aimed the fish gun at the shark's head, at whatever it had for brains. *Almost over for you, fishee,* he thought. A bad afternoon for the creature was about to end.

He pulled the trigger.

The bullet drilled right between the eyes of the fish. The tail slapped down onto the water, the flailing over. The mouth kept moving, but now with only the most pathetic gumming movements.

As if it was thinking, *I used to be a shark.*

Instead of twelve feet of dead fish meat.

Except it wasn't quite dead. Some involuntary muscle movements would continue.

He looked at Carlos. "Okay, Carlos. Let's bring her in."

The mate opened a door at the rear end of the boat, at floor level, designed for dragging the big catch in. Andy and Jack watched as Carlos took a big hook and, with a forceful swing, planted it inside the shark's maw. He unhooked the line from the reel.

Then Carlos ran back and used the winch to pull the mammoth onto the ship.

Everyone watched silently as the giant hammerhead slid into the boat, inch by inch, sliding its way home. Blood gushed from its maw, coating the deck with a slimy mix of seawater and shark blood.

And as soon as the shark was aboard, Carlos shut the entry door and then ran up to the pilot's wheel.

Time to get home.

Captain Andy turned to Ken—watching all the action from above—and yelled, *Come on down and check out your prize.*

Except Ken wasn't looking down here.

No—instead of watching the incredible spectacle of the shark being hauled aboard, Ken was looking out to sea.

"Ken," Andy said with a bit more excitement than he planned. "What is it?"

You don't work the ocean without becoming hypersensitive to each bit of cloud cover, to each ocean ripple or wave.

In this case, the ripple or wave was the chubby businessman, eyes fixed on some distant point in the horizon.

What the hell could he be looking at? Andy wondered.

He was about to shout and tell him to get his butt down here.

But Ken spoke first. "Captain." Then louder, "Captain! I see something out there. I see someone."

Impossible, thought Andy. *Impossible.*

"Somebody waving, waving right at us."

Andy turned to the general spot Ken was looking at.

The chop was high, two, three feet, and iced with foamy white surf.

But in between the chop—*damn* . . .

Damn if Andy didn't see what looked like arms waving back and forth . . . back and forth.

Except—and this part made his skin sprout gooseflesh under the hot summer sun—he saw what looked like *two* pairs of arms, waving, waving at his boat.

SEVENTEEN

The lifeguard pulled Daver back into the swimming zone and closer to the shore.

Quickly, Ted was there.

"What happened?"

The young lifeguard, a kid with streaked hair and a body toasted the shade of an acorn, squinted and looked up.

"Your boy here drifted away."

"I was okay," Daver said.

Ted turned to him. "What did I tell you?"

They stood in about six inches of water, but Ted could feel the strong, steady pull of the surf around his feet. He had gotten distracted for a few moments by the newspaper article. And in those few minutes his son had drifted.

"You best keep a watch on him," the lifeguard said.

Great, thought Ted, *getting "good parenting" instructions from someone who was what—seventeen?*

"I do. Just looked away for—"

Ted knew his excuse sounded lame.

"The surf's turning nasty. That's why we made the zone narrower. Gets hard to stay in, and throw in an undertow," the kid grinned, "stuff can happen fast."

"Yeah. I know. Hey, thanks. Really."

The lifeguard smiled back.

"It's why we're here."

Ted turned to Daver.

"Go get dried off, Daver, and I'll take you and your sister for some lunch."

For a second it looked as though Daver was about to protest. After all, the rougher the surf got, the better it was for boogie boarding. But their eyes locked, and the young boy obviously thought better of it. He turned and bolted for the umbrella and chairs.

Ted shook his head. "Kid loves the water . . ."

The lifeguard turned to the water, putting his eyes back on duty even as he spoke to Ted. "Yeah, and he probably thought he was okay. They always think they're okay. Until all of a sudden they aren't. Then . . ." a glance at Ted, no smile now, "sometimes it's a question of whether we're fast enough."

Ted looked back up to the umbrella, and Daver drying himself, Megan in the sand. Everything okay now. Everything nice and safe.

"You think that's what happened then? To those two kids?"

You mean Tollard and his girlfriend?"

"You knew them?"

"Sure did. Not buds, but I knew them."

"So maybe they went for a late swim, and they—"

But the lifeguard shook his head. His eyes still scanned the surf.

"Tollard was a better swimmer than any lifeguard on the beach. A champ at high school. Longtime Cape May boy. No way he screwed up in the water."

Funny, thought Ted, *how quick the instinct comes back.* Asking one question, then another, then—

"So you think maybe they ran away together? Just left?"

The lifeguard hesitated a moment.

Ted's question hit something. Ted knew the feeling, when the right combination of words . . .

"No."

"No?"

The lifeguard gave Ted a quick glance. "No. I don't think they left. Something happened to them. But damned if I know what."

Ted looked at the young boy scanning the water.

Something else . . .

And from the tone in the boy's voice, Ted guessed it was something that maybe scared him a bit.

The unknown.

Nobody likes the unknown.

"Okay, well I better get some hot dogs into my kids. And thanks again."

The lifeguard nodded. "No problem."

Ted trudged up the sandy incline to Daver and Megan, sitting and waiting on the sunlit beach.

What the fuck? Andy thought,

Two people out here, what the hell—out here! *How did they get here? How could they have stayed alive?*

Carlos was down below, securing the mammoth hammerhead to the boat as the choppy surf rocked him back and forth.

And that was another thing. The surf had passed way beyond the point that Andy liked, past that point where it's just a normal surf with some white caps and chop, to something else, something unpredictable, something dangerous.

Normally, it would be time to head back to Cape May *pronto.*

But now he was rescuing two people bobbing in the open sea, miles, goddam *miles,* from the shore.

Jack came up to him.

"Amazing thing, huh?"

Andy looked at him.

"Amazing?"

"Those two people out here, and we just happen to be in the area. What do you think happened to them?"

They were close now, and Andy made out a man and a woman, then—no . . . they were younger. He grabbed his binoculars from a small shelf below the wheel.

They were kids, teenagers.

He put the binoculars down. "I don't know."

The *Wanton Lady* slammed particularly hard into a wave, and it sent Jack rocking toward Andy. He scrambled to right himself.

"I mean, how did they get here? I didn't see any other boat."

Andy shook his head. He didn't see a boat either. No boat, nothing, just the two kids.

He eased up on the throttle. As he got closer, he could see the kids waving their arms, and then vanishing in the trough of the swells. There they were—and then they were gone.

Up and down, the boat closer, Andy easing up, until—

"Carlos!"

And Carlos left the giant shark and clambered to the front of the charter boat, grabbing a long metal gaffing rod, ready to extend it to the people in the water. They could grab it, Carlos could pull them closer, throw down a ladder and—

Now only yards away, and Andy could see their eyes.

Deep, sunken, scared—terrified. They looked right at him, pleading, begging for help—

Or—

Andy felt a chill. Something else there besides fear. Something besides begging for help.

An icy breeze ran over his forearms, raising gooseflesh.

The boat rocked left and right now with the churning of the swells. His two clients each held on to railings because otherwise they'd get thrown off, tossed right into the sea.

Andy moved the throttle into neutral; so hard to navigate, so hard to get closer.

The two teenagers rose on a swell, and then—

And then—

Right before Andy's eyes . . .

They slipped below the water, vanishing into trough.

Andy yelled, "Carlos, help them!"

But even Carlos had to hold on to a rail, lowering his center of gravity. Andy watched his mate scan the water.

The two people, the two survivors with hollow eyes, just vanished.

The wind turned chillier. Either that, or the cold feeling came from another ill-defined thought Andy had. They had raced to this location, to this spot, to save these two people—who then promptly disappeared.

And what does that sound like? Andy wondered.

He gave the engine a little power as he tried to circle the spot where he thought they had vanished. But that spot, wherever it was, had by now vanished in the foam and chop. There was no "spot" anymore, and neither he nor Carlos, apparently, could see anything below the churning water.

Andy heard someone hacking, the horrible sound of someone puking in an almost animal way, trying to empty their guts of any food.

He looked over to catch Ken hanging his head over the side, hacking, wheezing, bucking as he held onto the rail.

Which was when Andy felt the first bump.

That first nudge wasn't anything that came from the play of crisscrossing waves and water.

A different kind of bump. A bump that pushed the boat *up*. The first one subtle, as if testing.

Then a bigger bump, like something hitting the boat from below.

Andy's hand remained locked on the throttle.

With this second bump, he saw Ken go flying over the edge, head over heels, into the water.

Fuck.

"Carlos, *vamanos!*" he screamed. But Carlos was at the bow holding on to the rails like a human spider.

Gotta save him, Andy thought. And at the same time he thought of his condo on the south end of town. The living room with his giant TV, and the bar so well stocked with bourbon and vodka, the woman he saw from time to time, meeting her at Flanagan's for drinks before bringing her back . . .

Images of his life.

He scanned the water for Ken, and after a moment, he did see him, fighting the surf. Jack was on the other side of the boat, rolling on the deck, so close to the hammerhead, squatting a bit, then slipping, holding on.

Did he know that the bumps had nothing to do with the sea, that these bumps had nothing to do with the surf? That something else was rocking the boat?

Or, Andy thought, *am I the only one who has this bit of information?*

Another bump, and this time Andy watched the bow of the *Lady* dip right under the water, soaking Carlos, who held on for his life.

Andy looked around for Ken.

Gone.

Sure, how long could anyone fight that?

And in the next few seconds, amazing things happened.

When the boat righted itself, Andy looked down and saw that Jack had slid even closer to the hammerhead lashed to the inside of the boat, so close that his body pressed against the shark's body.

And as Captain Andy pulled back on the throttle, he saw

the hammerhead's mouth open—and then, watching it all happen, it closed on Jack.

A dead shark, twitching with reflexes, oozing blood from a bullet to the brain, now biting down on the man next to him.

Jack's scream was lost in the howling wind and the sound of the waves smacking the boat.

Andy pulled back on the throttle, but the boat didn't go anywhere. Were the propellers out of the water as the ship rode a wave? Or were they perhaps gone?

The next bump brought the sound of cracking fiberglass and wood, the scream of metal splitting. And then Andy was thrown forward, the boat's angle sick, almost looking down at the crazy sea, and he knew his boat had been split into two . . .

And his half was now relentlessly corkscrewing right into the water.

EIGHTEEN

Martin Bridger suddenly awoke.

His room in the Abbadon filled with a dull light. Sometimes the summer sun was so brilliant it would paint the room in a golden glow. And at those times he almost felt safe here.

But now the room was filled with a grayish light that made it impossible to tell what time of day it was.

Was it early morning, the sun barely up? Or had some Atlantic clouds rolled in, making the daylight a dull, gray glow?

He didn't hear anyone working down the hallway. But then he hadn't heard *anyone* working for days at the other end of the third floor.

The bits of his dream started to melt away. He could remember being in a room, and he couldn't breathe. And then, the room was filled with water, and people in tuxedos and dresses, partying in this sunken room.

So crazy . . .

One by one, the guests left the room to go somewhere else, walking through the gray-green water, walking through a door.

Until it was just him and a young woman. She looked right at him. Not exactly inviting him to join her, but not telling him to stay away either. Then she turned and walked through the door.

And in that dream, Bridger started walking toward the doorway.

And he remembered thinking, even in the dream, *I can use this! This is so strange, so terrifying, somehow I can use this!*

Until he got to the doorway and could see beyond.

Into total darkness. The blackest night, the absence of all light and color, a total abyss just past the threshold.

In the dream, he knew he couldn't go there.

Couldn't really follow everyone into that total blackness.

But he didn't have to. Slowly, as if seeping from the blackness in front of him, a cloud, a red filmy cloud of water came toward him.

He backed up, but the red cloud kept pouring into the room, surrounding him, filling the room. He clearly knew what the red cloud was. That was obvious from its color, from its filmy texture.

He tried to get to a spot in the underwater room where the blood couldn't touch him.

He fell to his knees, and now the cloud surrounded him. There was just this one small spot that wasn't red yet, as it closed in, swirling. He shook his head; he tried to scream.

But you can't scream underwater. The sound is too garbled, muffled, and strangled.

Until the red cloud finally touched his face, and it was complete.

He woke up sweating.

Now, he looked at a glass on the small table near the bed, filled with a mixture of whiskey and tap water, unfinished from the night before. He reached out and took a warm sip; he was so dry and parched, and he didn't want to get out of bed, didn't want to look at his watch on the dresser by the window.

One quick sip.

Then he'd go back to sleep. He didn't care what time it was. The last bits of the dream faded, like icicles melting in spring warmth.

Good, he thought. *Let it fade, let it go away.*

Some dreams he didn't give a shit about how good they might be for his writing.

Too damn high a price to pay.

He slid under the covers, the bed chilly now. He pulled a pillow close as he grabbed another one and wrapped it tight around his head.

There, he thought.

Like when he was a boy and the covers protected him from everything, all the monsters, all the creatures that waited down the hallway, under the bed, inside the closet.

He held the pillow tight.

And soon was back to sleep.

"Come on guys. Time for lunch."

Ted looked at the surf. The lifeguards had made the swimming zone even smaller as the breakers rolled in at an ever-increasing rate. And the clouds above the sea had turned nasty.

"I think it might even rain."

That made Megan look up. "Then no ice cream today?"

The disappointment in her voice was overwhelming.

"Well, maybe, if I can get you two to hustle a bit, we can get there, and then back to the inn before it rains."

"Come on, Daver! Hurry!"

Megan slipped on her jellies, her pink, see-through beach sandals, and then started gathering up her herd.

Daver also moved, but a bit more slowly, solemnly.

Was I too hard on him? Ted wondered. Nothing more scary then thinking your kid's in danger. Made the old testicles snap up tight to your groin. Not a good feeling. But still, he might have been too hard on him.

Ted reached out and tousled his son's sandy-brown hair.

"Ice cream sound good to you, kiddo?"

Daver nodded, putting on his flip-flops and then folding his Superfriends towel.

"Sure."

Guess I'll have to talk to him a bit, Ted guessed, *and undo any emotional bruises.*

Not an easy job this, he thought, *being a parent. Way harder then being a cop.*

Ted closed the umbrella and separated the two parts of the pole. He tucked them under one arm and then grabbed the aluminum beach chair and closed it with one hand.

"Okay, troops, let's go."

And they walked up to the road, while a steady wind blew at them from the water.

Andy gasped for air. Already he could tell that this pocket of air under the capsized hull was becoming foul, filling with carbon monoxide. The surf sent the chunk of the boat bobbing left and right as Andy held on to it.

Is this luck, he thought?

I fly off the bridge, and find a bit of the cabin that somehow is floating, that has some air trapped inside, and can protect me from the churning water.

But what happened?

For a moment, Andy pushed the thought away completely.

Best not to think about that now. Just hold on, breathe the fetid air, and hope that the chop doesn't turn the chunk over . . . because Andy figured that there was no way he could breathe on the surface, not with sea churning around him.

Best not to think about . . .

Whatever split The *Wanton Lady* in half.

Split it in two like a toy boat.

And, and—

He remembered seeing Jack, holding on for dear life, next to the hammerhead lashed to the boat, his body sliding close, and then the shark biting down.

What the fuck happened?

He pushed the thought aside again.

I'm alive. That's the important thing. Alive.

Like those two kids he saw bobbing in the water.

Those kids with their hollow, sunken eyes, who slipped below the water when their job was done.

Now I'm one of them. Just like them. Bobbing in the sea, a sea that might calm down. Could happen. The strong winds subsiding, the current turning, and the water settling down as fast as it came to life.

It could happen.

But as Andy rocked back and forth, holding on to the inside of what might be a piece of the galley or even the head, he knew things could get worse. The troughs could keep growing until they became actual breakers crashing over him, smashing this chunk of the boat right down on him. That would be bad.

But not as bad . . . not as bad as the alternative.

He thought back now. Whatever smashed the boat is still here, examining the floating wreckage to see what was still around.

Yeah, that would be worse.

Another swell, and the upside-down "cup" that Andy was under opened to the sea, letting in more fresh air but also sending a wave over his head. When the shelter settled, he could taste the difference in the air and took a deep breath.

Just gotta hang in there.

He thought of his condo, his friends, his life, and how much he didn't want to lose it, as if simply *wanting* it that badly would protect it. He didn't believe in any god, but yet somewhere in his thoughts, Andy was begging.

Don't take it away from me.

Which is when he had the strange thought. *Someone is doing this to me.*

His eyes darted in the artificial darkness of his floating shelter.

Just a feeling. *Someone is doing this!*

But it couldn't be someone. Not with the—monster?— below.

And as he was buffeted left and right, he could now see it down there. Nothing as small as the hammerhead, something bigger, something giant, twisting on itself, turning, before it started back to the surface.

From out of a movie, from out of book, from out of some twisted imagination—and yet totally real.

Andy could see the shark in the dark water below where all color and light started to vanish, working its way up to the surface.

It's work not yet done.

And Andy could only hope, as he started crying— weeping for his life, his world about to be lost—that it would be fast.

But when he felt the thing brush past him, teasingly, toyingly, he knew it wouldn't be fast.

His tears and sobbing filled his small sanctuary.

Another brush made him lose his grip, and he knew with a devastating horror, that, no, it would not be fast, that his terror and fear were all somehow part of it.

And when that first bite came, he screamed as if his voice, his plea, could carry to the mainland.

And in a way that he would never know . . .

It did.

NINETEEN

"Why so glum, chum?"

Daver licked his bubblegum ice cream and looked up at his father.

"I'm not."

"What's 'glum,' Daddy? Is that like gum?"

Ted rubbed Megan's head. They sat on a small bench outside Extreme Ice Cream, Ted between them.

"No, Megan. Glum, it means sad."

"Oh," she said.

"So, you're *not* glum, kiddo? Pretty darn quiet. Just because the lifeguard had to corral you? Happened to me a lot, back when my dad took us to Ocean Beach. Happens to every kid—"

Daver shook his head. "No. Not that. I don't know, I just guess—"

A small alarm went off in Ted's brain. Perhaps there's something wrong here that has nothing at all to do with the choppy surf, an undertow, and a lifeguard's whistle.

"Yeah, you guess *what?*"

Daver looked up at his father. "I don't know. I'm not sure I like it here."

Ted nodded. He had learned, thanks to Liz, that sometimes not saying something could be the best way to get information from the kids.

"Really?"

Daver's tongue worked the telltale drips that threatened to run over the lip of the cone and onto the boy's nicely tanning legs.

"I miss home. My friends, and—"

There. A fateful "and." Something unexpected there.

"And what, Daver?"

The boy turned to his·father. "I ran into this strange guy in the back of the inn." Ted's heart raced, like suddenly traveling on a speeding bullet train and not knowing where it's going.

"Some guy?"

Again, trying not to ask too much, to not cut off the communication.

"Guess he worked there. Did work. But he scared me. Grabbed me."

Ted wanted to crush his own cone at the words. He forced himself to keep steady.

"Then what?"

Daver looked away. "He let me go. I think he—well, he smelled funny. I ran away. Told Mom."

And Liz did not tell me . . .

Ted put an arm around his boy. "You told Mom. Good. And you're sure nothing else happened?"

Daver nodded.

"Things like that can scare you. But I bet Mom dealt with it, huh? And nothing like that will happen again. Mark my words."

"Daddy?"

Megan tugged on Ted's faded *Miami Vice* T-shirt.

"What Megan?"

"What does *that* mean? 'Mark my words'?"

He smiled at her. The little girl was listening to the whole thing—even the part about Daver being grabbed. It didn't interrupt her work on the ice cream cone. She just needed the occasional word check.

"It means my words—what I say—are good words. You can believe them."

It's odd to say that, Ted thought. *Such an important thing to say and mean.*

"Okay," she said.

Ted turned back to Daver. "So you understand? That won't happen again? Everything's okay. You're with us, safe and sound. And we're going to enjoy this little work/vacation thing."

Daver looked right at him then.

As if he could peer right into Ted's brain and see if there were any loopholes in the promise, anything that could be wiggled out of.

Then, like the sun finally creeping out from behind a cloud, he smiled. "Okay, Dad."

Ted guessed the boy felt better after telling him what had happened.

Question was, would Liz feel the same way?

But that little discussion would be for later.

Martin Bridger woke up shivering. Despite holding the sheet and thin blanket tight, he felt cold, almost feverish.

He looked around the room, still cast in a grayish pallor.

I have to get out of here, he thought.

Get some air, some food.

All he wanted to do was go back to the old woman. But she said she helped in the church, preparing meals for the well-hidden poor of Cape May. Food for those who some-how didn't get to share in all the tourist dollars that the re-sort town generated.

She didn't want to talk to him at all, he knew.

That's what she had said. But he knew she had the last pieces, the final parts of the puzzle. She'd have to tell him.

Bridger looked around the room, thinking about the le-gion of people who had stayed in this room in the Abbadon over the decades, over the century. So many sounds drift-ing in and out of the room, the lovemaking, the fights, the threats, the hopes.

So much these walls have been witness to.

And Bridger knew that the answer to the mystery lay here.

In the inn.

It was just a feeling, but tonight he'd get his answer.

About what happened back then, when the sea decided to send one of its own to Cape May, and beyond.

Bridger sat up, and the thin white blanket slid off his sweaty body, the air chilling him.

Of course he had just dreamed about that now.

Made perfect sense. You read about something, the wa-ter, the attacks, the faces of the people, the total horror of it. Made perfect sense that he'd dream about it.

At least, that's what he thought.

He reached out for a yellow pad, now with only a few blank pages left at the back. He started scribbling all the images he saw from the dream. The look of the water, the feel of the churning swells, and to be sure—almost as if he himself could feel it—the sensation of teeth *closing*. Now quickly, now slowly, the very act of being eaten prolonged, turned into this torture designed to take a mind into places a mind was never meant to go.

A place where all else vanishes.

Bridger scribbled furiously. The notes barely legible, one blank yellow page filled, then another, and another until there were no more images to transfer to his bulging pad filled with notes.

TWENTY

Liz stood in the dining room while Mrs. Plano averted her eyes, staring at the neatly set tables, the starched linen, the servers circulating in anticipation.

"What do you mean he's not coming?"

Mrs. Plano finally looked up.

"Mr. Plano—Billy—said he didn't, couldn't come here anymore. I'm terribly sorry."

"You're sorry? A little late for that."

Mrs. Plano's eyes narrowed. "I must tell you, Mrs. McShane, I have served this inn for many years and never—never—failed in any of my duties. Mr. Tollard's arrangements with Billy were his own. I'm just conveying the message."

Liz hesitated. She imagined if she pushed too hard, then Mrs. Plano would walk out. And that, quite clearly, would be a disaster of the first order. Mrs. Plano knew how everything ran, where—as the expression goes—all the bodies are buried.

Losing her would put the inn into crisis mode.

So she fought back her anger and then reached out and took the older woman's hand.

"I'm sorry. You're right of course. This inn couldn't run without you."

Did Liz see the trace of a smile at the woman's lips, acknowledging that what she just said was no compliment but merely fact?

"It does leave me in a spot. No barman, the inn nearly full."

Mrs. Plano deftly removed her hand. "There is your husband."

I see, thought Liz. As in: I'm not the only one with a husband problem. Mrs. Plano's is a drunk and useless, and Liz's—well who knows what the problem is there? Why isn't *he* working?

"I know he did fine the other night. But with my running around, the kids . . . it gets crazy."

Behind her, the new server, Julie, had been placing the flatware by the large Abbadon Inn plates.

Then she stopped and came closer.

"Mrs. McShane . . . couldn't help but overhear. I could end my shift after the first serving. That's the busy one, and I'd love to watch your kids."

Liz felt manipulated. First Mrs. Plano with her Billy report, now Julie so ready to shepherd the kids. Liz had to do some fast thinking. Did she know this girl—this young woman—at all? Not really, just that she was a local and seemed to know her way around a dining room and kitchen.

But what other options did she have? She had to be available and couldn't be playing ponies with Megan or talking the relative merit of different superpowers with Daver. Liz looked right into Julie's eyes.

Can I trust her? she wondered.

But her options were nonexistent. Though there had to be sitters in town, for now she was stuck.

"Th-that would be great. You don't mind? I mean, you'll miss the second dinner tips. But, I mean, I'll pay you for sitting. And—"

"I'd love it. They seem so sweet. I've baby-sat lots. And your kids seem great."

"Mrs. McShane, I best see to the cooks."

Liz turned back to Mrs. Plano. "Yes, you go on. I think we're okay."

She turned back to Julie. "Thank you. I'm sure they'll have fun, probably more fun than they'd have with Ted or me."

Julie smiled back.

"Great. I'll look forward to it."

Then Julie went back to her fistful of flatware.

She looked out the giant windows of the dining room. The puffy clouds had turned dark now, some rain surely coming, and—

Where was Ted?

Our new bartender.

Maybe that's not a bad thing, she thought.

Liz watched as Megan came out of the shower, shimmering from a coating of water. Her daughter looked up and grinned.

"I'm freezing, Mommy!"

And Liz was there, swooping down and wrapping Megan in a giant white terry cloth towel that swallowed everything but her head.

"Okay, sport, you're up," Ted said, sitting by the window now flecked with rain.

Daver had his nose buried in a magazine about video games. Amazing, Liz thought. After Atari, who thought video games would come back? Now Daver lobbied constantly for a Nintendo. Not that there was any place here he could use it.

"Daver?" Liz said. The boy looked up and rolled his eyes as best he could. Then he stood up and walked into the bathroom. Liz looked down to the sand dotting the wood floor.

She turned to Ted. "You did get them to spritz their feet before leaving the beach?"

"Yes," he said. "Duh. Of course I did. Their feet act like sand magnets."

Liz grabbed a broom from behind the door and began to sweep the grains into a pile.

"I'll do it," Ted said.

Liz laughed. "It's not that big a job, Ted."

And as soon as she said it, she regretted the tone. She could hear the faint implication . . . the charge in her voice.

I'm working my ass off here, and what the hell are you doing?

She stopped sweeping and walked over to her husband.

"Hey, I didn't mean that. Not the way it came out."

For a moment Ted's eyes stayed steely, narrowed. He had a temper, his famed Irish temper, and sometimes he could slip into a dark place. She'd lose him.

Like she did after that last dive.

Lost him for weeks . . . until finally, something Megan said made him grin. He had looked at Liz then.

That afternoon they made love, and all that pent-up feeling erupted in their lovemaking. And for a while the bad feelings were gone.

She looked over at Megan, now dressed in shorts and a pink blouse with a blue ribbon at the neck.

Liz went to Ted and kissed him.

"I'm sorry."

His eyes finally looked up, widened a bit. His dark cloud didn't come and stay this time. "No *problemo, signora.* Their feet will get the full treatment next time."

Another kiss, and this time she felt him return it. It would be good to just tumble back into the bed right now, with the rain flecking the window. Hold him as close as she could.

"Mommy, is it dinnertime soon?"

She pulled away.

"In a bit, Megan."

She started to walk away from Ted—but now he held her. Her eyes turned to his.

"There's something you didn't tell me."

Her eyes widened, thinking, *Did he already know about his new gig bartending, and Julie helping out? How could he?*

His hands still held hers tightly.

"Wh-what do you mean?"

Ted took a breath. "When we were having ice cream . . . Daver seemed a little distracted. A little quiet."

Small clicks of a tumbler fell into place, and she slowly knew what he was going to say.

"He told you?"

"Question is, why didn't you."

Now Ted released her. He could hear Daver in the shower making sounds, using the soap as a spaceship probably, fighting off aliens in the shower.

"Look, I didn't want to upset you. I know how you can get sometimes."

"How I can get sometimes? Just exactly 'how' is that?"

She grinned. "Don't stand there and tell me that you wouldn't have tracked that guy down and showed him some Brooklyn street justice?"

And Ted laughed at that. "Okay. You are probably right. And I may still do that. I just wish you'd have told me. I can show control."

"Sometimes. But I know how you love those kids."

"Well, as I said, that guy may still have his chance to meet me."

"I fired him and his partner. Didn't look like they were

doing anything anyway. The third floor, the east end—it's a mess."

"If I didn't have the kids maybe I could—"

She reached out and touched his arm. "Now that is something I did want to talk to you about. We have no bartender."

"Billy Plano?"

"Don't know whether he is drunk or just drifting away."

"What about the kids?"

"Julie, the new girl, offered to watch them. Frees you for the evening."

"She seem okay?"

"She's fine. I mean, the kids aren't that hard."

The sound of the shower stopped. Ted looked at the door. "Did you tell them yet?"

"No. But it's not like they haven't had sitters before. Probably be fun for them."

"Oh—and I'm not fun?"

She quickly smiled. "No. You are. They love being with you. But a young girl, someone new? It will be fine. Besides," and now she squeezed his arm, "I really need you to do it."

"Aye aye, lass. One bartender coming up."

"And you best get to it. I'll bring the kids down for dinner in a bit."

"Okay." He started for the door and then stopped and turned back to her. "Gotta tell you though—that guy better not walk into this place, or it isn't going to be pretty."

Liz laughed. "Go!"

And he did.

After dinner and the first sitting in the restaurant, Liz brought the kids into the sitting room. She saw Julie and gave her a nod. The kids stood side by side, little soldiers about to meet the new lieutenant.

"Okay, guys, this is Julie. You've seen her in the dining room?"

They nodded. Liz saw Megan studying the girl carefully. Megan, of the two of them, was the most likely to be suspicious of any new arrangement.

"Hi," Julie said. Then she bent down and gave Megan's shiny brown hair a gentle pat. "You're Megan?"

Megan smiled and nodded.

One hurdle passed, Liz thought. She quickly looked at Daver who wore the same expression he did on those few Sundays they took him to church.

"And you're David?" Julie asked.

She was half-afraid her son would say something rude like, *Of course I'm David.*

"We call him Daver," Liz said.

"So, Julie will be watching you guys. In the evenings for a bit, while I take care of things in the hotel and Daddy runs the bar."

Then she watched Megan reach out and take Julie's hand. "And what kind of things are we going to do?"

Julie laughed. "Oh, *tons* of fun things. You see, I know this old inn very well . . . lots of secrets I can show you."

"Secrets? Like what?" Megan asked.

"Hidden places, places that people just forgot about."

Liz leaned close to Julie and whispered. "Nothing scary. Megan scares so easily."

"Of course."

Liz smiled. "So, I'll see you guys later. Maybe you can walk to Delano's Market if it stops raining. Pick up some munchies."

"How about you guys show me your room for now?" Julie asked. And in a heartbeat, Megan led her away.

Liz stood there watching, thinking, *This is going to be fine.*

TWENTY-ONE

Ted dried some pilsner glasses and placed them on a towel on the bar. It had been quiet, but now the bar action was picking up after dinner. And since this was Saturday, locals would likely drop in to add a little kick to the weekend.

Someone cleared his throat from behind him.

Ted turned to see the writer, Bridger, sitting at the bar.

"The usual, Mr. Bridger? Gin and tonic."

Bridger made a small plastic smile. "Please."

Ted fixed the drink, sliding a curly wedge of lime onto the top of the glass rim.

"There you go."

Bridger took the drink quickly and downed half in a matter of gulps.

The man likes his gin delivered quickly to the system, stat, Ted thought.

"How's the writing going?"

Bridger looked up, and from the look on his face Ted

guessed it wasn't the most welcome question. Or maybe it was just a stupid question.

"I'm not writing. Not now at least."

Ted nodded.

"I'm researching. Got a lot of research to do before I start writing."

"Guess it's nice and quiet up there. The workers gone . . ."

"Workers? I never noticed. I guess it is quiet, I just don't . . ."

Wow, Ted thought, *wherever this guy is, he isn't* here. Maybe that went with the territory for writers. Like cops who have police radios in their own cars, glued to the reports, addicted to the job. Lost to everything but their buddies, and a few bats and balls when a shift was done.

Maybe more than a few bats and balls.

For a moment, Ted was back there, ferried back to the cop bars of Brooklyn by the smell of beer, the scent of freshly cut lemon and lime, the aroma of alcohol that hung in the air.

Steady, he thought. *Steady . . .*

"Well, if there's anything my wife and I can do to make your stay better, easier to work, or—"

Bridger downed the remains of his drink and put the glass down. "Another. I'll have one more before I go."

Ted took the glass.

"Heading out tonight? Still raining. Pretty hard, too."

Bridger looked out the window as if it were the first time he had bothered to check what kind of day it was.

"Yeah, I see. I'll need one of the inn's umbrellas maybe."

"No problem. They have a lot of them by the desk,"

Ted put the refreshed drink down in front of Bridger just as a young couple—laughing, chatting—drifted into the bar.

Good, Ted thought. *Some people to break the spell of the gloomy distracted writer.*

The gloomy distracted researcher.

Researching what, Ted wondered? *And why the hell here?*

He turned to the new arrivals, smiled, and took their drink orders.

Daver looked at his sister holding the sitter's hand.

He wished his dad was still looking after them. His dad didn't much care what Daver did. But this Julie always seemed to be watching him, real close.

She made him just sit there while she and Megan finished some dumb jigsaw puzzle.

For the first time in a few days, he wished he was back home in Brooklyn. And then the thought, *Are we ever going back home?*

Julie turned and looked at him.

"Jigsaw puzzles not your thing, Daver?"

He shook his head. "They're boring."

She nodded and made an O with her mouth.

"Guess they can be. Well, since you've been such a good sport, what do you want to do now?"

"I dunno. Maybe watch some TV. Not that there's ever anything on here. Least at home we had just gotten cable."

"People come here to get away from things like TV. To get away from a lot of things."

She seemed to look at him hard as she said that, as though there was a secret message in her words.

"So what else can we do?" Daver asked.

"Can we go to the store? Mommy said we could go to the store."

Julie nodded, glancing down at Megan, then up at Daver again. "Guess we could do that. But maybe . . ." and now she smiled, a slow smile that immediately had Daver wondering what she might say.

"Maybe we could do something more exciting."

"Exciting. Like what?"

"How about some hide-and-seek?"

Megan's face made a small frown, and Daver thought, *Oh great. Megan's gonna blow it. Just because she doesn't like hide-and-seek, or she's too little, or she's just such a stupid dumb little sister.*

Julie turned to her. "What's the matter, Megan? Don't like hide-and-seek?"

Megan shook her head. "'Cause . . . 'cause . . . I'd get scared hiding."

And now Julie laughed, and Daver saw she was some-one who liked secrets, keeping them hidden until opening them like a surprise package.

"Ah. Well, you see we're going to play in teams. You and me, we'll hide, and Daver will have to find us. Then Daver will hide, and we'll go find him. Sound okay?"

A smile returned to Megan's face. Then Julie turned to Daver.

"And okay with you, Daver?"

"Sure."

But even as he agreed, he wondered what other secrets and surprises the sitter might have.

Ralph passed the fifth of Seagram's whiskey to Ed, who took a big swig without wiping the rim.

"Christ, Ed. Wipe the damn rim. Where the hell are your sanitation habits? Goddam bottle has my germs."

Ed laughed. "The only germs that someone might catch from you won't be in your mouth, Ralphy baby."

"And fuck, don't call me 'Ralphy baby'. Shit."

All his life Ralph had lived in the shadow of the Great One, Jackie Gleason. Just because his old bag of a mother had an Uncle Ralph. So he became *Ralphy* to everyone who ever caught an episode of *The Honeymooners*.

Stupid-ass mother.

"Gimme!" he said to Ed, and his buddy passed over the bottle.

"So what the hell we going to do, Ral—" he caught himself, "Ralph."

Ralph awarded himself with another swig.

"We're gonna get back at the bitch. We're gonna make a big problem for the fuckin' Abbadon Inn."

Ed laughed, a laugh that turned into a cough that had him spitting on the ground behind the newly closed Esso station. Shit, there wasn't even any Esso anymore, was there? Used to be a decent gas station, now it had been abandoned for so fucking long.

After Ed's cough and spit, Ralph decided to kill the fifth. They could pick up another one later.

"Hey!" Ed protested.

"Sorry, *amigo.* All gone. We'll get some more."

"Okay. And what are we going to do?"

Ralph grinned. "Gonna be a *long* night. A hot time in the old town, know what I mean? But first," Ralph stood up. "We gotta find a fucking gas station that's open."

Ed looked up, his eyes dull and confused.

And Ralph thought, *Nothing the fuck new there.*

Martin Bridger could feel his excitement grow as he navigated the streets to the south section of the town, past the elegant homes to where—all of a sudden—the pavement sprouted cracks and the homes took on a disheveled look.

As if *disheveled* was the official building code for this part of the town.

So . . . excited.

Tonight he might get the last pieces of the puzzle. Tonight everything might become clear. What happened nearly fifty years ago, inside the inn and in the town.

He felt like Heinrich Schliemann, the discoverer of the lost city of Troy. Uncovering a city and a story buried for millennia.

But even as he neared the old woman's house, he had to wonder, *Why now?* When he tracked her down, and after finally getting her to talk, why did she continue to tell him things until he could barely keep up with—or believe— everything she said?

Though when he checked her facts, they all matched up. The names of the people, the dates—

She had been there. She had *seen* it.

But why was she revealing it all now? Was it just because she felt close to death?

Or was there another reason?

That might be his last question.

Why now? Why me*?*

He got to the house, guarded by a decrepit wooden fence and a gate that tilted at an odd angle off its hinges.

I couldn't make up a spookier seaside shack, Bridger thought. *Fiction can't hold a candle to reality.*

He lifted the metal latch and opened the gate, creating an alarm bell with the squeak as he slid it open.

And by the time he got to the front door, it was open— she was waiting for him.

III

Illusions and Secrets

TWENTY-TWO

"Hold the fucking thing *up,* willya?"

Ralph watched Ed give him yet another stupid look. The guy was full of them, a real goddam specialist in stupid-ass looks.

Then Ed followed it with a "huh?"

" 'Huh'? Is that all the fuck you can say? Hold the damn gas can up! You got that, numb nuts?"

Ed finally looked down and righted the can.

"Think we got enough?" he asked.

"What? We don't want to burn the whole freakin' place down, we just want to give them some grief, right? A nasty little fire that will ruin that bitch's season, okay?"

Ed shook his head.

"No. I meant booze. Mine's almost—" he reached down to his pocket and slipped out his pint of Old Grand-Dad, which promptly slid out of his shaky hand and to the pavement below, breaking.

"And now you got none, you dumb ass." Ralph shook

his head. Maybe getting some payback tonight wasn't such a good idea. Maybe they should just dump the gasoline somewhere, and head over to the Oak Leaf Tavern on White Street. Be packed tonight, Saturday night, all the good guys from the fishing boats, the white guys, hanging out, shooting pool, knocking back the bats and balls.

Maybe tonight wasn't such a good idea.

"Yeah, I'm a little low, too," Ralph said, laughing. "Though not as low as you!"

He saw Ed look around. Wouldn't take much to get Ed to bail on this little adventure. No balls . . .

"Tell you what. I'll go get us a couple of more bottles . . . and you just wait here."

"I gotta pee," Ed said.

"Then fuckin' *pee*. I'll be ten minutes, tops. Then we go toast some of that Abbadon's timbers, okay?"

"No one's gonna get hurt, right?"

"Right. Like I said. Just a little structural damage, some smoke. Maybe burn out the kitchen." Ralph laughed. "That would fuck 'em, right?"

Ed nodded.

"So I'll go get the booze, you go tap a keg, and then off we go."

Another nod, and Ralph turned and walked back to Washington Street.

Martin Bridger pulled his chair close to the old woman. She spoke so quietly that sometimes he missed words, and he couldn't ask her to repeat herself. She had a cup of tea on her lap, small plumes of steam rising from it. Bridger declined—brewing the tea would have eaten up precious minutes.

He knew she couldn't talk for long. She would grow tired very quickly. Then he'd have to leave, maybe to come back again.

But tonight Bridger thought he'd get the final pieces.

After all, here was someone who had been there.

He kept his eyes on the old woman's lips, dry, wrinkled things that barely moved as she spoke so quietly.

"Y-you sure you don't want some?"

Bridger shook his head. His steno pad, one of a dozen by now, sat open on his lap, his pen in his hand. He still had pages of questions.

Where to begin . . . where the hell to begin . . .

"You said, last time, that they *had* to use you."

The woman took a sip and nodded. "Once they knew that, well, that I couldn't be 'opened,' that Jackson Bell couldn't just look into me like a book, well, there was no other choice."

"And you always felt that power?"

The woman shook her head. "Not a power. God, I never thought of it as any kind of gift. When I was a little girl, I could sense things, almost like hearing things. I tried to make the voices go away. But they never did. I learned to live with them. Sometimes I could," she reached out now, her hands touched Bridger's hand, "turn it on and off."

"But the other part?"

"You mean, keeping my thoughts from him, from Bell? I discovered that accidentally."

"And he didn't know."

"No. He could understand only what I wanted him to understand. I could—it's like it was yesterday—almost feel him trying to dig into my mind, looking for more." She took a breath. "So when we acted, I knew I wouldn't have a lot of time."

"Time . . . to kill him, you mean?"

She nodded again, this time accompanied by a big sip of tea.

"I don't like to think of it that way. Not a killing. I was trying to save people, save those who thought that the inn was our last place to stop him."

"Why the inn?"

She looked up. Her eyes were small, set deep under wrinkled folds, the whites crisscrossed with red veins.

"The inn wasn't just a place to come for him. The Abbadon was old even then, and he fed off its decades of secrets, of people disappearing, of others who wanted to taste that evil. The inn became home to Bell and the others.

"And then it became their graveyard."

A final sip. The cup was empty.

Bridger flipped through the pages, going back to the previous night's discussion.

"But I don't understand—that summer, the shark attacks. How do they fit in? I mean, if Bell was somehow evil, how—"

"Listen to me, Mr. Bridger. *Listen!* That's the part none of us understood. And, and . . ." She looked around the room, as if she didn't recognize the place at all. Knickknacks lined the mantel, guarded by heavy aged chairs, thick with overstuffed padding and dotted with clumps of yellow cat hair. "Because this is why I want to talk with you. I don't really hear things, not anymore. But I sensed I could talk to you, that maybe it would help."

Bridger shook his head. "Help? Help what?"

The woman looked away, her thin lips trembling a bit. "This feeling that it's happening again, that something is making it all happen *again*."

The tiny hidden eyes started to water.

"That's why I've talked to you . . . why I need to tell you this tonight. I—I—"

Bridger reached out and patted her hand.

"I'm scared," she said quietly. "Please. Let me make you some tea."

Bridger put his pad to the side and smiled. Though he'd like nothing more than some icy vodka in a nice tall tumbler, he said, "Sure. Some tea would be great."

* * *

Daver could hear them walking down the hall. He tightened himself into as small a ball as he could and crouched
behind a hallway chair.

If his little sister bent down, she'd see him.

But this was a good hiding place. Maybe he'd even
jump out and scare them when they walked by.

That would be fun. Megan scared so easily. And though
Daver wasn't too happy that his dad had dumped them with a
sitter, Julie seemed okay. She knew the inn really well, secret
places she had said, places maybe nobody else knew about.

The footsteps grew closer.

From under the legs of the chair, Daver could see them
walking. Julie opened a door to one of the big hallway
closets, the place where the maids kept the towels and
sheets.

Nope, not there!

This was *so* cool!

They started walking again. Daver worked to control his
breathing; maybe they would pass right by. And then he
could run to a completely new hiding place, and they'd
never find him.

More slow steps. Daver closed his eyes.

Until . . .

"Peek-a-boo!"

He opened them, and there were Julie and Megan, lean-
ing down, looking at him curled into a ball under the chair.

"We found you!"

Daver scuttled out from under the chair. Maybe it didn't
hide him as well as he had thought.

"Still, that was a good hiding place," Julie said. "Just the
tip of your sneaker was the giveaway, that," she reached
down and gave the toe of his sneaker a gentle pinch, "little
bit of white we could just see."

Daver stood up. Next time, he'd get an even better hiding place. But for now . . .

"Your turn," he said.

Julie looked at Megan. "Want to hide and let Daver find us?"

Megan nodded. Julie held the girl's hand and gave it a squeeze.

"Alright then. You turn and fold your arms against the wall, lean in, and count to . . . how about . . . fifty?"

"Fifty? That's a long time."

Julie gave his hair a quick brush. "You want us to find a good space, don't you?"

"Sure."

"Then give us fifty, nice and slow, and we'll find a great hiding space."

Daver nodded.

"Ready? Close your eyes and start!"

Daver turned to the wall, folded his arms, put them against the wall, and leaned his head into them. He started counting.

"One, two, three . . ."

He heard the sound of their feet running, then a giggle from Megan.

Fifty was a long count. They could find a really great hiding spot, a really tough one. But that would be good, that would be fun.

"Ten, eleven, twelve . . ." Daver continued, counting slowly, resisting the urge to rush.

Ted walked over to Liz, who had slid onto a stool.

"Taking a break?"

She smiled. "Trying to. Guess Saturday nights at the Abbadon are a bit crazy, huh?"

The bar was more than half filled, some diners lingering

over an Irish coffee or a scotch. For now, everyone seemed armed with their drink of choice.

"Guess there isn't much action anywhere else in old Cape May."

"There are other inns, but this one must have that special faded seaside charm. Guess I shouldn't complain."

"If we owned this place, we'd be real happy."

"Yeah, but unfortunately we don't. Landlords for hire."

"Maybe some day. Get a place, maybe not this big. Could be fun."

She smiled at that thought. "Yeah. Could be. A somewhat smaller B-and-B some place."

Ted looked around. "Just as long as it has a nice wood bar like this one."

They both heard a cough from the other end of the bar. Someone in need of a refill, Liz guessed.

"I better get back to ye olde dining room . . ."

"I'll keep a stool free for you," Ted said.

Liz grinned. This was all going okay, Ted seemed to be moving past what happened, the kids were all set with Julie, the inn working, busy, bustling . . .

It's all going so well, she thought, moving back to the dining room.

TWENTY-THREE

Ed put the gas can down, and the gas in the can, which was only about a third full, sloshed around. He looked down the street, deserted, but he didn't want to leave the can just sitting on the sidewalk.

He pushed the can with his foot into the brush until it was off the concrete, and its bright red surface was masked by the tall grass.

There, he thought, *now to pee.* The empty lot would be perfect, he'd just walk in until the light from the streetlamp didn't shine on him anymore, and it would be *fine.*

He marched into the brush, stomping the grass down, his feet hitting potholes in the sandy dirt. He heard a crunching noise, and he wondered what he was crushing. Then, what sounded like glass cracking.

Sure, Ed thought, *everyone just throws their garbage in here—bottles, foam boxes from the hamburger joints, used condoms; a shitty dumping ground.*

Ed stopped. Only tiny slivers of light reached in where he was, even though the lamp, hanging over the road like some kind of blurry moon, seemed so bright.

Fuck it, Ed thought.

And he unzipped and started to pee. He heard the splashing sound as it hit the ground, slicing through grass, landing on sandy spots, nicking bits of paper.

Sure feels good.

Could anyone see him?

Who the hell knew?

Ed zipped up and started to walk out of the empty lot, toward the white light.

He walked quickly now, eager to get back to Ralph, who would be armed with some new booze.

He licked his lips in anticipation.

Anticipating that sweet burning hit. Goddam, nothing like it.

And Ed knew that he needed that hit to do what Ralphy baby planned.

I mean . . . a fuckin' fire? Torching the inn? Even though Ralph said it was only going to be something small, a little payback . . . the idea scared him. Could you really control such things? Could you really make sure that it didn't get out of control?

Ed shook his head.

Yeah—scary idea.

He stopped. The bright streetlamp still hung in the distance, but after his walking, heading right to it, Ed didn't it feel like he was any closer.

And now the brush seemed higher, as though he had gone deeper into the lot, deeper into the deserted fields and dumping areas that most Cape May tourists never saw.

Ed looked around.

No, the light was still there.

Booze was confusing him a bit, that's all.

He kept walking.

* * *

Ralph walked into Ford's Wine and Sprits.

The fluorescent light made the bottles lined up against the wall glow, as though they all had lights inside.

Shit, he never got over the excitement of entering a liquor store. No, and then pretending it was just another item to be picked up. Like eggs, or milk, or bread.

And—oh yeah—a fifth of Jim Beam. Or Seagram's, or . . .

The choices were dizzying, even in Ralph's normal bottom-rung booze shopping.

The store seemed empty.

Where the hell was Old Man Ford? Ford usually looked as though he needed the store just to keep a steady supply of booze pumping in his own veins.

Lights on, door open . . . where the hell was he? Taking a whiz in the back? Getting something to eat? Al Ford lived in a small room in the back. (And Ralph guessed that must be a pretty sight.)

He stood on one side of the counter, waiting.

"Al? Al . . . you here?"

Silence.

Shit, this was supposed to be a quick pick-up. Grab some needed supplies and get back to Ed before he lost whatever balls he had.

"Al?"

Again nothing. Ralph could hear the sound of a bug light just outside, zapping the moths that flittered by.

Okay, he thought.

He walked around the counter, and eyed his target shelf, the line of bottles at the very lowest price range.

He picked up two pints of Seagram's whiskey. The brownish amber liquid looking like syrup in the light.

Two of these babies should be fine.

And if Ford didn't appear, Ralph would just walk out with them.

Pay him tomorrow. Or maybe not. Maybe, fuck it, a little discount for a good customer.

Ralph started to move toward the other side of the counter.

"Now you just stop right there!"

Ralph froze. He turned to see Al Ford holding a handgun with a long barrel, pointed right at him.

Ralph smiled. Christ, Ford knew who he was.

Ralph nodded. "Where the hell were you, Al?"

He smiled.

But Ford didn't smile back.

"Forty-eight, forty-nine . . . fifty!" Daver said loudly. That was an important part of the game; let the hider know that the counting was done, and the seeking about to begin.

After having his eyes closed and buried in his forearms, the hallway looked so bright.

The green-blue rug looked like the ocean when it was sunny, and for the first time, Daver noticed that the walls were also green, but pale and faded.

Everything was still.

For a moment, Daver wished that there were some other people in the hallway, people going to their room, or heading down to dinner. It seemed so quiet here, so empty.

But the counting was done, and now the seeking had to begin.

He walked down the hallway to the big staircase that led down to the dining room. As he walked, he looked behind chairs, and then under a table that was tight against the wall—though he knew it was too small for both Julie and Megan to hide under.

He reached the stairs and looked down. He could see

people down there, talking, laughing. Could be they went down there.

Could be.

And maybe they went all the way to the basement.

He turned around.

At the other end of the hallway he saw the stairs that led up to the third floor.

And he suddenly knew—that's where they must have gone. They wouldn't go where there were a lot of people, people who could tell Daver where they went.

No. They *must* have gone up to the third floor.

So easy to figure out, he thought.

He hurried now, racing down the sea-like rug to the stairs that led to the top of the inn.

More walking, and now Ed started getting annoyed. What the hell was going on here? He kept moving, but never got back to the sidewalk.

And I keep heading toward the goddam streetlamp, he thought. How freakin' hard is it to get out of here? He took some more steps, but if anything the grass grew taller, the pits in the ground deeper.

He took another step, and he felt an ankle twist due to the weird angle of the cratered dirt.

"Shit," he said, tumbling forward.

His face hit the sandy ground hard; sand stuck to his lips, grains flew up to his eyes.

"Goddam!"

He dug his hands into the sand to push himself up.

But . . . but . . .

They closed on something. His fingers closed on something that for a few moments was completely unrecognizable.

Like sticks, and then something soft, followed by the crunching sound of sticks, breaking.

The light from the street barely reached down here. But Ed could look, and he saw what his hands were grabbing, fingers clenching tight.

The milky color of thin bones, the dirty white of—now he knew—feathers. He could even feel that his face rested against some feathers; he smelled the strange odor of the dead feathers, the meatless bones. In his right hand, he saw that he held a strange curved piece, shit—a bit of a beak.

He lay in a pile of dead birds, a scattering of bones, the flesh picked clean, a crazy pile of feathers.

"Fuck," he said, freaking out now, the fear for the first time penetrating his alcohol-addled brain, now only one thought racing through that brain. *Gotta get the hell out of here!*

He started to bring his knees up, to get to a kneeling position, to stand up, and get the hell out of this dump, this pile of dead gulls, this wasteland.

But as he started to get up, he felt something land hard on his back. Landing hard, and pushing him square into the sand. The weight pinned him to the sand.

Ed groaned. Like a crab trying to scuttle away after being pulled up in a trap, he tried to claw with his hands, dig with his legs.

But he went nowhere. The weight on his back pinning him securely, holding him tightly.

"Hey, what the—" Ed tried to say. But with his mouth buried in the sand, the words were muffled, unintelligible even to him. He kept squirming, the trapped crab, kicking with feeble legs, feeble arms.

Until he heard small sounds in the thick grass.

Things moving. Small things. Moving toward him. Slowly, pushing the grass aside, coming toward him.

Ed began to flail and kick even more.

But that only made the things hurry even faster until they got to the clearing Ed had made in the grass . . . and saw the great prize that awaited them.

* * *

"Hey Al. It's me, man. Just grabbing' a few of my usual. Didn't see you around, bud, and—"

But Ralph saw that Al didn't lower the barrel of the gun, that the barrel was pointed squarely at Ralph's chest.

Fuck, what the hell is wrong with the old man? He knows me, I'm a freakin' regular, and now he's standing there bug-eyed like I was some spook from South Philly.

Ralph took a step closer to Al.

"One more step, and I'll pull this goddam trigger."

The barrel wavered a bit now, but still well within range of blowing a good-sized hole in Ralph.

"You just stay right there."

"Okay, okay. Not going anywhere, Al. Staying right here. And you just stay nice and calm."

Ralph's mind raced. *What the hell is happening?* Why doesn't Ford know who he is? Has the man popped some loony pills, whacked out on something stronger than cheap-shit Kentucky bourbon?

Whatever it was, the old man looked terrified. And there was nothing worse than someone scared holding a gun pointed right at you.

"Okay Al. Whatcha goin' to do? Call the police. Go on. That . . . that would be a good thing to do."

Of course that would probably change the evening's plans. But there were other nights they could do some damage to the inn, screw up that bitch's life. Just had to end this little scene here.

But Al didn't move.

"Wh-whatcha got in your hand?" Ford said.

Ralph looked down at his hands, slightly raised, a pint in each.

"Just two of my usual, one for me—and one for Ed."

The old man's eyes seemed to go wider. He licked his lips.

"What'cha got there, what the hell do you—"

Ford's eyes went from Ralph's hands to his face, licking his lips, his gray stubbly beard making the store owner look ever crazier.

"Damn, you can see what the hell I got—"

Ralph raised one hand.

"No fuckin' way," Ford said.

Ralph saw Ford's eyes narrow, his brown nicotine-coated tongue snaked out and licked at his cracked lips, then, then—

Ralph could see the man's bony hand tighten. The slight movement of a finger moving, even as the gun wavered in its aim.

"No," Ralph said softly, not understanding what Ford was seeing, how he could think that Ralph was some kind of thief.

How the hell was this happening?

But Ralph knew one thing: Ford didn't see him at all.

A click, a blast, then—amazing pain.

Ralph heard the bottles fall to the ground. A moan, his own sound that turned into a groan.

He fell to his knees, landing in the new puddle of broken glass and brown liquid. Except, now that liquid mixed with something else as he fell forward onto the hard concrete floor.

He tried to mutter, "Why?" But nothing came out. He heard his own labored breathing, grunting, as he pumped out his life onto the stone floor of the liquor store.

His last thought before a filmy blackness covered his eyes . . .

Nothing would happen to the inn tonight.

TWENTY-FOUR

The after-dinner bar crowd thinned out. Ted started soaping and rinsing the pilsner glasses, hacked at the ice cubes that had molded into one gigantic block, and then checked that the bar was ready for any Saturday-night fans of a late cocktail.

He heard the porch door open.

A short man with a black beard and black close-cropped hair, stood at the entrance. He seemed to hesitate.

Then he walked to the bar.

Not someone Ted had seen here before.

"Hiya," Ted said, "what'll it be?"

Such a classic line. Almost corny, he thought.

What'll it be?

How about a blonde, a rare steak, and a brand-new Corvette?

But instead, the man nodded. "I, um, how about a beer. And, er . . . maybe something else, too."

Ted put a still-wet pilsner glass under the spigot of

Narragansett and waited. He now saw that despite the
man's sleek dark hair, it was flecked with gray like an old
tabby cat beginning to show its age. Ted looked down at
the man's hands, oversized for such a short man. Wrinkled,
powerful hands that did hard work.

The man's eyes seemed to scan the bottles behind Ted.
His eyes were a robin's-egg blue, striking in such a sun-
darkened face.

Guy works outside, Ted thought. *Under the sun, doing
heavy stuff. Lots of work with his hands.*

But he was no laborer. His eyes were taking everything
in with a subtle intelligence.

The man spoke, "How about a scotch. On the rocks, I
guess."

"You got it." Ted grabbed a tumbler, then turned to the
newly liberated ice cubes and, using the tongs, he tossed a
few in the glass. He poured the man a good solid drink and
placed it beside his beer.

"There you go."

The man nodded. And only then did Ted see that the
man's darting eyes, eyes that had roamed all over the bar
from the bottles, to the walls, to the dining room, to the
hallway, to the customers, finally seemed to land on Ted
with a degree of finality.

And Ted knew. *He's here to speak with me.*

For now, he'd wait for the man to start whatever conversation he brought into the place.

Daver stood by the door leading to the third floor.

Could they have gone up there? Only a few rooms were
open, he knew, and there was some building going on, or
something. But these stairs led to the top of the inn.

To that turret room that made the inn look like a castle.

Daver took a step into the staircase alcove and listened.
No sounds. But then, if Julie could get Megan quiet,

they could be in one of the empty rooms upstairs, waiting, hiding.

Daver fired another look down the second-floor hall-way. Empty, deserted.

So they were either downstairs, or up there.

He took a step. Though covered with the same blue carpet, the step creaked. *I didn't hear any creaks when I was counting, did I?* He wondered. But then, he had been counting loudly. So loudly, that he could have easily missed the tiny-mouse-squeaks of someone walking up the stairs.

Another step, another squeak, only now it sounded louder because he was on the staircase, heading up.

More steps, and soon he was closer to the third floor than the second floor, and Daver began to feel excited.

I'm going to find them! Show them how good I am at this game.

Bridger's cup of tea, a minty yellow-green brew, sat on top of his notebook. Together, he and Eileen quietly sipped their tea.

Will she get back on track, he wondered? She seemed so easily distracted, her thoughts veering off in odd direc-tions. And that was the other thing; how much of her mem-ories were true?

Some of it true? All of it true? Or was it all the crazy imaginings of an amazingly old woman who happened to be around a long time ago?

As the woman sipped, her tiny wrinkled lips made the same sound a straw does, a slow slurp of the tea through pursed lips. Then, amazingly, she continued . . .

"There was so much we didn't understand. They thought," she looked up at Bridger, "that if they could kill him, it would end."

Bridger moved his teacup and plate to a small table with

a lacy covering. He flipped open his notebook. "You mean, by killing Bell they thought all these . . . others would go away?"

The woman smiled at Bridger as if she doubted whether he'd understand. "They were nothing without him. Like mayflies, circling, entranced. Like the whole town."

"That night . . . you were there?"

She nodded. "Of course, he wouldn't have gone down there without me. I could feel him trying to, you know, 'read' me." She raised a clawlike hand to her head. "And I kept him out, had to keep him out, until it was too late."

Bridger looked directly at the woman's filmy eyes.

"You watched them do it?"

A nod. "So fast. So . . . terrible. Like hacking an animal to pieces. Before they sent him out to sea, thinking the sea would carry him away."

"And the inn? I don't understand. Why was the Abbadon so—"

Now the woman made a small laugh. "Old things have a lot of power, Mr. Bridger. Old buildings, old people. Memories, knowledge. The Abbadon back then had already been around for a hundred years. To someone like Bell, it was a magnet for those he'd attract. The inn became an extension of Bell, his office." She picked up a twisted napkin from her lap. "It seemed fitting that he died there. I almost—almost felt as if the inn had changed when Jackson Bell died."

"So it was over?"

She shook her head. "No." She laughed. "We were so wrong. The inn had secrets, phantoms, its strange history that wouldn't fade. But for a while, it seemed like everything had ended. The town, the sunlit town of beaches and lemonade and children, all returned to normal."

She reached out and tapped Bridger's hand.

"But every now and then, things happened. People vanished, someone died. Never given a big play in the sleepy newspaper. Things happened. And I knew," she looked into the distance, "that out there, something waited, still pulling people in, playing with their fears, their craziness."

Bridger tried to write down everything the woman said. In the quiet, musty room, just a single pale lamp on the table, he felt as if he had entered another universe. Someplace timeless, someplace terrifying.

"And of course, then there were the attacks. Couldn't tell anyone about them, now could I? No, people would just say they were normal. Such things happen . . . in the sea." Her voice rose.

Bridger looked up.

He thought about the ghost tale she was telling, a tale of a man with a strange power fueled by death and evil. And murders covered up by some of Cape May's finest.

But the attacks . . . ?

He needed her to explain this.

"What—I don't understand?"

"That year, it came. It wasn't the first time. But it was in all the papers. How strange it was . . . how the shark acted like it had a consciousness. Why there are even books about it. Look, there—"

She pointed to a distant dark shelf. Bridger got up and walked to the shelf.

"Next to the photo, of me. When I was young. I haven't read it. Couldn't read it."

Bridger picked up the book.

"Bloody Shore," he said quietly.

"Yes. Take it. The story is nearly all there. When that shark came and killed . . . when it took children, and took men and women, when it went up shallow harbors, when it almost seemed to search for a way onto the land. The strange shark attacks . . ."

Bridger walked back to his chair and, holding the book open, flipped through the pages, looking at maps, photos . . .

"I guess," she said quietly, "I was the only one who knew that . . ." she shook her head as if disbelieving how stupid people could be ". . . knew it wasn't just shark attacks."

She took a breath.

"It was so much more."

Another breath.

"Like now."

Liz watched Ted lean close to the man at the far corner of the bar, deep in conversation. It was hard for her to see from where she was, but the man didn't look as though the Abbadon was his usual stop for a few beers.

Then, with instincts born of being a policeman's wife, a stray thought entered her mind. *The man is here to see Ted.*

She glanced back at the dining room—quiet now, the last few diners slowly finishing up. And she then she turned and walked into the bar. Ted looked up at her, his eyes narrow, serious.

Liz smiled.

"Everything okay?" she asked. The man sitting at the bar turned and looked at her. His face was leather-brown, and he had blue eyes deeply set, almost hooded by his bushy sun-bleached eyebrows. He could have been anywhere from twenty-five to forty-five, weather having erased any logical clues to the man's real age.

Ted nodded toward the man.

"Liz, this is Brian Barefield."

Liz smiled as the man brought his fingers to the brim of a nonexistent hat.

"Hi," she said, not at all sure why she was being introduced to the rough-looking man.

She fired a glance at Ted, as if asking, *What's this about . . . what the hell's going on?*

"Have a seat," the man said, gesturing to a stool.

The bar was quiet, a few drinkers having wandered out to the porch, enjoying the balmy summer night.

Liz sat down.

"Good to get off my feet."

The man took a sip of his beer. She had clearly interrupted them. And Liz had to wonder how long it would be before someone said something.

"Honey, Brian—" Ted started.

"I was just—" Barefield said at the same time.

Liz laughed. "Okay, shall we start again?"

The screen door to the porch opened, and an older couple walked in with their empty port glasses. They put them down, smiled at Ted and Liz, and then headed to the stairs.

"Okay," Ted said. "Brian here, he's—"

"I run a dive shop in town. Though," he laughed, "I do a bit of everything. Diving, some fishing charters, whatever the traffic demands. When there *is* traffic."

"There's diving here?" Liz asked.

Brian nodded. "Got some nice wrecks out there. Most in pretty deep water, hundred twenty . . . hundred thirty feet. Not easy dives. But they're there for those who want them. For whoever can handle the depth. It doesn't get much deeper than that really till you hit the shelf drop-off."

"Well, who knew," Liz said, her antennae out, warning her that this wasn't good, that there was something bad about this.

"So—there's a reason I came here. Tonight, I mean."

Liz looked at Ted, a little I-told-you-so moment. "Really?"

Another nod. "I was telling your husband that something happened today."

"On a dive, something you—"

Brian shook his head. "No. There's this guy, with an old-time charter boat. Captain Andy Brickman. Funny enough, like you folks, Andy's from Brooklyn." Another sip. " 'Captain Andy' we called him. Knows his fish, knows the water. But today . . .''

Ted put down a foamy glass of draft beer in front of Liz. She wasted no time taking that first sip.

"Today something happened out there. The weather started clear, water calm, and Andy's radio report didn't tell us a lot—though we got a locator signal from it.''

"What happened?" Liz asked, since obviously Ted already knew.

"The boat, Andy, his two clients, his crewman—all vanished.''

Liz nodded. Another sip, the Narragansett beer bitter. "So you think—what? Some kind of freak wave, or—?"

But what Liz wanted to really ask was, *What the hell are you doing here, talking to my husband? What the hell do you want?*

"No. Skies were not bad, not much of a wind."

"So?"

Ted looked around the empty bar. A couple sat at one of the small tables by the wall, well away from them. Still, he lowered his voice.

"They went out for big fish, Liz . . . hammerheads, big hammerheads."

"One of Captain Andy's specialties," Brian said. "The clients loved it, the photo with a ten-footer dangling from a giant meat hook." He drained his beer. "A real crowd pleaser."

"So. Calm sea—and you think . . . ?"

The dive operator pushed his glass toward Ted.

"See, that's not all. These two teenage kids vanished a while back. Your husband heard the story. One of 'em the Abbadon owner's son. The town's been cooking up a lot of crazy theories about where they went, running off, God knows what. But, shit, they had been out in a boat. And there are others, too—a guy from Maryland who didn't bring a rental back.''

Ted refilled Brian's beer glass.

"That's when some of us began to get a little nervous."

"Nervous? Nervous about what?"

She looked at the two men. Already hating the fact that they seemed joined together, somehow *connected.*

Nobody said anything for a second.

"For Christ's sake, will someone speak?"

Ted nodded toward Brian. "He thinks it's a shark."

"What?"

"Something big. Something nasty. And hanging around," Ted looked up, in the direction of the porch and the clear night sky, "out there . . . staying near here."

And in that moment, Liz could finally put all the pieces of the puzzle together.

"Shit," she said.

TWENTY-FIVE

Daver looked down the third-floor hallway.

The light was dimmer up here, as though different bulbs were used.

Was that possible? Could they put different bulbs up here, and was that why the light seemed so faded?

Or maybe . . . maybe it was the carpet. It looked so old, frayed at the edges, a dark ugly green, matching the walls.

Maybe that's what made it look so dull up here.

And so *quiet*. Daver began to think that there was no way they could be hiding up here. No way.

"Hey," he said. Then again, "Hey, you guys, I know you're up here!"

Even though he didn't. He was starting to think that they were somewhere else, down in the smelly basement, or in a closet near the kitchen, maybe in the office.

"I'm going to find you guys!" he yelled. "You know that!"

He walked down the hallway, in the middle of the dark green carpet. The rooms were all shut. He passed one, and then stopped; he walked to the door and tried the handle.

If there was someone inside, he might get in trouble. Someone coming out, yelling at him. It wasn't a good idea to sneak into people's rooms.

But the doorknob turned only a little, and the door didn't open.

No good hiding places up here, he thought.

He saw the signs of people working at the far end. A big sheet of plastic hung from the ceiling, one flap partially open.

They wouldn't go in there, he thought.

No way would Julie take Megan in there.

With the dust, and tools, and—

But he couldn't really be sure unless he took a look.

It wouldn't hurt to take a look.

So he kept on walking toward the far end of the hallway, to the filmy plastic sheet, to the open flap—a last place to look before hurrying downstairs.

Eileen had spread the yellowed newspaper out on the ancient maroon couch, permanently dented by decades of sitting.

Bridger leaned over for a closer look.

"I don't understand. And these shark attacks in the fifties? What kind of connection could they have with anything?"

"You see, they never really understood Jackson Bell, what he did, who he was . . . where his power really came from. As if killing him would be enough." A small, shallow laugh. "As if sending his body streaming out to sea would end it. They thought that killing Bell would end it. They were so wrong. And I was so wrong."

Bridger had stopped writing. The story from this woman, maybe a crazy woman, had taken a turn that he hadn't imagined.

And Bridger thought to himself, *This makes no sense.*

"Bell wasn't the leader. He was only a follower, like the others. He served something else."

"Something else?"

"Something much more powerful. Something older, and deadlier. You see, that's the reason he did so much of his 'business' at the Abbadon. That place was important, is important. What used Bell, and the others . . . used that inn, too."

"So there's someone else who—what? Gave Bell his power?"

The woman's cracked lips seemed to tremble in the pale yellow light. A leathery tongue tip slipped out and licked at her lips.

"No. Not someone else. No. I doubt it's a someone. That's why you had all those attacks, you see . . . whenever it felt someone was there for it, someone it could reach, control, it came *close.*"

Now Bridger laughed—more of a nervous release.

"The shark? You're *not* saying that the shark somehow controlled—"

She reached out and touched Bridger's hand.

Then she said, "I thought you wrote about such things, Mr. Bridger. You see," she gestured at a distant glass-enclosed bookcase, "I've read many of your books. Yet you don't see this?"

Bridger shook his head.

"It wasn't the shark?"

Her voice rose, almost stern, almost the sound of an impatient teacher. "You write about familiars, and evil possessing good. Those attacks were *evil,* born of evil . . . however that creature, the shark, came under the control of that evil. Where it is, at what depths, whatever horrible blackness under the ocean hid it . . . it used Bell, it used the shark. Surely you could imagine that?"

"The shark was its . . ." he searched for a word ". . . its agent . . . its puppet?"

"Yes. It took me so long to understand, you see. But through that . . . agent, it could reach something else. Someone in that building, at the inn. I don't know, but someone would help it. The deaths fed it, made it stronger, made it ready to live again."

Bridger stood up.

He looked around the room and noticed amidst the array of religious articles, the photographs of people, the yellowed curling pictures of people on the beach, a shot of the Abbadon's porch, a happy couple sitting in a 1930s' roadster, and a later, faded color picture, some young men in a 1950s' convertible. Pictures from newspapers, pictures from ancient Kodak Brownies.

"It took me *so* long to see that it could reach someone at the inn, like it reached Bell. And when it did, the ocean itself would turn red, turn into a place of death. A place of horror."

Bridger had his back to the woman, looking at her small museum of images, books, maps almost invisible in the room.

Until he saw a picture of himself. In Manhattan. At a book party thrown by his publisher. A clear martini glass in his hand, a bright smile. Happier days, younger days.

An old picture that she must have had for a while.

His mind went down a trail.

Why did I come to the Abbadon?

What brought me there, and to this old woman and her crazy tales?

He turned back to her and saw her eyes locked on him.

Then, in her gnarled hands, a gun pointed right at him.

"I didn't know whether I could do this. No, not when we started. But I'm sure you understand. There's no question anymore."

The gun shook a bit in the woman's grip.

Bridger felt as though he had entered the psychiatric ward at Bellevue, an inner chamber for the maddest of the mad.

He was about to tell the woman to put the gun down when he saw her hand tighten, and then the beginning of her finger pulling on the trigger.

Liz sat there, staring at Ted.

"What? What is it?" Ted asked.

She turned to look at Brian, who quickly looked down at his beer.

"So now what? You're the great shark hunter? You're going to find out what the hell happened out there?" She turned away. "Christ."

For a moment Ted said nothing.

"Look, Liz. It's what I do. I'm a diver, not just a once-a-year Cayman Island day-tripper. I've dived in the worst conditions you can imagine; you know what I've seen. If I'm lucky, there's a body. But usually it's just bits and pieces—"

"Oh, give me a break."

A couple at the end of the bar sheepishly slid off their stools and walked out.

"Isn't this great for business . . ." she said.

"Brian came here because I could help."

She fired another glance at Brian Barefield.

Who was now her new best enemy.

"In this whole state, they don't have a dive team that can go down there?"

Finally, Brian cleared his throat. He rubbed his gray-flecked beard, and looked up to face Liz's heat.

"Sure, the state police has dive teams. But not for stuff like this. Murder, drugs, yeah. But a fishing accident? A shark attack? No way. An accident at sea is how they'd log it."

Liz took a step to the leathery skinned young man. He looked old but could easily have been barely out of his twenties.

"And isn't that what it was? Why not let it go? Why the hell do you need my husband?"

Brian took a sip of beer, tiny drops of foam sticking to his mustache.

"Yeah, I could do that, Could just forget it. Except, you see . . . the guy on the boat, Andy. He was a good guy. And he deserves to have someone find out what happened to him."

"He's a good guy from Brooklyn," Ted added.

"Well, isn't that special?" she fired back, and immediately regretted her mocking tone. Then, "I'm sorry."

"It's okay," Brian said. "I understand. There's that . . . he's a good friend and . . ."

"And?"

Brian fixed her with his blue eyes. "Your kids swim in that water. A lot of people's kids do. If there's something out there, I'd like to know. And I'd like something done about it."

She turned to Ted.

"It's just a dive, Liz. I've done hundreds in far worse conditions. I can help find out what happened. I'd want someone to do it for me."

And at that moment, Liz realized something else. That maybe this dive was important for Ted.

They had left Brooklyn because of what happened. But it was still there, still haunting Ted. Could it be that this might be something Ted needed? Something to send the ghosts from the *Andrea Doria* away?

As he said, it wasn't as though the open ocean was the worst place he ever dived.

She turned back to Brian.

"You'd be with him?"

"Yes, ma'am. And another experienced dive master.

Just that we have no training for something like this; we don't know what to look for. Your husband . . ." he tilted his almost empty beer to Ted ". . . he's the man."

"Yeah," Liz said. "He's the man, alright." She turned back to Ted. "Guess you don't need my, um, approval, do you?"

"If you don't want me to do it—"

"Of course I don't *want* you to do it. But go ahead. Help these people. And just make sure of one goddam thing, okay?"

"What's that?"

"You see any stupid-ass shark, you get the hell out of the water. And get your scrawny butt back to bartending as soon as you can."

Ted laughed.

"You know you *never* let me forget why I love you."

And Brian laughed, too, as he slid his empty glass toward Ted.

TWENTY-SIX

Daver let the plastic flap fall behind him.

Though the hall was lit, the paint-spattered tarps on the ground made the hallway seem darker.

He stood there for a second.

No way Julie would bring Megan down here.

It was too . . . too . . .

Scary.

No, they had to be downstairs.

Daver was about to turn around, though, when he thought he heard a sound . . . a small sound coming from the somewhere at the end of the hallway.

What's that? he wondered.

A mouse? Do they have mice up here, scurrying under the tarps, darting into a dark empty room?

Mice didn't bother Daver. They were cute. He had seen them in the empty lots near their apartment in Brooklyn, little brown guys popping in and out of empty cans of food, hiding under chunks of yellowed newspaper. They looked cute. He had even asked his mom if he could have one for a pet.

She had said no, of course.

He saw the end of the hallway and another door. For a moment he didn't know where that led. But then he remembered the castle-like tower that rose above the front of the inn. Yeah, it looked just like a castle, rising way above the inn.

The second-floor entrance to the tower had been locked.

But the door, right down there, must also lead to the tower.

No way Julie and Megan were there.

No way.

But he thought about the view from there. He could probably see over all the nearby buildings, out to the sea, and even inland. *Maybe it was the tallest place in this whole town!*

He started walking.

The tarp crunched below his feet, cracking as the dry paint split. It didn't look as though anyone had been working here in a while. It looked as though they had suddenly just stopped.

He reached the door to the tower stairs.

Okay, he thought. He'd just run up and take a look at the view, at how high he was, before running down and finding them.

(*The kitchen,* he thought. *Bet the cooks gave them a special hiding place down there!*)

He grabbed the large wooden handrail and started up the narrow stairs. There was no light here, just whatever spilled in from the hallway. Though when he looked up, Daver did see a glow. He looked right and left, searching for a light switch but couldn't see anything protruding from the wall.

That's okay, he thought. *Only a few steps, and I'll be in the small room at the top of the tower. Take a quick look around, and then hurry down . . .*

His hand slid along the rail as the light got fainter and fainter. He blinked, trying to hurry his eyes to adjust to the darkness. He didn't hear anything. And that was good.

In this darkness, even the small scurrying sounds of a mouse would be something he didn't want to hear.

Just want to hear my own steps.

And wait till he told them what he did.

Going up here, looking around . . . how cool is this?

He reached the top step and the small tower room.

He saw the windows, smeared, as if someone had spilled something on them. The light up here came from outside, maybe the streetlight below or from across the road, from one of the shops, or maybe even the moon.

Not a lot of light, though.

Just a glow. He walked to the window.

His plan to see everything from here melted away. He couldn't see anything from these windows, not the way they were, all smeared, all covered.

He wiped at a window with the elbow of his T-shirt, making a cloth bulldozer out of the white material.

And though it did clear a path on the glass, the window was still smeary, still hard to see through. He leaned close. Out there, past the blurry lights and the dark houses, was the ocean. He had hoped he'd be able to see it, the white waves crashing, the spiky bits where the swells bumped into each other. But it was all dark and dull.

Nothing out there to see really, and then . . .

In the glass.

His eyes changing their focus.

His eyes suddenly aware.

A reflection in the smeared glass, a blurry shape.

The reflection from something behind him. The reflection moving, shifting its position in the room.

Behind him.

His breath caught in his throat. He stopped breathing. He wanted to turn his head, to turn and look. But holding his breath, his heart thumping, he couldn't move.

The shape moved again, so slowly, but he could tell it was closer.

Until he knew that he had to turn—right now—turn and look at whoever stood behind him.

For Bridger, the room lost all air. The room became a chamber where someone had pumped out all breathable air, leaving a stale deadness.

That, and the old woman pointing a gun at him.

She's going to kill me, he thought.

She told me this crazy story, and now she's going to kill me?

He looked at her eyes, to see if he could gauge if she really was that crazy. Could she really pull the trigger, kill him in her own airless room filled with pictures and clippings and strange memories from decades past?

Bridger's eyes darted to the door, a path of escape.

He might be able to dodge the bullet, if he moved now, if he moved fast.

Or—

His eyes looked right and left, before centering on the woman's tightening finger, a finger moving to commit the most desperate act one human can perform on another.

Crazy lady . . .

He moved fast, a bit of a step to the side, her gun following, then weaving back as he reached under, and then scooped the gun barrel from beneath.

He was afraid that her finger would be so locked in a death grip on the trigger that the struggle would produce a gunshot.

But it was just too easy, her ancient hand slipping away

like tattered lace, fingers slipping off as though they weren't really fingers at all, but some dry, brittle crackers that crumbled to the touch.

And then Bridger had the gun.

Eileen started sobbing.

She began to wring her useless hands.

Bridger opened the chamber of the gun, a small snub-nosed revolver, and let the bullets fall into his hand. *How the hell did she get this gun?* he wondered. *How long has she had it? A vintage item maybe? Something she was saving for just this kind of rainy day?*

He put the bullets in his pocket.

The air had slowly started to refill the room, timed, it seemed, to the woman's sobbing, her head down, shaking.

Bridger didn't know what to say.

Something like, *Excuse me, but why did you just try to kill me?*

But seeing the woman there, as old as anything in this room, this once beautiful girl . . . he felt sorry for her.

He was tempted to go over and touch her shoulder. Comfort her. And say what? Sorry, I interfered with your plan to kill me. Chin up. Maybe you'll get another chance.

Instead, Bridger sat down on the chair facing her. He'd wait until the crying stopped.

And maybe then he'd get an answer as to why she wanted to blow a hole in the man to whom she had told her whole incredible tale.

Daver blinked again, this time not to adjust his eyes but to help make him turn and look. One blink, then another, a breath finally, then—

He turned.

Hoping with all his thoughts that there would be no one there, that what he thought was someone behind him would turn into nothing more than light reflected off one of the other windows. A car's headlights reflecting up here, hitting a bit of the glass.

That's all.

Not a person.

Not someone standing there, alone with him.

He blinked again, breathed.

Eyes now wide open.

And he saw her. So hard to make out her features. But in that moment he could see her dress that led down to the ground. The outline of someone young. And dark hair piled high.

A woman dressed so strangely, in the room with him.

He licked his lips. She didn't say anything. She just stood there. Looking at him.

He tried to find the courage to say something, to ask her, *Who are you? What are you doing here?*

But he had no voice. He *knew* he had no voice; he couldn't say anything.

The woman raised a hand out to him, as if urging him to take her hand . . . this woman who didn't say anything. And in that gesture there was something familiar . . .

Had he seen this person before? Had she been in the hotel?

(Not with that long dress, he knew. Nobody dressed like that, not in the inn, not now.)

The woman's hand remained outstretched to him.

Which was when it changed.

The woman's hand went to her throat. Daver could see her teeth, her mouth open as if she were screaming. But there was no sound in the room, nothing but Daver's breathing, fast, faster, sucking in the air.

The woman silently screaming, and the white dress darkening, turning a different color, and just enough light in the room to tell that the color was—

Red.

The dress now a deep red, shimmering with a soaked

wetness, the woman standing before him, writhing now, mouth open wide.

Until Daver's hands flew to his eyes, and he had to end the silence by screaming as loudly as he could.

TWENTY-SEVEN

Daver's scream filled the room.

But it grew even louder when he felt hands on his shoulders.

He couldn't remove his hands from his eyes. He couldn't look at that person again, red and . . . glistening in front of him.

But then, over the sound of his scream in the small room . . . A voice.

"Daver! Daver!"

He knew the voice. But for a moment he didn't do anything. Until there was another smaller voice.

"Daver! Stop! Stop it!"

Megan. His sister.

He stopped his yelling and pulled his hands away from his eyes.

Julie crouched down beside him, and Megan stood to the side. Daver realized that his mouth was still open, still gaping open.

He looked at both of them as though they weren't real.

He felt Julie give his arm a gentle squeeze.

"Daver . . . you okay?"

He looked at Megan. His little sister.

And he knew he couldn't say what he had just seen, not with Megan standing there. She had already wandered to a window, trying to look out.

Daver nodded.

"What happened?" Julie asked.

Her eyes locked on him.

Daver looked over to Megan again, as if trying to give her a message.

"Um, nothing. I was looking for you guys—"

Megan turned back. "We *said* we wouldn't hide up here. It's yucky up here."

Daver nodded. "I saw the door. I thought I could see things from up here."

"See things?" Julie asked.

It's as if she knows, Daver thought.

"The ocean. The town. It's so high. But I guess . . ." He looked around. "It's dark, guess I got a little spooked."

"Fraidy cat!" Megan said, laughing.

But Julie didn't laugh or smile. Even in the shadows, Daver could see that Julie's face was very serious.

"You got . . . spooked?"

Another nod.

Julie opened her mouth as if she were going to ask Daver another question. But she hesitated and gave his arm another gentle squeeze.

"It can happen." She stood up. "Old inns can be a little spooky, right? It happens to all of us. But," she turned to Megan, who immediately took the girl's hand, "what say you guys start heading downstairs, and seeing what cool desserts the Goudge sisters have left over?"

"Yay!" Megan said.

Funny, Daver thought . . . *little Megan didn't seem scared at all in the cramped, dark room. Not as long as she held on to Julie's hand.*

Daver almost reached out and took Julie's other hand.

But instead, he led the way out of the tower room, holding on to the big wooden handrail that led down to the third floor and back to the lights and people and noise of the inn.

Eileen looked up at Bridger, her eyes wet. She had seemed so strong talking to him these many nights; now she seemed crushed, a gossamer-thin woman that the tiniest of breezes could blow away.

"I—I couldn't do it."

"I don't get it," Bridger sad. "What the hell—"

He looked into the woman's eyes, the dark dots of her pupils looking back at him. And he could see that she was scared.

Why would she be scared of me?

"You wanted to kill me?"

The woman shook her head. "Not . . . wanted. I didn't *want* to. I had to. I had to try—but couldn't."

Bridger looked around the room. Maybe everything the woman said was nonsense. A crazy old woman's tale, madness from a woman who turned homicidal for no apparent reason.

Thank God she couldn't carry it out.

At least Bridger had material for a book.

If he could somehow make all this incredible material at all believable.

With the bullets safely in his pocket, he handed the gun back to Eileen.

But she kept her hands on her lap and shook her head.

"No. I—I don't want it. You keep it." Her eyes narrowed. "You keep it . . . keep it close."

Bridger nodded. Probably not a bad idea to take the gun out of the old woman's house.

"Sure." He slid the gun into another pocket. "But why, why did you—"

The woman grabbed the arms of her chair like a raptor digging onto a perch. She pushed herself upright with what Bridger thought was amazing speed.

She might be old but she can still move.

She walked with a looping, wounded gait that bespoke years of hip and back injuries, over to the tall secretary. She removed a skeleton key from a hidden pocket in her dress. She stuck it into a drawer, twisted the key, and slid open the drawer. Bridger watched her pull something out.

A small brown book, bulging with inserted papers. Some kind of diary, journal—

She turned back to Bridger.

"Here," she said walking over to him. "Take this. Read it. This will explain everything."

Even the gun? Bridger wanted to ask.

But he just took the book.

He stood up. "And after I read it, can I come back, ask you—"

The woman's hand shot up.

"No. No more visits. No more talk. All this . . . everything I've done with you . . . was probably a mistake." Her lips trembled with each word. "If I'm still here, if I'm still alive, I don't want to see you again."

"You'll be here," Bridger said. The words seemed hollow as soon as he uttered them.

"With that book," the woman said pointing at the journal, "you have everything." She turned back to her chair. "Maybe then you will understand."

Bridger looked down at the book wondering what secrets it held. "Thanks," he said, but the word seemed absurd. Then, "I'd better go now."

The woman nodded. She shut her eyes.

And with the woman's eyes closed, Bridger turned and walked to the door that led to the dark summer night outside the tiny house.

Ted looked into the adjoining bedroom.

"Where are the kids, shouldn't they—?"

Liz brushed her hair. The salty air made it go all wiry. If they stayed here long she'd have to get it cropped short.

And how long would they stay here? Was this just a distraction for a few weeks? Or was this maybe somehow the start of a new life? A life away from the streets of Brooklyn, the world of police precincts, squad cars, and late nights when your husband can't talk about what he did, what he's seen, for the past ten hours.

"I saw Julie. They were doing a late-night raid on the kitchen for some desserts."

Ted nodded, then looked at her. He walked over and stroked her hair just as she ran the brush through it.

"Hey, I know you're not happy about this—"

She looked up at him, eyes wide, mouth smirking. "Happy? Not exactly the word I'd pick." She started brushing her hair again. "But I agreed. You just keep your promise."

"I'll be meeting them early tomorrow. You'll be asleep."

"That's okay."

He reached out and grabbed her hand, stopping the brush. "No, its not." He leaned down and kissed her, gently at first, but when she responded, lips parting slightly, he kissed her hard.

When the kiss ended, she said, "The kids . . ."

Ted walked over to the door to the room and turned the lock.

"You just saw them, you said? Hitting the kitchen?"

Liz nodded, surprised by the feeling taking over her, feeling her cheek reddening. Ted came closer.

He smiled. "You'll have to be very, very quiet."

"I've gotten good at that," she said.

Then, quickly, roughly, but with very little sound, they made love.

Julie brushed Daver's hair.

"Cake good?"

He nodded, not pausing as he shoveled in another forkful.

"And you, Missy? The sherbert yummy?"

Megan's lips were two colors, Daver saw. The upper lip lime green, the lower like a really red berry.

Daver felt okay now, here in the bright lights of the kitchen, the metal surfaces gleaming under those lights. He knew that if he told his parents about going to the tower it might get Julie in trouble.

And now, he really liked her.

Besides, he probably didn't really see anything. Just a reflection, some lights, and then he thought he saw something.

That's probably what it was.

But . . . he didn't really believe that.

He just knew he wouldn't go up there again. Not even with his parents.

This bright kitchen was just fine.

Maybe I scare too easily, he thought.

He heard Megan slurping the melted sherbert, the last drops in the bowl.

She tilted the bowl like a cup and slurped loudly.

"You sound like a pig."

Megan lowered the bowl, her face now a mix of colors. "And you look like one!"

And all three of them laughed.

Then Julie said, looking around the empty kitchen, "Finish up. Time you kids got some sleep."

* * *

Bridger got back to the inn, and he saw the bar and dining room were dark. He'd use the side entrance for guests. The night had turned from sticky and humid, to almost cool.

And though he felt completely wired from the night's events, he also felt incredibly tired. He kept thinking about the too-soft mattress in his room, the fluffy comforter, the sound of the ocean waves just reaching his room.

Wired or not, he'd soon fall asleep.

He felt the gun in his pocket. *Crazy . . .* me *with a gun,* he thought. Maybe he'd turn it over to the police. But then that might get the old woman in trouble. Or he could toss it into the ocean. The classic mob way of disposing an unwanted weapon.

Or, maybe just put it in a drawer in his room.

For now at least . . .

As for the book he held tightly in his hand, he'd look at that tomorrow. See what else it explained about the strange stories about the inn, and the ocean, and the events from sixty years ago that so haunted the woman.

He opened the door to the inn—silent, sleeping, such a quiet place with everyone in their rooms. Maybe a few guests reading, most of them sleeping.

And Martin Bridger tiredly walked up the stairs to his room.

TWENTY-EIGHT

Eileen sat in her chair, nodding off.

Too tired to walk to her bed, so drained from talking, from her crying, from her life.

And when she woke, she knew that there might be another reason she still sat in the chair.

Tonight was different.

She felt it, in the room, in talking with the writer.

She could sense things, and what she sensed now made her afraid.

Her eyes scanned her room, looking around at the little islands of light made by her floor lamps. She felt as if she had melted into the chair.

I wish, she thought, *that I'd never have to leave this chair.* It felt so comfortable to simply sit there, not making her bones ache with every painful step to her bedroom.

Sit here forever and—

She stopped. That thought . . .

She felt a chill.

Where did that thought come from? A thought of stay-ing here, thoughts of forever, and now, amidst the tired-ness, her complete exhaustion—fear.

And then she knew.

She had become too weak.

And it, the evil out there, the evil that could now reach her again, had grown strong.

And why had it grown strong?

She knew the reason for that.

If only she had been able to use the gun. If only she wasn't old, if only—

The light began to recede from the small islands of yel-low made by the lamps. Like a tide pulling back for the shore, the light receded while she watched.

"No," she said to no one and nothing. Just a feeble protest.

Not that death was coming for her, but that now there was no one to watch, to record.

Except for the words in her book . . . now in the Abbadon.

The light seeped away, slowly, steadily.

Until Eileen was in darkness. And the darkness of the room shifted.

She had resisted her entire life, she had been—yes, she knew this—a *hero*. Fighting back.

But not now, not anymore.

The darkness shifted until she knew it was a darkness miles and miles away, and miles deep, where an ancient evil sits and broods and now could claim victory over her.

The icy chill of water.

The air all gone.

Her old, red-veined eyes blinking as she tried to find air.

The blackness, a physical feeling, cold, sickening, sum-moning a revulsion that made her tiny body shake.

No power to resist anymore, it claimed her in such a special way, bringing her there . . .

There!

To a deep hell even she could never imagine.

And as was its wont, that evil would now take *so* long squeezing the small amount of life out of her tiny wizened body, destroying and torturing the last person to know about the evil, to fight it, to resist . . .

And out on the desolate street, what small animals there were—the lone tomcat, the Norwegian rat scrounging for garbage scraps, the big-winged moths in love with light— they all knew to stay far, far away.

TWENTY-NINE

Ted woke up early, with only a dull morning light filtering through the windows. He was tempted to push open the shade and see what the day looked like. But then the light would fall onto the bed and maybe wake Liz.

He had long practice in getting out early in the morning without waking her. Vanishing silently so that she never even knew he had been there. Though she had always told him, *Give me a kiss good-bye. Even if I don't wake up.*

But he ignored that.

If it was me, he thought, *I'd like to sleep well into the morning—and hold the kiss.*

Now he stopped for a second and looked at her, the white sheet pulled up tight under her chin.

She could have told him, *Don't go. Forget about helping these people, with their missing boat, their shark tales.* But she let him, and he knew why.

Though she totally hated the idea of his going out, she thought it was what he needed.

And was it true?

Is it some kind of version of getting back on the bike after falling off?

Some fucking bike.

Amazing thing for her to do. And all Ted had to do to keep his part of the bargain was come back.

And after all the nasty dives, from the churning waters of Spuyten Duyvil looking inside a car sunk by the mob, to the murky, scummy water of Red Hook, where the muck holds secrets better left forgotten, this dive today should be easy.

He scooped his wallet and car keys off the bureau and headed downstairs.

Ted pulled into an empty space just past the edge of the dock. A few charter boats already had lines of guys outside, holding their fishing rods up like ill-equipped warriors.

He looked around for Brian's dive boat, which he said, was at the end of the row of charters. At first Ted didn't see it, but then, with some of the bridge sticking up, he spotted it.

He walked past the loud crowd of day fishermen, some already knocking back brewskis. Some sportsmen . . .

As he walked along the concrete dock past the charter boats he glanced up at the sky. Still gray, but not a dark, ominous cloud cover, laced with black rain clouds. No, it still had the look of a sky where the cloud cover would burn off, opening pockets of blue.

Ted assumed that Brian would have checked the weather. Not too much fun to go diving in choppy surf that made it impossible for your BCD to keep you afloat.

He reached the dive boat, a good thirty-footer that could easily handle a dozen divers and their tanks.

For a moment the boat looked quiet, and Ted wondered

if Brian had slept in. But then he saw him emerge from the small cabin at the front, wearing a CBGB's T-shirt stained with what could have been a mix of fish guts, chili sauce, and coffee gone cold.

He didn't notice Ted.

"Hey, Brian—how you doin'?"

Brian looked up. "Oh, great, Ted. Glad you got here. Thought I still had some time. Got the nitrox tanks all set, guessed your size for a suit. Large do it?"

Ted laughed. "Unless the Abbadon's food has already taken a toll."

Then another guy, thin with skin the color of burnt toast, came up to the boat with a tray of coffees and a bag.

He smiled at Brian, then nodded at Ted. "Provisions," he said laughing. "Name's Ally, *mon.*"

Ally put down the bag and stuck his hand out. Ted shook it.

"One of these coffees is for you, and I have every donut the Cape May Bakery had.

Brian hopped off the boat.

"Ally's a great diver. Dove everywhere in the Caribbean."

Ally laughed. "And the Pacific, *mon.* Don't forget that. With those giant rays, twenty feet across. Like being in heaven." Then he let the smile slip, and his eyes locked on Ted's. "Real good to have you with us. We find out what happened to Cap'n Andy, to his ship. Find out . . . just what's going on around here."

"I'm a police diver. Search and Recovery. Not much of a shark detective."

Ally nodded. "My guess is you've seen a lot. Whatever happened, you'll have some ideas."

"Could be."

Brian took one of the coffees and removed the plastic lid. "I'm thinking we should get out of here as soon as we can. Maybe have time for two dives, with recovery time. I don't trust that sky."

"Doesn't look like a storm," Ted said.

"Yeah. Well, things can change fast here. Too fast."

Ally laughed and hopped onto the boat trailing pow-
dered sugar from his snowy donut. "That's the truth . . ."

Brian pointed at the boat. "Be my guest."

Ted jumped onto the boat just as Ally started the engines.

Ally was at the wheel, flying right into the wind, while
Brian and Ted set up their dive gear.

"You have a good fix on where the boat went down?"
Ted asked.

Brian seemed quiet since leaving the dock. Strangely
quiet, especially after recruiting Ted the night before. Maybe
he was one of those guys who just got real *still* on the sea.

That could be . . .

Or it might be something else. Ted had felt something
similar when going out on a patrol or a particularly nasty
recovery, and the guys could feel something bad coming.

Was that it? Did Barefield feel something bad ahead?

"When they went down, their GPS sent out an automatic
signal. It's on battery so it keeps sending out a signal. So, at
any rate, we know where the hell that is."

"Which is hopefully where the boat is."

"Yup. At about a hundred forty feet. They weren't too
far from the shelf. Another mile or so, and the boat could
have been a few thousand feet down."

"And then we'd never know what happened."

"Exactly."

Brian fiddled with the tanks, checking hoses, giving the
mouthpieces a little push to make the air shoot out.

"You checked our gear three times already," Ted said.

The dive master laughed. "Sure did. Guess I just want to
get down. Get in the water. And see . . . what we see."

Brian got up and went to the small storage area under
the fly bridge. He came out with two long metal poles.

"What are they?" Ted asked.

He handed one to Ted. "Never saw these? Kind of underwater guns. Brand name is Harpoon, fires a nasty spike. Designed to take out a big fish with one shot—that is if you hit it in the brain."

"And if you miss?"

Brian laughed. "You have one angry fish."

"Fish? You mean shark."

"Yeah, I guess that's what they're designed for. Shark killers, with good aim. Of course, if we see something on the surface, I have my rifle."

Ted looked up. "Just like *Jaws*?"

"What?"

"You know, when Roy Scheider has his gun and says something like 'die, you motherfucker.'"

"Yeah, just like that. Except, that was the movies."

"Tell me—why are you so convinced that a shark did this?"

"It's not just what happened out here, or the missing kids, who I think no fucking way just ran away. This place . . . Cape May . . . has history . . ."

"Shark history?"

"You bet. Not sure what it is about these waters. Can have years with no problem, decades even—then something happens. First time was in 1916. The railroad brought people from the cities to places like this. Swimming in the ocean became a pastime. Fun at the shore. For a while."

"What happened?"

"So in 1916 people discovered the shore . . . and then there was a series of attacks. During just a one-month period, three men and a boy were killed. At first no one knew what happened, they just vanished like human bobbers. But then during one attack, the fin was so clear, so close . . ."

"A great white?"

"Apparently. A rogue. Who, against everything we seem to know about what sharks like to eat, decided to start preying on humans. The thing even started heading into the goddam canals, water so shallow the monster could barely get in and out. Like it was looking for something. They never caught that shark."

"What happened?"

"People stayed in shallow water. Time went by. Things went back the way they were. Until 1929. And those attacks made the others look like a warm-up. From Montauk on down, seemingly unrelated attacks."

"Different shark, no doubt?"

Brian looked up and grinned. "No doubt? Had to be, right? Yet, God, it seemed like the same thing. Like it wanted to go for innocent people."

Ted looked up at Ally piloting the ship. "'Course I know about the ones in the fifties. Heard all about that from my dad."

"Yeah. The ones that inspired *Jaws*. But you know," he tapped Ted on the shoulder, "tip of the iceberg, man. Tip of the fucking iceberg." Then he handed him one of the harpoon guns.

"Hey, no. You keep this. I never fired it."

"Ally has one, I have one, we each have one, okay? Humor me?"

Ted's hand closed on the gun. "Okay. I'll take it."

"Good."

"Yo!" Ally yelled. "We're almost there."

Ted looked up at the sky, and, no question about it, it had darkened some. He stood up on the rocking boat.

"And not that I don't trust you . . . now it's time for *me* to check the gear."

Brian laughed. "See, a good diver is never satisfied."

THIRTY

Liz had planned on spending some of the day with the kids.

With Ted gone, she had hoped she could steal some time away from the inn. But like some stern stepmother, Mrs. Plano showed up at the door of the office while the kids were outside wolfing down Cheerios.

"Mrs. McShane," she said, "I really need to go over the orders with you today."

Liz looked up, feeling the first attack on her resolve to get out of here with the kids.

"Can't we deal with that tomorrow? My husband had to—"

"I'm afraid not, Mrs. McShane. I have to call the orders in today, and there are things that you have to decide. Of course, I will talk to the Goudge sisters about menus and so on. But we need to do this today . . . ," the woman hesitated, as Liz heard her deliver a well-rehearsed blow, ". . . it's all part of the job."

"Yes, I guess it is. Okay. Maybe after—"

But the woman was shaking her head. "Then the new workers will be coming by for you to interview. I think we've got some good ones there. But again, you need to talk to them, decide."

Liz smiled, game over. "Gotcha. Lots to do." She picked up the phone. "I'll see of I can get Julie to come over, pronto."

Mrs. Plano smiled, then she turned and left the cramped office.

And Liz thought that maybe it might be a good thing to be so busy, with Ted under the water.

Keep her mind off things.

Maybe . . .

Brian had anchored the dive boat from both the front and rear, a classic technique to give the boat the maximum stability and also guarantee that the boat would be there when the three of them surfaced.

Always a good thing to hope for.

The dive suit felt a bit snug, but nothing he couldn't live with. Brian had explained that he had considered diving in dry suits. But a dry suit was bulky, and its "Michelin Man" style cost maneuverability. And getting in and out of tight spaces with a dry suit on could be tricky. If they had to explore the sunken fishing boat, if it was upside down, a lean neoprene would work a lot better.

So they were going to be a little cold.

But again, nothing that he couldn't live with for forty-five minutes or so.

Though diving with the nitrox mixture meant that they had a longer dive time. Longer dive time, and less concern about decompression.

"Weight good?" Brian asked.

Ted tugged at his weight belt that held twelve pounds.

"Should be fine. Maybe a bit heavy, but I don't want to waste any time getting down."

Brian nodded and turned to his partner. "How we looking, Ally?"

"We drifted some setting the anchors, *mon* . . . but nothing too bad. The GPS signal is twenty, twenty-five meters— due east."

"Okay," Brian said. "So we'll go straight down and then head east. Not sure what the bottom is like. I imagine it's pretty smooth. But we're close enough to the shelf that there could be some rock, some protrusions."

Ally, amazingly thin in his suit, appeared next to them.

"Looks flat on the screens," Ally said.

"Yeah. Good. Okay." He looked at Ted. "You all set?"

Ted nodded. He wished he had the underwater radio setup that the NYPD divers used. If the Jersey state troopers were diving, no doubt they'd have it. Bit crazy jumping into this without being able to communicate.

But the troopers weren't coming.

And every day that passed would make it harder to find out what happened to Captain Andy, his crewman, and his two missing clients.

"Okay. Once down, let's stick together. Scan left and right as we head east. If we find the boat, I guess it will be important for you, Ted, to get a good look, right? See what happened. Then maybe we can come up, talk about it as we off gas, talk about what else we should take a look at. Then a second dive."

"If we need to," Ally said laughing. "Gonna be too cold down there, *mon*. This isn't the Caymans."

"Right. *If* we need to. I forgot to mention one thing," Brian said. "It's a bit unlikely, but, well . . . if we find some bodies, I'd like to bring them up."

A little surprise, Ted thought.

"You have any problem with that?"

"Nope. Seen enough waterlogged bodies in my time.

No problem at all. But I gotta tell you, out here, with all the big fish down there, not too sure you'll find anything much resembling a body."

"Yeah. That's what I figured." He took a breath. "Okay. Let's hit the water."

Ted looked up at the sky. Definitely a smoky-black gray now. *Some local squall rolling in,* he thought. This cloud cover was about to ruin a lot of people's day at the beach.

And he thought of Liz, the kids, just as he did every time before he hit the water, every time he was away from them.

Liz took Julie's hand.

"God . . . thank you. I had hoped I could get away. But," she smiled at the girl, "evil Mrs. Plano cooked up a nice little agenda that ended that fantasy."

Julie smiled back warmly, and for a moment she seemed so much older than her years. Liz thought, *Guess that makes sense . . . the girl has been around, and now she's saving my butt.*

"We'll be fine. I love being with them."

"And they with you. So, maybe the beach for a bit? Though it looks a little cloudy. I could also give you some money for the arcade."

"Daver loves his Skee-Ball."

"I know, I think he has a couple hundred prize tickets already. Maybe some lunch at Extreme Ice Cream?"

"Great. Don't worry, Mrs. Mc—"

"Liz. Please, the 'Mrs.' makes me feel so old."

The girl laughed. "Liz. And don't worry. I'll make sure they're fine."

For a moment the choice of words seemed off.

I'll make sure they're fine.

Of course they'll be fine. It seemed strange.

But Julie smiled quickly, and then turned back to the

two kids, patiently waiting outside in the dining room for the day's adventure to begin.

No longer was there air in the room.

Where once was air, now something else seeped into the room from the walls, the ceiling, from the dark shaded windows. Something smoky, a deep, dark smoke that started to suck out all the light in the room until the darkness became total.

Under the sheets Martin twisted, knowing that once again he was dreaming.

But that knowledge was no help at all. He was a prisoner of whatever vision his mind wanted to create.

The smoke filled the room, but now when Martin saw himself—and strangely he could see himself in the bed, twisting, writhing—he could *feel* the smoke.

And it was wet.

The smoke was water.

Then the room itself, the walls, all vanished, and Bridger could start to see again.

He watched the darkness begin to lighten.

He watched ripples move, streaming through the water.

The lightening water. Turning from an utter black, to purple, to something gray, lightening even more.

As if . . . something was moving into shallower and shallower water . . .

Marian Setlow loved it here.

So much of her life seemed to have somehow gone wrong, losing her job at the advertising company, then losing her husband to his secretary. And her two kids didn't seem to have any time for her, though she did get the obligatory call once a month.

Their begrudging attention.

Not to be confused with affection.

There wasn't much of that in her life these days.

Much? None.

Unless a few kind words from the guys at Scaliano's Deli could be taken for affection.

Still, coming here had been one of the best things she ever did. Once they sold the house in Irvington, cashed out big time, she was left with a nice bit of money. No husband, but he didn't fight her on the settlement. Gave her half.

Bought her off.

The way such things work. You get some money, and the husband gets a younger woman for his golden years.

But here, in her house on the canal that led to the bay and the harbor, she could almost forget about all that.

Not forgive the bastard. No, she hoped his testicles fell off some night during whatever athletic lovemaking his new wife put him through.

Here there was water, and the calling of the gulls—a constant soothing sound. And the ship horns when weather was bad. Fresh seafood. The absolute best seafood, all year round, which was good even when it was cold.

As she snapped the lower half of her one-piece bathing suit into place, Marion reminded herself that she best watch just how much of that good seafood she ate. Her suit, a relic a good six years old, now felt more than a bit snug.

Screw it, she thought. *Not like there's anyone I need to keep in shape for.*

At least not now.

She walked to the end of the small dock that edged out into the canal.

She loved her morning swims, the water a bit chilly but so refreshing.

She had little aches. Tiny things really, popping up here and there. Something on her left side, near her hip. A knee that sometimes gave her a pinch as she walked. And when she woke up and tried to sit up in bed, something painful was slumbering near her lower back, pinching her there.

The swimming made all that go away, for a while at least.

She grabbed a splintery mooring pole, and dipped her right foot into the water.

Chilly, as usual. No matter—once she was in, and swimming full out to the open bay, she'd warm up.

She had been a champion swimmer back at St. Mary's in Baltimore. And now, years later, she could still move pretty fast.

She took a breath.

And then smoothly dove into the water.

THIRTY-ONE

Megan squinted up at Julie.

Julie looked so magical this way, the sun behind her, just like a beautiful princess with a halo.

"You're pretty," Megan said.

She couldn't see if that made the girl smile. But Megan bet it did.

"Why, thank you, Miss Megan. You're very pretty, too."

Megan heard Daver laugh. She turned to see him take another bite of his hot dog. Then he spoke with his mouth full; that was always so gross.

"Can we go back to the beach soon?"

Megan saw Julie move, the sunlight now landing right on Megan, and the girl turned away.

"You were the one who said he was hungry, mister. Something about not having breakfast?"

She saw Daver take another bite, almost as if he couldn't speak without some hot dog in his mouth.

"I wasn't hungry then. But then I got hungry."

Julie laughed. It was a nice laugh, a clear, light sound. Not like her daddy's laugh, which always seemed rough, almost like a bark. Or even her mommy, who laughed so quietly.

"Well now, guys," Julie said, "you must be full, so I guess some beach time is in order."

Julie turned back to Megan. "Okay with you, little miss?"

Megan nodded. She didn't much care what they did, as long as they were with Julie.

There was something about just *being* with Julie that felt good.

Megan slid off the bench outside the snack place and took Julie's hand.

Liz ripped open the envelope. It was addressed to her and came from the management company that hired her.

She read the letter, immediately confused. After making sure she understood it, she went in search of Mrs. Plano. First she checked the dining room, only now recovered from the mayhem of breakfast. But none of the waitresses there knew where the woman was. Then she headed into the kitchen, already bustling with peeling and slicing.

At first she didn't see the short woman, but then, over by the massive sinks at the back, she spotted Mrs. Plano talking to the Goudge sisters. Though nothing had been said, Liz got the definite feeling that there was no love lost between those three pillars of the inn.

She walked over, interrupting.

"Sorry, Mrs. Plano. I wonder if I could speak with you?"

Mrs. Plano turned slowly, not one to be so easily moved. "I was reviewing some things with the cooks, Mrs. McShane—"

The woman said 'cooks' as though the Goudges' cuisine

wasn't the mainstay of the inn that it quite clearly was. People loved the rooms, the nearby sea. But without that old-fashioned home cooking, the place would probably be deserted.

Estella Goudge waved a hand. "You can talk to us later. We *do* have work to do right now."

Mrs. Plano nodded. "Fine then." She turned to Liz. Liz forced a polite smile and led the way out of the kitchen, and into the small office.

"Would you mind shutting the door?"

Mrs. Plano reached behind her and pushed the door shut. The windowless room immediately felt warm, dry, and airless. Liz would like this to be fast. But she feared it wouldn't be.

"I got this letter," Liz said, holding it up.

"Yes?"

"It's from Onshore Realty, the management company."

Mrs. Plano took the letter without enthusiasm.

Then, again, "Yes. I see."

"It says that the owner, Mr. Tollard, will be having a prolonged recovery at the Noble Medical Center. They want to extend my contract."

Mrs. Plano nodded.

"Well then, that's a good thing, I guess."

"I don't know. But I thought that Mr. Tollard had just gone away. Some family problem, I thought. But this hospital in Pennsylvania . . . is there something wrong? How come no one told me?"

Mrs. Plano handed the letter back.

"You see, Mrs. McShane, they probably didn't tell you on purpose. They probably didn't think it was important. But Mr. Tollard did have to go that hospital. It's a . . . special kind of hospital."

"And exactly what kind is that?"

Mrs. Plano fixed Liz with her eyes, so small, like her frame, and nearly hooded in her puffy face.

"It's a hospital for those with a mental illness, Mrs. Mc-Shane. Something happened to Mr. Tollard. That's why he had to leave, you see. Something happened to him."

Liz held the letter, now like the tip of some dark iceberg. The first door in a house of secrets.

"Something happened to him? Something happened to him *here*?"

"You could say that. Now, I best get—"

Liz reached out and—very gently—put her hand on Mrs. Plano's right forearm, stopping her.

"I'd like to know what 'that' is. What happened here? If I'm to stay . . ." She took a breath. "Can you tell me?"

Mrs. Plano didn't look happy at the prospect. But then her eyes seemed to open a bit, widen with memory, with perhaps even excitement.

"Very well. I can." She took a breath, sighing. "But do you mind. Let me see that everything is good for lunch, the dinner plans, too. Then we can talk?"

"Okay." Liz nodded. "Later then."

And Mrs. Plano left the office.

Marian took pride in her long, smooth strokes. Even young kids looked awkward next to her powerful movements. Pretty amazing about swimming, she thought. Years . . . decades later, you can jump in the water, and you're still a seventeen-year-old swim champ.

Though those arms *did* have to move more weight and a less sleek shape through the water.

She scanned the small bay that led to the ocean for any sign of jet skiers.

That was the biggest problem. The boats usually watched for swimmers, even the day-trippers out for blue fish or hunting the perfect spot to crab. But the kids on the jet skis acted as though they were on crack. One of them could come from nowhere and plow right into her.

Not that she hadn't complained,

But the coast guard told her it was a town problem, and the town's harbor police consisted of three men who only smirked when she complained.

So she just had to be alert, careful, watchful.

The water had felt as chilly as usual after that first plunge. Prickly gooseflesh rose on her arms. But once she started swimming, once she locked into her rhythm, she felt heat growing from within. Such a great feeling, to go from that cold, the water trying so hard to chill your body, then building up that nice warmth from the intense exercise.

She looked up. Through her swimming goggles the bay looked deserted. By this time of day, all the fishing boats out for the morning were well gone. The afternoon charters, the lazy-man boats, wouldn't leave until two . . . boats for those who cared more about their sleep than catching fish.

Her hand brushed something. Something white and slick. She gave it a sideways glance.

A plastic bag.

They seemed to be everywhere. A thousand years from now, the planet will be covered with white bags.

She pushed it away.

Marian kept plowing ahead to her turnaround point, midway in the bay.

Ted kicked down, equalizing his ears easily as he dove deeper. He hadn't gone down twenty feet before he saw just how bad the visibility was. He had expected terrible visibility, and the North Atlantic—true to form—delivered just that.

And he had to wonder again about the wisdom of doing this without an underwater communications system. While it was understandable that Brian's dive operation wouldn't have such gear, it still might have been a good idea to locate a radio.

Maybe the state police could have loaned some gear.

But then, how long would that take? A few days? And a few days of deep currents could work wonders with the wreck.

Ted turned on his headlamp, hoping that it would make the murk a bit more transparent. But the light seemed to only highlight the "snow" of debris swirling around him as he kicked down.

He checked his gauges, nitrox looked good, depth forty . . . fifty feet. Nearly halfway there. He looked to his right and saw the outlines of Brian and Ally, dark shapes to the side, but now also dotted with their pale yellow lights atop their heads.

Getting cold, too, Ted noted.

One gets used to the fireside warmth of a dry suit. No amount of neoprene would ever make this wet suit a pleasant experience.

He hoped they found what they were looking for fast, figure out what happened to Captain Andy and his poor crewman and clients, and get back to shore.

And if it was a big shark?

Well, that would be interesting, Ted thought. Trying to convince the town that something that's happened quite a few times in the past is—guess what, boys and girls— happening again.

Another glance at his gauges.

Seventy-five feet. Getting well into the red zone. Ted always explained to any new divers on the force that there is a big difference between a dive at sixty feet, and one that goes deeper. You can always bolt for daylight from sixty feet. Deeper than that, it all changed.

Ten . . . twenty feet . . . could make all the difference in the world.

The murk, as he expected, thickened. With his light on the visibility, had to be eight . . . ten feet. Might as well be blind down here.

He felt something touch his side and looked to see Brian, and next to him, Ally. They gave each other the okay sign. It was a good idea to bunch up as they neared the bottom. Cumbersome way to dive, but at least they'd start together and—with luck—carry out some kind of search-and-recovery dive plan.

Ted checked his wrist computer for depth. One hundred ten feet.

The bottom had to be close.

Instinctively the three divers began to slow their heads-down descent.

Wouldn't do to crash headfirst into the sandy floor.

At least, it should be a sandy floor. Though there might be outcrops of rock. Strange, exposed chunks connected to some massive underwater bit of bedrock.

Their three headlights pointed straight down.

Give me the Bahamas, Ted thought. But he had done so much diving in water like this that the blue-green crystal clear water of Caribbean seemed like a fantasy.

Then, just ahead, the murk changed.

Ted pointed. Bottom coming up.

Another foot or so, and the bottom, a smeary grayish terrain even under the headlights, was clearly there.

Ted turned smoothly and righted himself. He checked his buoyancy, always a tricky thing when diving with someone else's gear.

He felt himself start to slip down just a bit, so he gave his BCD the tiniest injection of nitrox. He waited again, and all felt good—neutrally buoyant. He looked to Brian and Ally, hovering nearby, waiting. Brian made a symbol signaling that Ted should lead.

It occurred to Ted, *They're depending on me. This is not the usual recreational dive that they do. Both probably a bit anxious, hearts racing a bit. Stressed. Something to keep in mind.*

A concern . . .

He swam ahead slowly. In this low visibility they could go flying by the wrecked fishing boat so easily, missing it. Then they'd waste time going back and forth, even moving farther away from the dive boat.

Slowly, with only the slightest fin kicks.

He thought of his family. Could they be any farther away? Ten stories of ocean sealing him off from their world. A sea that has hidden more secrets, swallowed more deaths than he would ever know.

Giant, lumbering, hungry.

It ain't the Hudson, Ted thought.

He glanced behind and saw the other divers close, scanning left and right.

Ted turned back.

Thinking, *Come on. Be here. Don't play with us today.*

And then . . . there it was.

THIRTY-TWO

Ted stopped as soon as he saw something ahead.

It took a few minutes for some recognizable form to emerge from the murky water. But then he saw the shape of what looked like a boat, and then, twisted at an odd angle, the stern of the vessel, twisted into a kind of V.

The boat looked like it had been snapped in two like a toothpick.

He turned to Brian, who was checking his underwater GPS.

At least they had no trouble finding the pieces.

Ted used his arms to signal that the other divers should circle around on either side. Get as many views of the thing as possible.

Ted wondered, *Where was Captain Andy, his mate, the fishermen?*

Long gone, he imagined. Down here food didn't go to waste for too long. And as if confirming that fact, Ted saw a black eel scurry out of the wreck, performing a few jagged moves before swimming away.

I was never big on identifying animals, Ted thought. *Black ugly eel will do. I'm good on how to get into a locked car buried in sixty feet of water. But eels and fish?*

Someday, he promised himself. When he retired to the Caribbean.

As Brian and Ally went around the boat, Ted moved ahead slowly, aware there could be any number of jagged points sticking out. Could be a ragged piece of floorboard jutting out, or some metal from the superstructure. Maybe a bit of engine lodged like a trap in some nasty spot.

You had to be careful.

He moved closer, now only feet away from the wreck.

He had sent Brian and Ally around to the side because this was the tricky part. Better that someone experienced with wrecks did this. Someone who knew that a wreck could have teeth, teeth that bit and trapped.

Yeah, he thought. *This is my job.*

Ted hesitated a minute.

He noted where his thoughts were leading. Thoughts to his last wreck dive.

When he lost a good friend.

A few quick images of that dive. The panic growing, the fear, and all of sudden, no matter how many dives they'd done, they became something for the great ship to eat.

But after only a few of those thoughts, Ted forced himself to stop.

All that was a distraction down here.

Distractions killed.

And with that realization, Ted cleared his mind.

Above the boat he could see the pale glow of the other divers proceeding slowly around the edges. Good.

Now to move ahead, into the open mouth of the wreck, the broken splintery gash of the boat.

A slight kick—and it carried him slowly ahead. Ally, buoyant, floated a few inches above the ship.

Ted saw the break.

The boat looked like it had smashed fucking hard onto a rocky shoal. Smashed, doubled up—and sank.

But there were no rocks out here.

Gliding slowly, he looked down, into the darkness of the small open cabin area. He saw things floating around. A bit of a life preserver, some rope swaying in the small play of currents, both looking alive when there was only death here.

Something tapped his head.

One of the other divers, he assumed, done with their circuit.

Ted looked up, the light falling full-square on what just hit him.

There, trapped in the ropes, pieces missing . . . but still recognizable.

Sure, with one eye, most of the head, most of the torso, and what looked like a leg. Yeah, had to be a leg.

Someone from the boat.

Ted knew enough not to kick back.

Wouldn't be good to kick back in shock, backing into something that could cut a gash into his suit or cut a hose.

He had to hover there with this thing, hardly human, bobbing there in front of him.

Not much left of it.

Ted fought to get his breathing under control. Even under nitrox, it wasn't good to breathe too deeply. He looked to the side and saw Brian coming close. In a few moments the other diver would see Ted's prize.

Ted put a hand up, stopping Brian.

He looked around for Ally, who appeared beside him.

Ted put his hand in front of his light and pointed to the surface, a signal that they should head up followed by the "ok" sign.

He saw them signal "ok" back.

Good enough for the first dive, Ted thought. *Now that we know where the ship is and can plan a second dive.*

Though Ted thought he already knew quite clearly what the hell happened out here . . .

There, thought Marian looking left and right, and finding her landmarks on the shore that signaled that she had hit her turnaround point. Though she felt she could easily do another hundred meters or so.

Still, this was enough of a workout.

She swam in an arc that took her away from the glare of the morning sun and had her heading back to the canal entrance and her home.

A few strokes, and then her leg hit something.

Another plastic bag, some floating wood, or—

Another kick, and she hit something *hard.*

She looked left, expecting to see—somehow—the hull of a boat. Because that's what it felt like.

Nothing there,

Then she looked right.

For a moment she didn't see what it was, the thing right next to her. Not through the spattered lenses of her swimming goggles. Something sticking up. Like the blackish single sail of a small skiff, except this was close, right *there.*

Then it instantly became clear.

The fin of a shark. Only yards away, keeping pace with her, going at her speed.

She kept swimming.

It wouldn't be good to stop.

Stopping wouldn't be good.

Stroke.

Stroke.

Stroke . . .

* * *

Tyler Gage stepped out of the kitchen of his clam-and-fries place, the Sea Shack, to the small dock at the back. He lit his Marlboro and looked out to the water, the surface shimmering even under the overcast sky.

And he saw, as he often did, Marian Setlow doing her swim.

He saw her.

He took a drag of his cigarette.

The he froze, seeing what was next to her.

"No fuckin' way," he said.

Thinking, *What should I do? Call someone, get some help, do . . . something?*

But what?

So he stood there for what seemed like such a long time but in actuality was mere seconds, and he *watched.*

Stroke, stroke, and—

She looked right.

The shark was gone.

God, it was gone. And in those moments Marian told herself what a tale she'd have to tell people, about the encounter, how close, how lucky, how bizarre.

Giddy with her survival.

When ahead, she saw it surface. Seeing, sweet God, sweet Jesus, its open maw.

Stopping now—not as if that did anything. Then the eyes.

Expecting the dull eyes of something that didn't have any feeling.

But that's not what she saw in those eyes.

The eyes looked at her, studied her, as its teeth moved forward, and so quickly closed.

* * *

"Hey!" Tyler Gage yelled.

He looked around at the few fishing boats at the docks, a few being scrubbed. He screamed as loud as he could.

He saw the shark hit, going at Marian from the front, looking as though it bypassed her head and went for her side.

It hit, and a puffy red cloud exploded—*exploded!*—into the air like a balloon.

"No!" Tyler yelled, as he watched the shark, now with Marian between its teeth, twist and turn in the water.

As if . . . as if . . . playing with her.

The agony was total. She felt everything, the teeth biting down hard, but not as hard as they could, not cutting her in two. The feel of the white hardness of the teeth, so many teeth, a vice, a prison. The rough texture of the gray skin close, tight wet skin above the teeth, and the smell—so many sensations, all competing for attention above her screams, her shrill, desperate, and constant screaming.

And when she had no air left to scream, when her mouth eerily opened and shut like a puffer fish, soundlessly, open . . . shut—that's when the teeth started at last to tighten, and finally all the sensations thankfully ended.

The woman was dragged underwater.

The red cloud seemed to hang suspended in the air for a few moments, only to be replaced by a red pool that now caught the dull sunlight.

It was over.

"Jesus," Tyler said, not yelling now. He looked at one of the boats across the bay, and he saw a few men standing there, pointing.

They had seen it.

So it wasn't a dream. Wasn't a nightmare.

It had happened.

"Jesus Christ . . ." he said again.

And now he turned, racing to the phone, to call—who?

The police?

Who the fucking hell did you call?

He'd start with them.

They'd know.

God, he hoped they'd know.

"I'm going in the water," Daver said.

Julie looked over at Megan playing in the sand, safely under the shade of the yellow-and-blue-striped beach umbrella.

"Okay," Julie said. "But stay close, so I can see you."

Daver looked as if he barely heard the instructions.

"I will," he said, racing to the water, kicking up a flurry of sand as he did.

Julie looked back at Megan, then back to Daver hitting the surf. She looked up to the sky, still overcast.

Everything felt safe.

Julie could only hope that . . . that meant everything was really safe for now.

She kept her eyes on Daver, as the boy dove yet again into the churning water.

THIRTY-THREE

Ted looked at Brian, then Ally.

"You guys okay?"

"Yeah. I'm alright," Brian said too quickly.

Ally laughed. "Maybe *you* are. But I now have enough bad mojo for a year of nightmares. Shit, man, that was too freaky."

Ted took a giant gulp of water. The boat rocked crazily despite being held by the twin anchors.

He could see that the other two divers were shaken. Good idea to come back up, not just to off gas, but to get a plan for what to do next.

Brian looked up at him, backlit by the sun.

"You ever see anything like that?"

Ted decided to lie. "Yeah. I mean bodies get pretty funky when they've been underwater for a while. So, yeah."

Ally laughed. "*Funky*? You call that funky? That dude has sailed way past funky. Half-eaten, half-fucking-*eaten*!

And then wrapped in all that rope like some goddam Christmas present from hell."

"Okay. I think we got the picture, Ally," Ted said, smiling, wanting to get the mate to tone down his language. Bad enough they had to go down there again. They didn't need Ally painting pictures of just how bad it was down there.

Not when they had to go back down.

"It was a fucking shark, right?" Brian asked.

"Guess so. Had to be big. The ship broke in two. A monster. But—"

Ted hesitated. He didn't want to say anything to add to the jitters of the other divers.

"But what, *mon?*" Ally said, his ever-present smile now evaporated.

"Well, why would it attack, and leave someone down there? It doesn't make any sense."

"You mean, why didn't that old white shark eat the rest of that dude?"

Ted smiled. "You could put it that way. Doesn't match anything I know about sharks. It's like the shark was crazy."

"More crazy than hungry," Ally said. "Maybe we should forget about going back down."

Brian cleared his throat. He had been deferring to Ted; but this was *his* boat, his deal after all. Still, he knew what *he* wanted. "We came here to see what happened. Now we know, and we can tell people, and everyone can keep their eyes open. All the hell the way from here to Asbury Park. But I need to go back down . . . grab some pictures. And try to get Andy up."

Ted looked up. "Bring the body up?"

Brian nodded. "It's what I'd want done."

"There ain't that much of it to bring up," Ally said, making no secret now of his jitters.

Ted stood up.

"Alright—we've had enough time topside. Let's do it. Got something we can use . . . I mean, to put him in?"

Brian nodded.

"Then we'll go down and get him, cut away the rope. Get some pictures of the damage. Just in case the local authorities don't believe what happened. Show them what the fish did."

"Right," Brian said.

"One more thing," Ted added. "Let's do it fast, okay?"

Ally laughed. "No argument from me, *mon,* no fuckin' argument from me."

The three men silently put their gear on, the only noise the sound of weight belts being clicked, hoses being checked, face masks being swirled in fresh water. Not for the first time Ted noted how medieval this was. Knights suiting up. The silence hanging over the boat, a silence that came from each man checking his personal mental inventory, checking gear, checking his state of mind.

In minutes they were ready.

The boat bobbed and rocked in the choppy water, but the twin lines kept it tethered.

Ted looked at Brian, who gave him a thumbs-up.

Ted grabbed his mouthpiece.

"Here we go," he said.

He popped the mouthpiece in, and then the three men rolled once again into the ocean.

Martin Bridger opened his eyes.

He felt so cold, as if icy wet air had suddenly filled the room.

He pulled the sheet and the thin terry-cloth blanket tight, but that didn't stop the chill as he lay there, shaking.

Fever, he thought. *I got some kind of fever. Not been taking care of myself, getting all caught up in this story. Not eating right, not sleeping right, drinking too much.*

But as he lay there, the chill started to fade.

It's not really cold, he thought. No, in fact the room now felt hot and airless. He reached over to the side table, passing over a glass with some whiskey from two nights ago, for a glass of what he thought was pure water.

He took a sip. No alcoholic buzz.

Success.

He took another sip, finishing the water.

He sat up in bed, the chilled feeling from just a few minutes ago fading. The fragments of his dream, the feeling of cold and motion and . . .

. . . all started to fade.

He ran his tongue over his teeth, as if there was something to clear there. But he hadn't eaten since a late lunch yesterday.

I have to eat, he thought, *get a decent meal.*

He looked at the bureau.

He saw the book that Eileen had given him. *Amazing,* he thought, *it could be that all the secrets of this place are in that book.*

The writings of a crazy lady. Does age do that? Pulling a gun on him. Scared, crazy lady imaging demons from decades ago.

Now he had the gun.

Never had a gun, Bridger thought.

He stood up and walked over to the bureau. He picked up the gun, feeling its weight. Though compact, the gun felt heavy and dense in his hand.

The bullets were still in his pocket. *I probably should toss it, lose the gun. Who knows whether it even works?*

He picked up the book. The leather binding cracked, small flakes of leather sprinkling to the bureau top just from picking it up.

I should go eat, he thought. *Get a good meal. Take better care of myself.*

But instead he walked back to the bed with the crumbling

diary and sat down. There was just enough light to read, despite the faded lines of ink; he could decipher the flowing penmanship of a young woman from so long ago.

He could open the shade, get more light . . .

But somehow this darkness felt right.

He grabbed a yellow pad from the floor and flipped past the first few pages.

He opened the diary.

He started reading.

Julie turned around, sensing movement behind her. She checked Daver, jumping in and out of the surf, then looked back to the street.

A police car . . . people turning as two policemen started down the stone steps to the beach.

Back to check Daver, nicely between the red flags, and not too deep.

Once more to the police, in their dark navy blue uniforms, walking on the sand, looking so strange.

One of the lifeguards jumped off his chair and turned to the two police officers.

Julie looked back to the sea. For a moment she didn't see Daver. Then his head popped up, a magical elf, rising out of the water, grinning wildly, lost to his fun.

The police talked to the lifeguards. They pointed at the water. The lifeguard turned to look at the ocean.

Julie stood up.

She turned to Megan. "Megan, stay right here. I have to get Daver."

The little girl looked up. "Why, did he do something bad?"

"No, I just need—I'll be right back. You just wait here, okay?"

The girl nodded, and Julie ran down to the water.

"Daver!" she yelled just as he disappeared into the

waves. Julie kept running, her steps wobbly in the wet sand and the pull of the surf.

Running to where Daver vanished, now aware that the police were here because something happened. Something happened, just as she knew it would.

Daver didn't surface.

But then, like a seal, Daver popped out of the water, the salt water cascading off his sleek body. Julie resisted the urge to grab him and pull him out.

Instead, with an exaggerated gentleness, she reached out and touched his shoulders. Daver's eyes squinted, avoiding the water dripping off his mop of hair.

"Daver, you have to come out."

His face sank and scrunched up into a mask that was part protest and part confusion.

"Why?" he spat out some of the salt water, then continued. "I stayed," he looked around to make sure what he was saying was correct, "right where I should be. I didn't go out too far."

Her hand tightened just the slightest on his arm.

"Come back to the blanket. I'll explain."

"But I—"

Julie leaned close. "Daver, I need you to come out of the water *now*."

Daver hesitated, looking at Julie, his eyes finally clear. Then he nodded begrudgingly and started to walk out of the ocean.

"I don't see why I have to come out of the water. I was having fun, I—"

Julie let his complaints fade into the background. Megan sat in the shade, as if she hadn't even taken notice that Julie left. The police stood next to the lifeguards, but then one of the guards ran down to the surf with a megaphone.

He grabbed first one, then another of the poles with red flags indicating the safe swimming area. He started yelling to the bathers.

"Everyone please—out of the water . . . now!"

The guard kept repeating the instructions as the swimmers struggled out, a few looking over their shoulder for whatever boogeyman might be chasing them out of the water. But the sea looked calm and peaceful.

As Julie got to the blanket, she saw the guard race down to the other lifeguard station.

The police started trudging back to the street.

"See," Julie said. "Everyone has to come out of the water."

Daver looked back at his former playground.

"Yeah, but why?"

She tossed him a *Beauty and the Beast* towel. "I don't know. But you see, everyone is out. Maybe there's an undertow."

She almost told him, *Look at the police*—visible evidence that something was indeed very wrong.

But Daver started drying himself and, in that way kids always have, he moved on.

Julie sat down.

"Can we go to the arcade then?" Daver asked.

"Maybe. Maybe we can," Julie said.

"I don't like the arcade," Megan said. "My ponies don't, either."

Julie reached out and brushed Megan's shiny brown hair, so soft and smooth.

Maybe the arcade isn't a good idea. Maybe they should go back to the inn.

It's all happening now, Julie guessed. She wouldn't leave these two children.

And she could only hope that that would be enough.

IV

The Inn Lives Forever

THIRTY-FOUR

If anything, the poor visibility had taken a turn for the worse.

Now, whether because of currents moving toward the shore, or just the regular ebb and flow of these waters, the sea was filled with tiny flecks of debris and sand. Their dive lights did little but make the snowy scene glow.

Almost fucking festive, Ted thought.

Ally and Brian took pictures of the boat, though now Ted wondered if there'd be enough detail to show the coast guard and the police what had happened here, and how they better get some warnings out.

But the body . . .

That would speak volumes.

Ted hovered near it, the eyes wide open, a loopy grin on its face. The mouth hung partly open, a gasp for air, a scream . . . maybe both.

The jagged bit from the captain's midsection had turned a puffy white, laced with pink, the blood long drained.

How come nothing else came to feast on it?

Free food, this far out to sea?

Should be *nothing* left of the guy.

Nothing.

Ted reached down and slid a dive knife out of its sheath. No touristy three-inch blade, his knife had a big blade, with a well-maintained edge.

Quickly, he cut the tangle of rope crisscrossing the head and the man's pulpy body. He tried not to let the knife hit the skin. *The guy's been through enough,* Ted thought.

Ted's eyes focused on cutting as the body bobbed back and forth, waving, the left arm rising slowly when freed.

I've seen and done some bad stuff underwater, Ted thought. *But nothing like this, nothing—*

Slice—

Suddenly, with one big cut, the body was nearly completely free. Only something was pinning the poor bastard by his feet. Ted looked down to see what had to be moved.

No, that wasn't the problem. The guy had no feet. The legs ended just below the knee. Something pinned a chunk of bone, though. Ted would have to go into the boat a bit, try to pry it loose, and—

He had a thought. Something that made him hesitate.

What is this like, he thought. *What does* this *feel like?*

And for some reason it all became very clear. Why, it's just like a lobster trap, baited with a chunk of fish sitting in the mesh to lure the lobster in, draw it deeper.

Like the ship that ate his friend . . .

Ted pulled back. He felt something close by. Ally, maybe, hustling his butt to finish. But when he looked around he could see the pale light of their headlamps still on the other side of the wreck.

Ted held up his hand, feeling the motion of water, a current, something stirring up the bottom, the silt, the debris. Or—

Something moving.

Ted ignored the nearly freed corpse.

The tempting bait.

He kept looking at the lights only yards away. Watching as something eclipsed one of the lights. It vanished, reappeared, and—

A fog appeared before the light, muting it even more, so that Ted couldn't see its color.

Not from this distance.

But he could guess. He kicked with his fins and glided over the body, its hair floating wildly, giving Cap'n Andy's crazed look an added bit of madness.

Ted sailed over the maw of the wreckage, his big knife held out in front.

Until he was close enough that his light caught the fog, close enough that its deep burgundy color was clear. Clear now, as was the shark that held Ally between its teeth.

Ted couldn't see the man's eyes. But he could see the way Ally's limbs kicked, how he struggled madly.

Fuck it, Ted thought. *Bite him, kill him.*

It was like a cat, playing with a toy.

Enjoying the kill.

Ted turned to see Brian, backing up. Ted pointed to the surface.

The shark was a monster. Bigger than any great white Ted had ever seen. And the three of them had been lured here so easily.

But then another cloud exploded as the shark bit through Ally, popping his body, a bloody piñata.

Gotta get the hell out of here, he thought. *Get the fuck—*

But out of that fog, the shark emerged, first its bullet-shaped snout, then the rows of teeth, tinged with red, dripping flesh, and Ted knew that he was a dead man.

There was not a movement he could make fast enough that would do a single thing.

But in that moment, his mind still alive with crazy-faced

corpses and thoughts of human lobster traps, his light caught the animal's eyes.

Shark's eyes.

Always so dull, black, empty.

Ted had had close encounters with blue sharks and great white sharks. The eyes were always empty, single-minded, resolute in their desire to do one thing: eat.

But these eyes . . .

They weren't like that at all. These were like the eyes he'd seen on some cracked-up guy with a gun on a deserted street in Red Hook. Not lifeless, not dead—but alive with madness.

Almost . . . human eyes.

Merciless human eyes.

Ted saw movement from the left. Brian, bolting for the surface, about as uncontrolled an ascent as Ted had ever seen. Pure panic.

The creature turned, spotting Brian getting away. The movement of its massive body turning sent an underwater wave flying toward Ted. Then, the razorlike tail fin slammed into Ted, knocking the air out of him, making him spit out his mouthpiece.

He grabbed it quickly, and when he looked up he saw Brian with his two legs well-buried in the shark's maw . . . again, not biting down, but holding Brian with those dagger teeth, torturing him.

Christ, Ted thought, *what the hell is going on here?*

The red fog was everywhere.

And though he knew it was hopeless, Ted started for the surface. No safety stops, as he bolted for sky at twice the safe speed.

He had no doubt that he'd fail to see daylight again.

Daver felt Julie's gentle push at his shoulder.

He tuned around to her. "What's the hurry, Julie?"

He saw her look back to the beach. A strange look, as though something was coming, chasing them. Like when he used to play freeze-tag in Brooklyn, running, looking over his shoulder to see if someone was gaining on him.

All the time taking care not to trip and fall on the sidewalk.

He'd done that plenty of times.

"Nothing," Julie said. "I just want to get back to the inn. You guys must be hungry, right?"

"I'm not hungry," Megan said.

But Daver had a feeling that there was something else . . . something Julie wasn't saying.

The way she tugged him out of the water, then the way she packed up all their stuff—so fast!

And the police . . .

He was sure Megan didn't notice. But he did. He saw the police on the beach looking out of place in their dark blue uniforms. The police, talking to the lifeguards. Something happened, and Daver guessed it had something to do with Julie pulling him out of the water.

And there was this: Julie seemed scared.

In that way adults do, when they pretend that everything is okay, everything's fine. But you could tell something was wrong.

"And what are we going to do there?" Daver asked, as they took the stone steps and walked up to the street. Usually they stopped here and rinsed off their feet.

But today, no stopping, no rinsing.

"What will we do? I don't know, maybe play some games, there's cards, and—"

"But what about exploring the inn? You said you knew a lot about the inn, knew lots of secrets."

"Yes. Right. But I think we've seen enough secrets. Remember the tower room? You got pretty scared—"

She looked at him, and Daver suddenly felt embarrassed. He had gone looking for them and gotten scared.

"It was dark," he began in his defense. "I couldn't see—"

"Still, I think we should just do something quiet this afternoon. It will be fun."

Daver felt a lot of things at that moment. Confused, because he had to leave the water, but then even more confused that they had to leave the beach when police showed up.

Maybe . . . maybe that's something I should tell Mom.

Maybe she should know that.

But he also felt something else, something that kept swimming around his brain, a feeling he couldn't really identify. He had been scared when he went to the tower room. He had gone somewhere, and seen something— something that really wasn't there.

He wanted that feeling to go away.

And he realized, as if discovering a really cool idea, that there was only one way to make that feeling go away.

Of course.

One way . . .

Maybe today he'd have a chance to make it go away. To show them and—

No, to show himself—

That there was nothing to be scared of.

So, okay, quiet games, quiet afternoon. But Daver started thinking about a plan—something to do that would make the feeling just go away.

But he had to keep it secret.

It would only work if he kept it secret.

THIRTY-FIVE

Liz heard a faint knock at the door. She had started looking at the Abbadon's bills, all the accounts for the inn. Most of these would be paid directly by the management agency, but she had to check that they all looked right.

Based on the various bills, it didn't seem as though the inn could be making much money, if any.

Still, she imagined that there were tax write-offs . . . so who knew?

"Come in," she said.

Mrs. Plano opened the door, walked in, and stood opposite the desk.

"Everything okay outside?"

"Oh, fine. Just that . . ."

The woman's eyes looked away as though reluctant to pass on some bad news.

"Something wrong?"

"The weather. Taken quiet a nasty turn. Clouds, wind, maybe rain soon, I imagine. These Atlantic storms . . . they just pop up from nowhere. Chase everyone off the beach. People go to the bar, they want food . . . it can get a little overwhelming here."

"Well, can we put one of the girls on the bar? I mean, until Ted gets back."

"Yes, but we had that stupid Susie girl call in sick. So we're already a little understaffed."

Liz let the papers fall. "You know what, I can do some tables, or run the bar if it gets crazy."

Mrs. Plano laughed, something that sounded more like a humorless harrumph. "Oh, it will, it will."

Liz took a breath. The letter from the hospital about Tollard still sat on her desk, the words chilling in their coldness. "But not now? Everything's okay now?"

"Yes. Everything is okay. I mean, until the rain, until everyone comes running off the beach."

"Then . . ." she pointed to a wooden seat with a long, dark blue ledger book on it. "You can sit a minute. Can you explain," she held the letter up, "this a bit?"

Mrs. Plano picked up the ledger book and put it on top of small bookcase sitting against the side wall. The woman sat in the ancient wooden office chair as though lowering herself into a trap.

She doesn't want to talk about it.

The woman waited.

"So what did Mr. Tollard do?"

Again, the woman's eye looked away. "At first I wouldn't have known anything. I mean, bills all got paid, he answered my questions. But then he started to sleep in so late . . . never saw him before noon . . . sometimes even later."

Liz smiled. "Sounds good to me."

"But the way he looked. I mean, he started looking scary. His clothes, always the same, always looking as though they were thrown on. And his eyes . . . dark circles around them, sunken . . . and up close I saw the red lines. The eyes of someone who didn't sleep. And when he started asking me strange questions—well, that's when I got scared."

"What kind of questions?"

Mrs. Plano hesitated as if they were about to talk about something delicate. "I really don't—well. He asked me . . . if ever I saw things."

The words—so simple—rolled off Mrs. Plano's tight lips. *Saw things.*

"What did he mean?"

The woman shook her head. "I didn't know, not really. But he wanted to know if I ever saw anything unusual, when I was alone, up on the second floor, or third floor, or—and he'd lean real close and whisper—in the basement or the tower." The woman laughed. "I never went to either place, certainly not to the tower with those two drunken workers wasting the inn's money. But I got the feeling he had gone there."

"To check on them?"

Mrs. Plano shook her head slowly.

"No. I think that was furthest from his mind. He went there because he saw something; I got the feeling—and this is going to sound crazy—that he followed something up there."

Liz sat back. The air in the windowless room felt stifling. "The haunted Abbadon Inn?" She ended the words with a smile, as if that could dispel such nonsense.

Mrs. Plano's eyes looked up. "You've read the history, then?"

"What? No. A history? Not at all."

"You can find it in some Cape May books in the library. This house always changes, and some of those changes over the years gave birth to stories. Strange stories."

"Ghosts?"

"And worse. But I just do my work, Mrs. McShane. I don't know anything about that. But when Mr. Tollard opened that room downstairs, when they found him there . . . well . . ."

"Downstairs? The basement? I haven't gone there. You said that there's nothing—"

"Nothing there? Of course. Nothing there *now.* But there were two rooms, and one led to another through a narrow stone hallway. But it was sealed. To keep out the dampness, I imagine. The cellar. There's an old pipe for waste down there. Lot of the inns used them. Sealed tight how. Until that day, that is . . ."

"Mr. Tollard opened it?"

Now it was Mrs. Plano's turn to smile. "Open it? You could say that. Everyone heard the noises. I wouldn't go down there. But I did call people. My cousin Tim's on the force. Told him about how odd Mr. Tolland had been getting. They came. Later . . . a lot later . . . he told me what they saw."

Liz sat there. Her lips dry, her tongue barely able to moisten them. *This goddam room . . . so suffocating.* And Plano making her ask. Knowing she had to ask.

Love to can her ass, Liz thought.

"And your cousin told you . . . ?"

Mrs. Plano nodded. "Mr. Tollard had pulled open the boards, old damp planks nailed together as though it had been done fast. The smell . . . they said it must get water down there because the smell was so bad." She looked up at Liz. "But that's not what really got to them."

Mrs. Plano's fingers were entwined, tightening, and Liz could see that simply telling this story went beyond upsetting her.

The woman looked scared.

"Mr. Tollard was on the ground. He was kneeling, almost as if praying. And he was mumbling, talking—"

"To the police?"

Plano shook her head. "No. To nobody. Talking, moaning, sobbing. In that room, that horrible room. He didn't even turn to look at them. My cousin said it was as if he was begging, pleading . . . talking to absolutely *no one*."

She stopped talking.

Liz studied her face, the usually impassive eyes now a little watery, the fear and confusion rattling Mrs. Plano's face now.

"Then what happened?"

"He didn't talk to them. No, he kept jabbering down there, until they took him away. And then—then—" She took a breath. "I really don't like talking about it."

"I know. But . . ."

Plano nodded, agreeing to continue.

"They took him away, and he screamed, screamed all the way out of that room, all the way upstairs. The guests. Those we had, wanted to leave immediately. They thought something terrible had happened. And of course it had, you know. Mr. Tollard had gone mad. And his madness had something to do with that room, with what he saw . . ."

"Saw? But it's just an empty room, that's all, right?"

Now, a more tentative nod.

"Empty. I imagine so. But it had been sealed for over seventy years. Someone sealed it. My cousin said he wanted to gag when he entered the room. The smell, the air. The damp horrible smell. A few days later, he told me something else. That down there . . . it wasn't just the smell of the old stone, the floor, the dampness. He said it smelled like blood."

Mrs. Plano looked away, as if searching for a window to look out of.

"I don't know what Mr. Tollard thought he saw down there. We never saw him after that. They took him away. And then we all managed—until you came. To take over."

The air . . . so dry, stifling. But despite that, Liz looked down at her bare arms and saw gooseflesh, as if a chilly breeze had shot through the windowless office.

"I suppose," Liz said, "they sealed the basement room up again after that."

Mrs. Plano raised her eyes gain, looking right at Liz.

"No, ma'am. It was left open. Exactly the way Mr. Tollard left it. It's open right now." The woman held her gaze for a moment. "Now," she stood up, "I best be about my work."

Liz stood, too. She had to get out of this room, get some air, maybe go to the porch and look out at the ocean.

Think about Ted, the kids, and this place she brought them to.

"Thank you," she said, but it sounded like a strange thing to say as she followed Mrs. Plano out.

Ted looked up at the mirrorlike sheen of the surface. He raced during his ascent, but not so much that he'd definitely get the bends.

He'd have a chance.

If he did get the bends, then he'd be useless getting the boat free, getting back to Cape May.

And that's the only thing that mattered now.

He tried not to think of what was going on below. The shark, with its unearthly eyes, ripping the other two apart, distracted enough for a moment so that Ted could get away.

But did he have enough time to get to the surface and free the boat?

Stop the fuck thinking, he ordered himself.

He kept breathing steadily, so important on the ascent. If he was sucking normal air in a regular tank, this ascent speed would be seriously hurting him. With nitrox, he stood a chance.

Slim, but still a chance.

The surface . . .

Maybe ten yards more.

He looked at his depth gauge, moving too fast. But he knew that already. Best not to look at how fast, or—

He saw something ahead, rising with him.

First one shape, then others.

What the—

Not the shark. Something like . . . a person. Then another.

And he saw the mutilated body of Captain Andy rising with him, the body with its gutted midsection, the tendrils of sinew where a leg once was. Captain Andy now raising his good arm to him, waving, smiling.

Can't be, Ted thought. *Can't be fucking narcosis. We weren't down long enough, didn't go deep enough with nitrox. This can't be a hallucination.*

And if not that . . . then what?

And as if reading Ted's mind, Captain Andy waved, a big broad wave. Friendly, open, warm—

Ted gagged, and for a moment he thought he was about to throw up into his regulator.

He kept looking straight ahead, kept kicking, and now the animated corpse of Captain Andy was joined by two other figures, a young boy and a young girl, each perfectly fine in some spots, but then with weird chunks missing.

No fucking way, Ted thought.

He looked straight up. The shimmering mirrorlike surface very close. The shape of the boat tethered to two lines.

Yes, Ted had been too much of a cop not to see this for what it was.

A trap. Carefully planned, built, and executed.

And why trap me?

Why?

Maybe . . . so that I wasn't somewhere else.

Crazy, he thought. These insane ideas. But no more insane than seeing mangled bodies surfacing with him.

Just a matter of mere feet now, his head about to break the surface.

He reached down and removed the knife from its sheath attached to his calf.

He surfaced . . .

THIRTY-SIX

Ted hit the air valve on his BCD for buoyancy, then used fast broad strokes, the knife in one hand, to swim to the back of the dive boat. He pulled the release latch for his weight belt and let it tumble to the bottom.

Every fucking second counted now.

He did a quick scan of the surface, looking for the half-eaten friends who accompanied him on the way up, and also searching for the telltale knifelike black-gray of a giant dorsal fin.

With his free hand he grabbed the aluminum platform of the back of the boat. He released his vest, freeing the tank, and spit out his regulator.

Like a frantic eel, he shimmied free of the vest and kicked with strong strokes to get out of the water. The abandoned tanks and vest drifted away.

Ted wasted no time. He slashed at the stern mooring rope with his knife. The first hack did nothing, a mere nick.

"Shit," he said, taking a fraction of a second to scan the surface of the water.

How many seconds did he have?

Not a goddam lot . . .

He put his full weight onto the blade and made sure that he had the rope positioned at the back of the blade, near the serrated teeth. He sawed with as much force as he could and after the third hack, the rope split.

He ran to the bow, stepping onto the narrow outer ledge of the boat that led to the front deck.

Again, he looked at the water.

Nothing yet.

He grabbed the metal railing at the front and began sawing the front rope. This one was even thicker, but he kept hacking at the rope, sawing, pressing, cursing at the tightly gnarled line.

Until it too popped free.

Still holding the knife, he ran to the bridge. He turned the key. The engines coughed, groaned, but he kept the ignition key turned, and finally they roared to life.

The ocean now played with the boat, the choppy surf, wind, and swells below rocked the boat back and forth so badly that he had to grab the wooden dashboard to steady himself.

He took the throttle, yanked it out of neutral, and threw it into forward as far as it could go.

The powerful dive boat rocketed forward, throwing Ted backward; he held on to the wheel with both hands.

But the boat was moving fast, the fucking boat was *racing* over the choppy sea, smashing down on the whitecaps, flying.

He couldn't escape that image . . .

That thought . . .

Jesus, the things we carry, the things that stick.

From a goddam movie.

Quint steering his ragged boat, face set, grim, nodding,

while behind him the shark follows, just waiting for the boat to break down.

Don't break down, Ted thought. *Don't you even think about it.*

He looked back. No shark. No fucking shark. Did it give up? Was it busy enough with everyone below? Or maybe it was playing with the same hallucinations that Ted saw.

"I'm outta here," Ted said, turning around to the bow again.

And saw . . .

A dark gray shape rising right in front of the boat, a giant. The shark had to be twenty feet, maybe longer, its tail whipping the water, its dorsal fin a fleshy knife.

And Ted was heading right toward it.

Of course it had followed the path of the boat and planned to surface right in front of it.

Ted cut the wheel hard, turning it so severely that the boat leaned starboard at a sharp angle, and the water splashed over the side, laying down inches of water on the deck. For a moment, Ted hoped that he hadn't done anything to screw up the engine. Get some water in a line, then it starts to sputter, cough—while the shark goes for the boat.

Please, Ted thought. *Please.* Not that he believed in God. Not that he believed in prayer. Still, he begged.

But not for himself.

He thought of Liz, the kids, his instinct telling him that all this meant *something.* The attacks, those eyes, the trap.

The boat righted—at least as best it could in the rough sea—and Ted steadied the wheel.

Now the shark was back, moving at its top speed. But there was no way it could catch up.

Ted could feel his face lock into a grimace.

His teeth clenched hard.

Scared, determined . . . scared.

But now having this one merciful thought:

I escaped! I escaped the trap.
And with that thought came hope.

Two waitresses went from window to window in the dining room, closing them tight, banging the long, heavy louvered windows shut. The wind hitting the last two remaining open windows kicked up the curtains wildly.

"Where's Mommy?" Megan asked.

Julie had her hand resting on the girl's shoulder.

"I don't know. Maybe checking the rooms."

Daver ran to the window. "The storm looks cool." He turned back to them. "Look at those clouds!"

But Julie stayed where she was.

She could imagine the clouds, and the way the waves at the beach rolled in with an anger and ferocity that made it seem like such a foolish idea that you could ever even *think* of playing there, of running in the gentle waves.

"I can't wait until the lightning comes!" Daver said.

Megan looked up at Julie. "Will there be lightning?"

Julie smiled. "Could be. Why? Don't you like electrical storms, Megan?"

Megan looked confused. "Elec—elec-it-cal. What's that?"

Julie caught herself. "I mean lightning. You don't like lightning?"

Megan shook her head. "No, they wake me up. Back home they would wake me up when it made those big bangs."

Daver shook his head. "That's thunder, dopey."

"Daver . . ." Julie said.

"Anyway, you don't always get thunder and lightning, do you?" he asked Julie.

"I—I think they go together. I think so."

Where was their mother? People were coming into the inn; guests, but also people escaping the gathering storm.

The dining room was filling up. Lots of people here, lots of strangers.

Julie looked around at the people already eating, the gentle clink of cutlery against plates, the sound of teacups being placed down.

The inn would be full, the bar, too.

"Hey, guys," she said to the kids, planting a smile on her face, "let's go upstairs. We can play some games, and . . ."

Daver wasn't thrilled with the idea. She looked at him.

". . . you'll get a great view of the storm, all the way to the beach."

Megan took her hand. Daver nodded.

And Julie led the way up to their room, away from the growing sea of people gathering in the dining room, the lobby, the bar . . .

Liz walked up to Ariella at the front desk.

"The people keep coming," Ari said. "That guy at the bar? He's a TV news reporter!"

Liz looked into the bar. She had one of the waitresses on it, and from the impatient look on some of the customers' faces, she wasn't doing such a good job.

"You'd think we were the only bar in town."

"Actually," Ari said, "there aren't a ton of restaurants with liquor licenses. They're expensive . . . though the Abbadon has always had one, I think."

Liz nodded. She wasn't in the mood for an Abbadon history lesson. The place was getting busy, the restaurant, the bar, and even the rooms.

But more than anything, she wanted Ted to call and say that he was back, that he'd be there in a ten minutes.

She looked at the girl. "Do you know why the reporter is here?"

The girl looked left and right, with almost a look of guilt, it seemed to Liz.

Then she nodded.

"And . . . ?"

Like pulling teeth, Liz thought.

"This woman, in the harbor, she was attacked by a shark. Killed. Now people are saying—"

The girl stopped herself again, and Liz thought, *I'm glad the kids are here. That's good—but Ted's out on the water.*

"What are they saying, Ari?"

"That the other people who have vanished—maybe it was the same shark."

Liz looked at the bar and the overwhelmed waitress.

She entered the bar area and went to Elaine, one of the more experienced waitresses, who now was surrounded by an army of impatient drinkers.

"Everything okay here?"

The girl's look answered the question.

"Okay. Let me help a bit, alright?"

The girl smiled, nodded, eager for the help.

Liz started taking orders. Fortunately most of the people just wanted a beer. The local news guy asked for a club soda with lime. He gave Liz his best surely-you-must-know-me look.

Liz smiled at the blond newscaster with vapid blue eyes. She did recognize him, but didn't have a clue what his name might be. Rod, Tod, Tab . . . something that went with the dark blue cotton blazer and crisp khaki pants.

She put the glass of club soda down in front of him.

"On the house," she said, smiling.

Since I don't know your name.

"Why, thank you." Rod-Tod-Tab took a big sip, then leaned close. "Say, getting a bit crazy in here, isn't it?"

Liz nodded. "Too crazy."

His eyes widened a bit, and Liz was suddenly aware that

he was actually flirting with her. "I wonder . . . maybe we could interview you. Get the local businessperson's perspective on the thing."

"The thing?"

"Yeah—we're calling it the Jersey Jaws. Nice, huh?"

Real nice. So catchy—

"I can get Hector to set the camera up in here, wouldn't take—"

Liz smiled and held up a hand.

"Um, as you said. Things are busy. And besides, I'm pretty new to Cape May, to the inn here."

Tod-Rod-Tab took the turndown with a look of genuine disappointment.

"Well, I still think it would make for a good sound bite."

"Yeah—" she looked around the Ten Bells, everyone now finally with a drink. "I better see to the rest of the inn. Like you said, getting crazy, you know?"

The newscaster smiled as Liz walked to the back exit, out of the bar well.

She hurried to the kitchen, which looked more chaotic than usual. The Goudges were a blur, moving from the stove, to the prep area, to the counters while the servers streamed in and out.

It appeared as though there wasn't even any room for her to stand.

But she slid past the procession of servers over to where the two cooks were moving pots and trays, filling plates with a scary precision.

"Everything okay, ladies?"

One of the sisters—Estella?—brushed past Liz.

"No, everything is too crazy today, Liz. But we'll manage. Not the first busy dinner we ever had."

The other sister laughed as she flipped what looked like some chicken cutlets in a pan.

"So I guess I better leave you to it?"

Goudge One turned and said, "Right."

Liz gave the mayhem one more glance, and then walked out.

The front desk was clear.

Good time to check the kids, she thought. With the storm building, the Abbadon and its coziness would get well tested.

But first—

She walked over to the desk again. "Any calls for me?"

Ari shook her head.

Liz chewed her lower lip.

Ted said he'd call as soon as he was on his way back.

She turned and started up the stairs. Liz wished they had one of those new cellular phones. So expensive—but to call Ted, or know that he could call anytime . . .

It would be a relief . . .

She started up the stairs, telling herself, *Stop worrying. He's fine.*

THIRTY-SEVEN

Daver looked at the Chutes and Ladders game board.

"This game is dumb. D-U-M, dumb!"

Raindrops were pelting the bedroom window and Daver knew that they couldn't go anywhere. He was trapped here.

"Your turn," Julie said.

"I don't want a turn," Daver said.

"I'll take his turn," Megan said.

His sister grabbed the dice and tossed them onto the board.

"Oops," she said. "You landed on a chute."

"No," Daver said, "you landed me on a chute." He turned and looked out at the window. The sky was dark now, the clouds black, small puddles starting to grow on the street. "You guys play. I wanna look at the rain. And all the beach people getting wet. That's funny."

"Okay," Julie said. "We'll finish. Then maybe we can—"

The door opened.

"Hey, gang. Everything good here?"

Daver turned. "Everything's boring here, Mom. I wanted to go to the arcade."

"Well, you can't go now. It's miserable out and getting worse. Maybe some late lunch?"

He saw his mother look down at Julie, but Megan spoke up.

"I'm not hungry, Mommy. Besides, me and Julie are playing a game. Daver, too, but I do his turns for him."

" 'Julie and I,' " his mom said. Then she walked over to Daver by the window. "The rain will end soon, Daver. Then you can do something."

"Doesn't look like it will end. Looks like it will rain forever."

She stroked his hair. "I doubt it will last that long. Maybe," she turned to Julie, "you guys can do some arts-and-craft things later? Make some things . . ."

"Yes," Julie said. "That would be fun."

Daver nodded, turning back to the wet street, the thick clouds.

Arts and crafts . . . like it was kindergarten.

But he had another plan, another idea.

To show them he wasn't a little kid anymore, that he didn't really get scared so easily.

To show himself, too.

So he said, "Sure. I guess so . . ."

Then his mom said, "I better get back downstairs. Getting crazy, with the rain and everything."

"Bye, Mommy," Megan said.

"Bye, Mom," Daver added, already thinking about his secret plan for an adventure.

It would be so busy downstairs, he imagined, that no one would even notice.

For a moment, the room became something moving, something *alive*.

When Bridger walked over to the small bureau and picked up his bottle of Four Roses, it was as if he were walking on one of those sliding floors in a funhouse. Panels of wood shifting this way and that while he stumbled toward the bureau.

He grabbed onto the bottle as though it was attached to the bureau top and could somehow steady him.

Instead, the sensation increased. He let his hand slip away from the bottle and with both hands grabbed the edge of the bureau to steady himself.

He looked at the walls, and instead of looking a dull, sea green, they slowly changed color, brightening, the hue shifting . . .

What's happening? he wondered. *Something I ate, something I drank . . .*

Or what I just read.

He hadn't finished the diary, there were more pages to read, more to digest, to understand.

But he knew enough now—about this place, about this inn, about what had happened.

He knew that its history had been filled with years when it became home to something strange and deadly. People died, disappeared—and the Abbadon had a connection to it all.

And yet there were years when it was just a sleepy inn.

And to think that Eileen had witnessed such a time, when the inn was home to something that killed people, feeding a darkness that, after all these years, she didn't understand.

No, she didn't understand it—but she acted to stop it, despite being so young, really just a girl. They needed her because—somehow—she couldn't be "read."

They couldn't see into her mind. She could keep the secret of what was about to happen and lure the man down there, trick the man with her beauty, her sweet innocent beauty.

Down to the basement where he would be brutally killed.

She had been the one who brought Jackson Bell down there, to the basement.

The wind rattled the windows.

It had gotten so bad out, Bridger realized. Wind, rain, the sky so dark. So strange . . .

It all happened here, nearly sixty years ago.

Bridger took a step back to the desk, to the flimsy wood chair. The floor still felt as if it were moving, a psychedelic shifting of the planks, the light slowly shifting on the green walls.

When he reached the chair, he pulled it away from the small desk and sat down.

He had to read more, there was still so much he didn't understand: Bell ran the town of Cape May, and no one questioned his wishes. No one asked about the people who disappeared.

And those disappearances . . . a summer of missing people. Maybe those who questioned Bell were killed by him?

But what of the children?

And what happened in the water?

Were they somehow all connected . . . back at a time when seashore bathing was still a new phenomenon? A creature from the sea arrives to feed, to kill.

It was crazy. How could there be a connection?

The ancient diary open before him, he looked up at the windowpanes, sloppily painted, the smeared green paint straying to the outer edges of each pane. Almost impossible to see through with so much rain.

Bridger thought of his dream, swimming through the ocean.

I dreamt of a shark, he thought.

Moving though the water, cutting through the water.

And not for the first time, he had to think: *Am I losing my mind?*

Most writers are a little crazy anyway, all that time living inside their heads, carrying out conversations with the phantoms they created, imagining bad things happening, then having those things turning even worse.

Had to make you a little nuts.

He put his hand out on the diary page.

He'd return the book to her when he was done.

He didn't want this book. Not at all.

But first he had to finish it.

Another gust of wind. God, almost like a hurricane.

He looked at the whiskey bottle. No, he couldn't do that, he needed to be clearheaded.

Bridger flipped to a page he had skimmed. Now he'd read the pages carefully.

The section had a title given by Eileen.

"Secret of the Abbadon."

He took a breath and started reading . . .

Secret of the Abbadon

When they first attacked Jackson Bell, when they made that first cut, I backed away. I wanted to run away and hurry upstairs. No one would have thought me weak to do so. I had, after all, lured him down there. I was the one who allowed this to occur.

And so, even though I could leave, I didn't.

I stood there, my eyes transfixed by the man's pain, the man's suffering. I found it odd that all that pain, his moans and cries—not for help, but cursing—left me unmoved.

I thought of those who had vanished, killed in what I knew had to be a horrible way. I had only to think about the children . . .

I thought of Clara, such a sweet-eyed girl, my friend, someone born to revel in the play of sun and water. A mermaid, I called her, made for summer.

All I need do, I told myself, is think of her.

Think of her mother watching as her shining face and long, dark curly hair, straightened by the seawater, bobbed under the water, vanishing forever.

Her mother sobbed against me for an eternity, and I sobbed, too.

She kept mumbling, "Why . . . why did God do this?"

But they knew then it was not God's work. Far from it. But even then, with Bell in his death throes, on his knees as each one of the men grimly ran their blades into him, I didn't understand.

At last, when it was done, someone spoke. I don't know who it was. Just a voice echoing off the stone walls.

The words clear though, words hopeful. "He's dead." Then, "It's over."

Such hopeful words, and yet I still couldn't move as they began the even more grisly part of the work. Like many of the old inns, the Abbadon had great pipes that ran to the sea, pipes that once carried sewage and now went unused. A long metal pipe that ran out to shore.

This one could be pumped by a tank down in the basement. Whatever you put into the pipe could be flushed to the sea by the pressure of the water cistern.

The work grew ever bloodier as I watched the men pick up what were now just pieces of Jackson Bell. And though I backed up, I stayed there. I watched.

I did this, I thought. They might be the ones who have turned the basement into a charnel house, but I brought the man there.

I didn't say then what I was thinking. I didn't ask were they all so sure that this would end it.

We all had to believe that it would work.

That this would end it.

Bell's followers would hide or flee. The town would return to normalcy. The town would become safe again. The sea would become safe.

But later I would realize how mistaken we were.

The men put the pieces into sacks, then into the pipe, feeding it from above, the blood on the floor so thick and dark, dripping off the men's hands, staining their clothes.

Once in a while, one would look at me as if wondering why I stayed there and why I watched.

I didn't explain. I didn't say that I couldn't leave, that I must see how this ends.

And when the great pipe was filled, someone went to the cistern and pulled a chain that flushed the pipe . . . a pipe that hadn't been used in a decade or more.

We stood there, listening. My beautiful friend's father was there. They had him pull the chain that released the water. As he let it go after his one strong tug, I could see him crying. All this wouldn't bring her back. Another man put his arm around him, holding him up.

We listened for the sound of the water hitting the pipe, the sound of movement. We waited.

Until it was quiet.

The men looked at each other, their eyes looking guilty from what they had done. Guilty, and maybe frightened. None of them looked at me. But I understood that. If they felt guilty with the horror they had just committed, how must I feel?

Then Mr. Flynn walked over to me, his tears having ended, but with eyes that might never be completely dry again.

"We will change now, Eileen. Can you go back upstairs . . . on your own?"

I nodded.

It was done. We thought it was over.

But we missed the real secret. We were so ignorant in our plan, so stupid in our confidence.

Until, as it always does, time revealed the truth.

The truth?

How much of the truth can we ever really understand?

I write these lines so many years after that night, years after I thought I understood what we did and what we didn't do.

True, Jackson Bell was killed. His followers dispersed. Some simply mysteriously disappeared. The town slowly slid back to a state of peace, the nightmare was over. Not to be spoken of again.

And yet . . . how to explain what happened to the people who killed Jackson Bell? How to explain the accidents that occurred over the years? Each and every one connected to the sea . . . as if the sea itself was reaching out for them.

And the Abbadon Inn? Over the decades, as the massive building changed owners, changed shape, a chameleon, growing and changing, I could see the signs that something was still there.

Forever in the inn.

But how to tell anyone that? Some of the events—like the murder of that congressman (the papers spoke of his "secret life" as if that explained everything) now seemed all too clear to me.

The inn, the sea—connected. We had stopped something important. But slowly it came back; it would wait, and then reach out. I'd walk past the building, and my skin would sprout gooseflesh.

I'd stand there and say aloud . . .

"You won't have me."

Of course, then I could turn, and see the ocean shimmering under the sunlight.

And in the way that we just know things . . . in the way that we can sense the truth well before there is evidence, I knew the truth.

With so many of the men dead, I knew what horror lived in this town.

Still lived.

Lived . . . because how can you kill what's eternal?

I knew that I had to be the one here, that if I lived, I had to.

Bridger turned the page and saw the next two pages were torn out.

His trembling fingers went to the ragged spot from where the pages had been removed.

No, he thought. *Why would she tear pages out? Why would she hide things now?*

He looked around the room. The walls seemed steady for a moment, and then—when he simply thought of them shimmering, nearly bending—they did.

Then, he looked down at the floor, the funhouse floor of shifting boards, bending and buckling hundred-year-old planks.

He stared at the floor as the jiggling wood slowed, steadied.

Did anyone else hear this, this sound of the wood shifting, moving?

He smiled.

No. Not unless . . . he wanted them to.

The truth. Becoming clear to him, even with those missing pages.

He took a deep breath. His excitement was beyond anything he had ever experienced. He thought, *I sit here at the heart of a mystery so massive, so powerful, I am truly blessed.*

But then he realized that no, *blessed* was not perhaps the right word.

He flipped past a blank page, to one of the last entries in this journal.

The room calmed. He wanted it calm, and it became so.

And he read Eileen's words.

This time, addressed to him.

I didn't know, at first, how I should feel about you.

I am so old. When I'm gone, the secret of the inn would also be gone. The things that have happened, the things that—God forgive me—I have done over these many decades, trying to stem the tide.

Stem the tide . . .

Like the waves that race to the shore and break, crashing down on the sand, on a shoreline already turned into tiny granules of rock after a million years of pounding.

That's all I could do.

But what would happen when I was gone? What would happen when there was no one to know, to understand?

You came to me. And I had no choice but to trust you.

The secret of the inn . . . the secret of the sea . . . could not just die with me.

But then—I am so easily confused—I had to wonder: Was this a trick? Was I—after so many years—making a mistake?

And then I knew that it had to be a trick, and I resolved that there was one more act, one more murder that I had to commit.

If you are reading these words, I couldn't go through with it.

Not that I couldn't kill again. I told you . . . there have been decades of watching and acting. And if there is a God, he may not forgive me.

But I was unsure. Was it too late to stop you? Or could you till somehow help?

So old, so easily confused . . .

I didn't use the gun. Not when that act itself could have been a mistake.

But I also couldn't tell you the last secret for fear that it would give you to the inn. You will have to find that out yourself.

You have the gun I gave you.

Just a weapon. But that, and the truth, is all I can give you.

You may want to see me again.

You may want to ask even more questions—though by now you surely can answer those questions yourself.

But I am sure that as you read these words—and my heart feels terror for telling you all this—I am dead.

And there is no more help I can give to you, to the town, and to the people who will continue to come to that cursed building and face a horror from across time . . .

Bridger shut the book.

The air in the room no longer stifling, but swirling with colors, and electric, narcotic, waves of energy that surrounded him.

He stood up.

In the many years of writing stories that took people into realms of imagination and terror, now, to be *here*.

He walked over to the bureau, no longer unsteady, the room in service to its master.

To its master!

He picked up the gun, the ancient snub-nosed revolver. Did it even work?

Did he even care?

He turned the revolver and opened up the chamber.

And with great care, enjoying the way each cartridge smoothly slipped in, he loaded the weapon.

THIRTY-EIGHT

Liz rushed past the entrance to the kitchen—things were getting out of control in the Ten Bells. Where the hell was Ted?

Mrs. Plano reached out and grabbed her arm.

"Mrs. McShane—"

"What? I was just—"

But Liz saw the woman's eyes, darting away, embarrassed, or—

"What is it, Mrs. Plano?"

"It's just this, Mrs. McShane. Maybe now isn't a good time. But I had placed some calls to those places, the other inns, you know, to check—"

"What are you talking about?"

"The new girl, Julie. To check her references. She said it was a while ago—there might be new people, new owners at the places she worked in. But I called. Everyone's so busy . . . they didn't get back. Then, just now. Two of the places called me back."

Mrs. Plano had Liz's full attention now.

"And?"

Mrs. Plano finally looked up.

"That's just it. They don't have any record of her ever working in their places. None."

"She said it was a while ago."

Mrs. Plano started shaking her head well before Liz finished the sentence.

"No, you see, that's why they took some time. These old inns, they keep such terrible records. Not like the big hotels. It took a while." The woman took a breath. "They say they went pretty far back and there was no one by that name. I figured you'd want to know right away."

"Christ, yes. Okay, okay—I'll deal with it."

Right, she thought, *my kids are upstairs with someone who lied to get a job.* But was that so bad? To lie to get work? Liz hadn't always been totally honest on her job applications. Everybody did it, didn't they?

Still, two references, both bad.

That couldn't be good.

Mrs. Plano continued to stand there. "Can you put someone else in the bar? That poor girl is drowning."

"But the dining room—"

"Just get the people in from the storm their first round. Please."

It was an order this time, not a request.

'Yes, certainly, Mrs. McShane.

The front door of the inn opened, and a breeze raced down the hallway, chilling Liz. She turned to look. More people. This was crazy.

"Is this normal weather? A storm like this?"

Mrs. Plano ignored the question.

Liz looked up the stairs. She had to go talk to Julie. What a horrible day to become unsure of her.

She took a step.

"Mrs. McShane!"

It was Ariella at the desk, shouting. Liz turned.

"It's your husband . . . on the ship-to-shore."

Liz left the stairs and ran to the phone at the front desk.

The handset lay on the front desk counter, right on top of the register.

"Hello."

"Liz."

Ted. God, she was overwhelmed by how much she had worried about him. Worried, and now here he was calling—and maybe with some demons exorcised.

She heard the sound of the boat engine, wind whipping. He was on the ship-to-shore, using a relay. But then why hadn't he called her sooner?

Then, Ted was quiet. Nothing but the engine sound, the wind making a roaring sound on the handset.

"Ted? Ted . . . is everything . . ."

"Liz, something happened out here."

Christ. What could have happened? What was he saying? He was all right, wasn't he, calling from the boat, safely on his way back . . . ?

"Listen Liz, something happened . . . and—" he stopped. "Where are the kids?"

"They're here, upstairs, with Julie."

Liz almost told him what she had just learned, but she forced herself to be quiet.

"Ted, tell me what happened."

The radiophone broke up. He said something, but she had no clue what it was.

"—down, but then it came at them. I watched it, God—" again it broke up. She heard the crackle of static electricity. How far away was he? Her hand held the handset tightly as though sheer pressure could make his words clear, understandable.

"Ted, I'm losing you. Something came?"

"Yes. The shark. I watched it come for them, Liz. I *watched* it, and I—" Another burst of static.

"Damn," Liz said. A few people in the lobby heard her and looked, drawn by the volume of her voice, that and her obvious tension.

No. Not tension, she thought. *Fear.*

"—in its eyes. I tell you, Liz, I'm not crazy."

"I know," she whispered, not telling him that the connection was still poor.

Then quite clearly, during a few moments free of static, "It was a trap, Liz. Waiting for us. Waiting. That's why I asked—"

The lobby felt airless, a room filled with expressionless mannequins watching her, the walls and the carpet turned sickeningly strange while she had this surreal conversation.

"Asked me what, Ted?" She said the words gently, wondering if she said them loud enough to be heard on the boat, over the crashing waves, over the steady roar of the engine, over the rumbles of thunder.

But he heard her and repeated what she said.

"About the kids. It all felt so pat . . . to get me there, to have you . . . and them alone. Because of what I saw in—"

His voice was cut off again, and this time she thought the signal was lost for good.

"Keep them there, Liz. With you. I can see the harbor. So fucking bad out here. I—" a loud blast this time, then, "—soon. Okay?"

Liz nodded. Such a silly thing to do. To nod.

"Okay, Ted. I love you."

"—you, too!"

The phone went dead.

And now Liz felt cold. The people standing in the library continued their movements, to the dining room, to the bar, and some guests headed up the stairs.

All of them seeking shelter from the storm.

Standing there, she heard the rumbling outside, still distant, like Ted. But with each rumble drawing closer.

She didn't tell Ted . . .

. . . About Julie.

Is that why I'm so cold? she wondered.

Or because—though it could all mean nothing—I'm scared.

"Do you want to hang up the phone?" Ari asked.

Liz turned and looked at the girl. Right, hang up the phone, take a breath. Then—

She had to talk to Julie. Away from the children.

That's what she had to do, and she needed a plan.

Another low rumble rattled the dining room windowpanes.

Closer . . . and closer . . .

Liz picked up the handset again and dialed the number for her own room.

THIRTY-NINE

She heard Julie's voice.

"Hello?"

Liz fought to keep her tone normal, with no sign of tension or concern. Except she had to think, *This young girl is watching my two children, and everything she told us is a lie.*

"Julie, hi, it's Liz. How's everything up there?"

"Oh, fine. Megan is playing quite happily—Daver's a bit bored, but I told him I would teach him a card game, Crazy Eights. He liked the name."

"Yeah—good. Um . . . if they're all settled, I wonder if I could have a quick word with you down—"

A clap of thunder sounded outside. Liz heard it even in her office, and also through the phone line. For a moment the static made her think the connection had gone dead.

"Julie—"

She heard Julie talking to the kids. "Just thunder, guys," she said.

Then, in the background, Daver's voice. "Cool. That was so *cool*!"

"Okay—think that one startled them a bit. But they're fine."

Maybe this wasn't the time. Maybe she should wait till Ted came back. But Ted would want her to deal with it right away. He was never one for waiting.

Not if his kids were involved.

"Just a quick word. The kids will be fine in the room for a few minutes."

"Okay, I'll be right down. In the office?"

"Thanks."

She hung up. Now Liz thought, *What am I going to do? What the hell am I going to say?*

"Christ," she said, waiting . . .

Bridger walked down the hallway to the stairs, barely aware of the storm raging outside.

Because nothing compared to this.

After all, what could compare to *this*?

With every step, he could *feel* the Abbadon waiting for him. The decades of history, stories, lives and—he now knew too well—deaths.

All here. Waiting . . .

Everything that happened here, only now he could *see* it.

Not only see it, he heard things as he passed each room. Whispers, sounds of love, sounds of anger, sounds of laughter.

And the way the floor and walls seemed electric—no, not electric, *alive*. Amazing that having written about such things, but always as fiction, he was now here, at its center.

Feeling that living power course through . . . what?

A building.

Wood, paint, stone.

It might as well be its own planet, a world removed from the sun and sand of the beach.

He was almost at the stairs.

He could feel the walls urging him forward. A warmth emanated from those walls, soothing, calming, almost . . . erotic.

Like the warm breeze on a Caribbean island at night. So luxurious, filled with the perfect amount of warmth to keep even the slightest chill away. Sometimes laced with the scent of flowers, the distant scent of exotic plants.

He took a deep breath.

Amazing, he thought. To finally see what this place really was.

And, as he took the first step downstairs, he didn't ask why he was the one who could see and hear all these wondrous things.

The chop of the water rocked the fishing boat, and navigating the boat into a slip seemed impossible.

Ted had taken boats out, but never in weather like this. Water streamed off his face, his clothes soaked. He could see a few people scrambling, covered in green and gray slickers, trying to secure their boats with extra lines, hoping to God to protect their investment.

A sudden surge sent the dive boat smacking against the outer lip of the dock. He heard the sound of wood cracking, the boat probably taking a gash above the waterline. He threw the engines into reverse.

It's like the fucking sea is working against me, he thought.

He pushed the throttle forward.

The boat's powerful inboards pulled it a few yards back from the slip.

Only one goddam way to do this, he knew.

Wait for a trough between the swells, then gun the boat forward.

Going to fuck up the bow, but at least he'd be in the slip.

Jump off with a line, and then . . .

Get to the inn.

Brian's dive boat would be totaled, but at least Ted would be ashore and the boat wouldn't be drifting around the harbor.

He waited. The water churning; no sign of a break in the whitecaps, no sign of a trough that might allow him to get the boat into its slip. And if no trough between the waves appeared, then . . .

He gunned the engines forward, aiming as best he could into the slip.

The dive boat rocked left and right as it shot forward. It entered the slip, but then smashed hard to one side. Ted had to hold on to the wheel so he wouldn't be thrown to the deck.

The bow rammed the end of the slip, and he cut the engines.

Ted hurried to the lower deck, and he grabbed the stern mooring rope still neatly coiled.

It would be better to moor both the bow and stern, but Ted didn't have time for that.

He grabbed the rope, and as the boat dipped low, he jumped onto the dock. Despite wearing sneakers, he slipped, nearly careening off the other end of the dock. A tug on the line told him that the sea was already pulling the dive boat back out.

He quickly tied the boat to the stern mooring pole, looping it, knotting, and then looping some more. The unfettered front zinged left and right, a seagoing bronco eager to be out of its stall.

Another loop and knot.

Ted considered going for the other mooring line. Not only would the front of the boat turn into a chopped-up mess, but the dock would also get smashed.

The rain came down so hard that he could barely see through it, and he decided to leave the boat as is. To hell with it and the dock.

Ted turned and started running for his minivan.

Julie knocked at the door.

"Come in," Liz said.

The girl walked into the office. Liz smiled.

"This will just take a minute. It's just that—" The girl stood there, stiff and straight as if she might be sensing something was up. There was another clap of thunder, muffled in the room.

"Sit, please. Is Megan nervous about the thunder?"

Julie shook her head. "No. I think she's so absorbed in her play. And with Daver thinking it's so cool . . . it all sounds like fun, I guess."

"Right. That's good." A beat. "You've been a great help with them."

Damn, Liz realized that she just used the word *been.* Past tense, as if something might happen now to change that.

"I just need to ask you a few questions. About something we learned, Mrs. Plano learned—and told me."

The girl nodded; her face solemn, eyes locked on Liz, awaiting the question.

Daver had his nose plastered against the chilly glass, looking at the streams racing down the outside of the pane. It was raining so hard that he saw curtains of water racing across the road outside.

Like a snake, Daver thought. A snake made up of rain.

But though the storm was so big, so cool, he was getting bored.

He turned and looked at his sister, still talking to all her toys.

Part of him thought, *That's just so stupid.*

But he also had another thought: *I wish I could get lost in my toys like that. Wish I could play and not think about anything else.*

They were alone.

Nobody here . . . for a few minutes anyway.

Megan wouldn't even *know.*

Yes, he could walk to the door in the other room, open it really quietly, and she'd never even know he was gone.

He could explore some place that he hadn't been to before.

Daver also knew it was more than about being bored. It had to do with his being scared last time.

About being embarrassed.

I'm not a little kid, he thought.

I'm like my dad. And he's not scared of anything.

It would just be a little adventure, that's all. Somewhere that nobody ever went.

Someplace secret.

He could walk downstairs, go past the lobby, past the kitchen, watching for his mom or Julie coming back.

Secret like . . .

Just like my dad probably does when he chases bad guys.

Though he didn't really know much about any of that since his father never spoke about what he did.

But he probably did exactly that.

Eyes open, listening closely . . . listening for someone coming.

I can do it, Daver thought.

Go down into the basement. Look around, see what's under this big old inn.

Then come back up.

No one would even know.

It would be just his secret.

And funny . . . when he had that thought, it was almost as if—just like Megan—he was talking to something.

No. That wasn't it. More like . . . something was talking to *him*. Telling him how cool it would be. How he would be just like his dad.

No one knowing.

A secret.

He moved away from the glass, his breath leaving behind a small cloudy spot.

He walked out of one room, to the other bedroom.

His eyes on Megan, and now he smiled. She didn't even look up.

He went to the door to the hallway, turned the knob as silently as he could.

Like a police officer, or a spy . . . slowly turning until it couldn't turn anymore.

Then he pulled it open.

He looked out to the hallway. He couldn't just walk out if Julie was hurrying back.

But the hallway was empty.

Another blast of thunder; this one made him jump.

He took a breath.

The hallway was empty.

And he stepped out into the hallway, taking care to shut the door very quietly behind him.

FORTY

Bridger looked at the front desk of the inn. Some people stood there talking. Then, to the left, the servers went in and out of the kitchen, feeding the people chased here by the storm.

For a moment, Bridger let the feeling of this room surround him. Waves of color and light, and still the heat, all seemed to surround him. He looked over at a small mahogany table; he reached down and touched it and, suddenly—

He heard the faint sounds of music, a saxophone playing, a bass, something slow, moody, the clink of glasses.

Bridger grinned. No one else is feeling this.

No one. Just him.

To everyone else, the Abbadon was merely a building.

He walked into the lounge, past the few people sitting there, then to the small corridor that led to the back of the inn.

But it also led somewhere else.

Though he had never been down here before, he knew

exactly where to go. He walked casually, so as not to draw any attention.

No reason anyone should know where he was going.

Is this why Eileen gave me the book? he wondered. *So I would know what the Abbadon really is . . . and maybe discover the last secret she wouldn't tell me?*

Such an incredible gift . . .

Then, at the south end of the room, he reached a small corridor. Some boxes stacked to the side made the narrow hallway look like a storeroom.

But he saw the door at the other end. A wooden door.

The door to the basement.

Nobody went down there.

The passageway now glowed with a light that didn't come from the lamps in the room behind him. The wood was now a golden yellow, the red oriental carpet brilliant, flaming.

So welcoming.

Inviting me.

He walked down the hallway. The warmth grew, and again more of that seductive warm breeze, his face flushed as if he had been drinking.

But now, today?

Why, he hadn't had a drop.

He reached the door.

He turned the knob.

It wouldn't turn.

He kept trying, pushing on it.

He heard the sound of the TV in the lounge behind him. A newscaster talking about the storm, the rain, the tides. So sudden, so surprising.

The sound of the storm would mask an even stronger attempt to open the door. Now he twisted the doorknob so hard that he thought he might yank it off.

Still nothing.

He looked at the knob.

He looked at the keyhole.

Then . . . why it was so *obvious*.

Why hadn't it occurred to him before? It was now so clear what he had to do, what he *could* do.

He pulled his hand back and stared at the keyhole, imagining the darkness within, seeing the narrow chamber, and the metal grooves designed to accept a key.

Then as he stared and imagined that darkness, he thought of those metal latches and grooves, turning, twisting until . . .

There was an audible *click*.

He reached for the doorknob again and turned it.

It opened.

Of course it opened.

He pushed open the door, closed it behind him, and started down the stairs.

Daver put his hand on the railing. He heard the voices from below . . . so many people here. He'd have to hurry. How long would Julie be with his mother? Not long . . . maybe minutes.

And the point of his mission was to do it without getting caught.

He'd see something secret, something dark and hidden, and not tell anyone.

Especially not tell Megan. She told Mom and Dad everything.

He took the steps slowly, his hand holding the rail. He had to think of something to tell Julie if he ran into her coming back up.

Something like, *I went looking for you.*

Or, *I wanted something to eat.*

Something so she didn't ask what he was doing.

With each step, he heard the voices downstairs more clearly. People eating and talking and laughing. The noise made Daver hurry now, taking the steps a bit faster. The thunder wasn't so loud here, away from the windows.

A man started up the stairs, taking them two at a time. He looked up at Daver and nodded.

No one will think about what I'm doing, he thought.

Funny, though, how he felt as if everyone *could* know, as if they *could* read his mind.

So . . . funny.

Megan reached out and took a plastic teacup and plate off the rug. She took a pretend sip, then went to each of her ponies and gave them a sip, too. She tilted the cup so they got a good, long drink.

And when another loud blast of thunder exploded outside, she spoke to them.

"Now don't be afraid, little ponies. It's only a little storm, and we're having a nice picnic. Want a cookie?"

Another plastic plate held invisible cookies. She scooped one off the plate, took a bite, and chewed it. "Mmmm, they taste so good. Here, have some!"

She broke off a bit of the invisible cookie, a yummy oatmeal and raisin, and gave a piece to the pink pony with rainbow-colored hair—her favorite.

"It's good, right? Now for the rest of you."

She gave each pony a bit of cookie, bringing her fingers up to each rubbery mouth.

Megan hadn't noticed that Daver was gone.

She hadn't noticed she was all alone.

All she knew was that, with the nasty rain outside, she and her ponies were having such a *nice* party.

"Mrs. Plano checked your references. You know, the other places you said you worked?"

Liz proceeded slowly. The girl didn't say anything. She sat there, her lips pressed tight, watching, listening.

"She called them all, and it took some time. They came back with answers."

Liz took a breath.

"*None* of them knew you, Julie. No one remembered you ever working at their inns. Not one."

Julie sat perfectly still, her eyes on Liz. Liz hoped that her words would trigger something in the girl, a quick defense, some rationale as to why no one seemed to know her.

But instead, the girl kept silent.

"I guess you understand why I'm concerned. It's one thing to lie about your background . . . but you're watching my kids. I—I—"

Liz looked away. What the hell was she going to do? Fire the girl? It was the only thing she could do.

"I'm afraid I have no other choice than to let you go."

"Mrs. McShane . . ."

And when Liz looked back at the girl's face she could see a glistening in her eyes, a wetness, the beginning of tears.

"What is it, Julie?"

But instead of answering, the girl turned behind her to the small bookshelf in the office. A row of old books on the top shelf that Liz hadn't even glanced at.

The girl slid one book out.

Then she turned back to Liz, putting the book on the desk.

Liz looked down.

The binding was old, frayed at the edges, the brown cover faded to a pale dusky cream.

A History of Cape May.

Liz touched the book.

"I d-don't understand . . ."

Julie stood up. "What you need to know is in here. Page

137. I'll go, say good-bye to the kids. That is, if you still want me to go . . . after you look in there."

She turned back to the office door. Liz wanted to stop her, ask her why she had nothing else to say in her defense.

She looked down at the book again.

The answer's in there?

"No," Liz said. "Go on up. But don't say anything yet."

The girl nodded. Liz should have been the one in control, but it was so clearly this young girl instead.

"Yes," Julie said.

The girl's eyes glistened, her cheeks streaked with the trails of tears.

Julie opened the door.

Liz opened the book as the sounds from outside, loud, too crazed, came into the office.

"I'll wait for you upstairs," Julie said.

She had meant to simply ask the girl to leave. You can't lie about what you've done, hiding who knew what.

The girls' tears, Ted's call—and suddenly Liz's skin felt icy, her fingers cold as she opened the book, flipping through the pages, looking at pictures from so long ago . . . racing to page 137.

A page.

With a picture.

The Abbadon Inn from 1929.

And there, next to it . . . *God* . . . there, *next* to it, another picture.

The stairs turned, then ended in a small room with curved rock walls. *Is this bedrock here?* Bridger wondered. Or just a massive chunk of granite pushed by the last glacier to end its run here, at the edge of the sea.

He reached out and touched the cool stone.

A fine sheen of wetness, as his fingers slid over the

smooth surfaces. A single lightbulb with a metal pull chain hung off to the side. Though the glow from the stairwell light let him see, he reached out and gave the chain a pull.

The bulb filled the small room with a garish light, as though it might be the site of a strange excavation, some unknown ancient tomb.

Bridger now saw that the dull gray rock had spots of dark green, perhaps algae, or a fungus.

He turned around.

And at the far end of the room, another narrow passageway. And at the entrance, planks that once sealed off the passage, now tossed to the floor, off to the side.

Such a narrow passageway . . . as if the inner room was secret.

A perfect place for secrets.

Bridger licked his lips.

That's where it happened.

And though the room had no air other than what drifted down from the upper floor, he felt chilled. He looked at the opening.

But he had no fear now, nothing to be concerned about.

He walked to the passageway. The bright bulb lit the first few feet of the corridor, but Bridger was sure that once he walked in, his eyes would adjust. He'd be able to see it all.

He heard the creak of steps above him.

People walking around, hurrying to their room, or for a meal.

Totally unaware of the secret underneath the house.

This secret place.

Bridger walked into the passageway.

FORTY-ONE

The light vanished after his first few steps.

He put his hands out to the side and felt the mix of stone and planks that made up the passageway's walls.

He stepped slowly, not sure if there might be something in front of him, something he could trip over, using the front of his shoes like bulldozers.

But he felt nothing, save for the irregular bumps and indentations of the stone floor.

A massive piece of stone, he thought.

Massive . . .

The passage opened up to another room.

At first he could only make out a few points in the room, spots that caught what little reflected light somehow filtered in. The swollen belly of a large rock, the bleached, splintery end of a plank, the undefined shape of something metal at the other end.

Too dark to see.

Too dark, Bridger thought.

Then, he remembered . . . it didn't have to be dark. Not at all. Not once he understood what was going on here.

He blinked, and when he opened his eyes he could feel a warm yellow glow begin to build in the room, almost as if someone stoked an invisible fire, with yellow-and-orange flames, sending light into every curved space in the room.

For there were no corners in this room.

Only curves, dips, the smooth rise and fall of stone.

Ancient stone.

He could see the room.

And then . . .

He could see *them.*

Daver slid past the open door and shut it behind him.

Perfect, he thought.

He had snuck onto the stairs with no one seeing him. He had thought that the door would be locked.

(And a small voice in his mind said, *Maybe I wished the door had been locked . . .*)

But it wasn't, and now he was on the stairs leading down to the basement with no one knowing. He wasn't scared. He was just like his dad. Just like him. He could be brave and do things.

The bright light made it easy to see the steps, to walk down.

Daver grabbed the handrail and started down.

Bridger realized that he stood in the center of the room, and the others stood around him. Three people. Dressed in summer suits, old-fashioned and strange.

But one person he knew. He had seen the picture many times.

Of course . . .

That person smiled, nodded.

"Welcome," he said.

I should be afraid, Bridger thought. But instead he still felt warm, peaceful in the orange glow that filled this room, this secret chamber that was so soothing.

Bridger had so much to ask the man.

So much to ask Jackson Bell.

Was he the first to discover the secret of the inn, the power it held, how it was *so* much more than mere wood and stone and paint?

"We're so glad you're here." The others surrounding Jackson Bell, a man killed, hacked to pieces a half century ago, also nodded and smiled.

"I don't understand," Bridger said. "What has happened to me?"

Jackson Bell laughed, and it filled the room. "Amazing, no? We knew you'd be perfect."

Bridger looked at the other two men, nodding in submissive approval at what Bell said.

Then Bridger said, "Perfect . . . for what?"

They laughed again, the sound even louder, and Bridger thought that they must hear this upstairs.

But, no.

How could they hear . . . when they couldn't see?

Bell took a step closer to Bridger. "But you felt it, Mr. Bridger, didn't you? When those two young people died, when that fishing boat was split . . ." he leaned even closer to Bridger . . . "*split* right in two? The woman swimming. Oh, the horror of all those people, their muffled screams, the blood. You felt it all, yes?"

Bell put a hand on Bridger's shoulder. "So can't you imagine what's out there? With *your* imagination . . . out there, in the depths. Using this inn, waiting for someone like me . . ." a broad smile now ". . . or someone like you. You *can* imagine that, can't you?"

He clapped Bridger's shoulder.

"Imagine . . . what is it that has reached out to us? And to think, Mr. Bridger, it's real." He leaned close and whispered. "*Real* . . . "

Bridger nodded. The glow grew dizzying, a carnival-like mix of brilliant red and orange.

"But why?"

More laughs from the other two, scornful chuckles, but Bell only narrowed his eyes.

"Oh, I think you know that, Martin. If I may call you Martin . . . ? I think you know."

And in some sick way, Bridger did know.

The last secret.

He heard a step from behind him, from the other room.

And he turned.

Liz bolted up the stairs, two at a time, as fast as she had ever moved in her life.

The stairs seemed endless even as she ran full speed, panting, finally reaching the hallway, running down to the room.

It's impossible, she thought as she ran. *Impossible. I made a mistake . . . the picture . . . I'm hysterical.*

She had nearly reached the door when Julie came out, her tears dried, but her eyes wide . . . frightened.

And before Liz could say something, to try and ask a question that didn't seem completely insane, the girl spoke.

"Daver's not here."

"What?"

"He's not here. I think . . . I think he went exploring."

"Megan—"

Julie stepped aside so Liz could see that her little girl was still playing.

"She's fine. We have to find Daver."

Liz nodded, as the madness swelled.

She looked upstairs.

"There, you think he—"

Julie shook her head.

"No. Not this time. I think I know where he went. A place he thought he picked. Come—"

She grabbed Liz's wrist, and Liz felt the girl's cool fingers on her wrist pulling her down the hallway, back to the stairs, down, racing past guests, not caring, racing, anticipating the horror, anticipating the unknown . . .

Bridger saw the boy.

"Sorry, mister. I was . . ."

Bell stood alongside Bridger, his arm around Bridger's shoulder.

"Tell him it's okay, Martin. Boys will be boys."

Of course.

Of course . . .

The boy couldn't see the others. The room probably looked dull and dingy . . . the boy was scared.

"That's okay, son. That's perfectly alright. Doing a little exploring?"

Daver's eyes were wide, looking around, taking in the strange room.

"He's scared, Martin," Bell said. "Very scared. Make him feel better. Go on . . ."

Bridger smiled. "I was, too. Never been down here. I wanted to see it." Bridger feigned looking around. "Kind of cool down here, isn't it?"

He could see the boy clearly, but the boy would only see shadows. Had to be scary for him.

Then, Bridger felt the boy's fear.

His growing fear . . .

And it was exciting.

* * *

Daver looked around. He couldn't see much in the room, just the outline of a rock, and a big metal pipe.

But he knew one thing.

He shouldn't be here, not with this man down here.

He had to turn around, run, and bolt back upstairs.

And . . . and not tell anyone. Not tell anyone that he got scared again. Not tell Mom, not tell Dad—

But then the man spoke again . . .

"What a strange room, hmm?" Bridger asked the boy.

He took a step to the side, looking around.

Bridger felt Bell's hand still on him.

"We have to do this, Martin," Bell whispered. *"You have to.* There's no free lunch, Martin. And you have to do it fast. We don't have a lot of time."

Bridger turned and looked into Bell's eyes. In the glow he thought he saw things swirling in the green-blue pool of the man's eyes, blue-green like the sea. For an instant, Bridger looked into the depths.

To whatever had used Bell.

Used the others.

And now, used Bridger.

Feeling its power, its ancient indescribable power. So strong, but also something that needed . . .

He turned to the boy.

Knowing what it wanted him to do. Knowing what he had to do.

"Guess we better get upstairs, what do you say?"

The boy nodded.

Upstairs.

Good, they'd go upstairs, and Daver could just vanish into the inn with all the other guests.

This was okay, he thought. *Coming down here. Okay,*

*because I went someplace hidden, some place cool . . .
and . . . and*

Daver turned toward the stairs . . .

When the man grabbed him.

The others clapped.

Bell slapped his back.

"Well done! Well done, indeed. Don't pay attention to
the boy's struggles. They'll end soon, right?"

Bridger was faintly aware that the boy was fighting him,
kicking his legs. He tried to scream, but Bridger had his
hand locked on the boy's mouth so that his screams and
yells were muffled.

Another clap from Bell.

"I'm afraid now's the time, my friend."

The boy's kicks were painful, but Bridger only felt the
heat from the light that filled the room . . . and now he heard
music as though there was a party upstairs . . . then—

The screams of people, screams from different times,
merging, melding like waves joining . . . until he knew that
the Abbadon had come fully alive.

Across the years, the decades, the sounds of those who
died here, growing louder, louder—

"Come on, my friend. It's not fair to hesitate. Just do it,
and we can join the celebration."

With his other arm, Bridger reached under the boy's
neck. So small, so fragile.

Another harsh whisper, "Just *do* it!"

He tightened his grip around the boy's windpipe.

Ted pulled the minivan up to the curb and bolted out. Giant
puddles filled the street.

Lightning flashed overhead, and it was nearly impossible to see in the steady downpour. He ran into the
Abbadon.

Thinking, *I avoided a trap.*

Not knowing what awaited him when he entered the inn.

* * *

Julie released Liz's hand as they took the steps to the basement.

Liz hurried to catch up, but the girl flew down the stairs. And as she ran down, Liz heard sobbing.

She's crying. Crying, running down the stairs.

Liz tried to hurry, to catch up.

But the girl was too far ahead.

The noise swelled to an insane volume now, screams, howls, the rattle of chains, violins playing a disjointed melody, insane laughter—

Bridger blinked, trying to force the sounds away. His grip hadn't tightened, distracted by the cacophony.

"It will all stop, once you finish," Bell said.

Yes, Bridger knew that, there was only one way forward now, one way out of this.

The boy gagged, the horrible sound muffled . . . but his struggling weakened.

Until—somehow—a woman's voice soared over the crazed din.

FORTY-TWO

"Stop. You must stop now."

The girl—he recognized her from the dining room. Just a serving girl.

"You can't listen to them. You're just feeding this place, and feeding what it's really connected to, what uses this place . . . what's using you."

"Bitch," Bell said. "Stupid bitch. You—"

"You can see them?" Bridger asked.

She nodded.

Bridger's hand slipped off the boy's mouth. But the boy was too dazed, too frightened to do more than cry and whimper. Bridger still held the boy with his other hand.

"The bitch lies, Bridger. You just kill the boy now—"

Then Bridger saw the boy's mother beside the girl.

He looked into her eyes, and saw her terror, the loss of her child so close . . .

The glow that filled the room began to dim.

"Y-you can see them. How can you—"

But it was the boy's mother who spoke.

Liz saw Daver, his terrified eyes locked on hers.

Her Daver, alive, breathing.

Liz turned to Julie, her eyes so watery, the tears rolling down her cheeks. It was too late for her, for the others, but not for Daver.

To Liz, the room was dark, only the three of them.

But not for Bridger, and, she knew, not for Julie.

"Why can she see? Because—" another look at Daver, listening, not understanding. Now Julie's tears fell full force.

Liz had seen the picture of the inn 1929, and then the picture of the beautiful girl killed that year by the shark.

"She was there . . ."

The man's eyes went wild. She saw him look around, as if seeing the other people here.

Insane, Liz thought.

She took a step closer.

"Let my boy go. Please."

Bridger looked around.

He started to shake his head. Then Julie, through her tears, spoke, softly, comfortingly . . .

"It will keep hunting for those it can claim and use. You see that don't you? Tell me you see that?" She looked at Daver, and Liz knew she was trying to speak carefully. "I'll always be here, but I can't stop it. But you can. Now."

Liz waited, watched.

Then, steps behind her.

"Let my son go," the voice said.

Liz didn't take her eyes off Daver's, even with Ted behind her.

But instead of letting the boy go, with his right hand, Bridger took out the gun that Eileen had given him.

Liz reached out and her hand dug into her husband's arm. She shook her head, begging some god she didn't believe in, *Please, don't let this happen.*

Yes.

The last piece, Bridger thought.

Why Eileen gave me the book. Why she gave me the gun. So clear.

Others may come, or the house may sleep again . . . and the thing out there, in the depths, that uses it . . . would move on.

But not as long as it still had me.

He released the boy.

He looked at Bell, who scowled at him, his face twisted as he bellowed Bridger's name.

But it was too late. He saw blood erupting from Bell's neck, as the—what . . . spirit, ghost, fantasy?—oozed blood yet again, gushing from all the places it had been cut and hacked.

The boy ran to his mother.

I was so close, Bridger thought.

The boy's face was pressed against his mother. The girl sobbed beside him, but she, too, was turning into what was her final state, that day in the ocean when something dark and gray came and took her.

"I'm sorry," Bridger said to them all.

He didn't need to be told what to do.

He looked at the mother.

The boy's face was hidden, he wouldn't see.

Bell and others became misty shadows. The girl, too . . .

Until the only people there were the parents, their young boy, and himself. Four people in the damp stone room.

Bridger raised the gun to his temple, again thinking how amazing that the old woman knew how it would be used.

He pulled the trigger.

And with the deafening report of the gunshot, there were only three people left in the room.

EPILOGUE

"You guys ready for a pit stop? Got a Burger King coming up."

Daver looked out the window and didn't answer. But Megan spoke up.

"Yay! I'm hungry!"

Ted looked back at her. "You're *always* hungry, sprout. Okay, next rest stop we *mangia*."

"What's *mangia*?" Megan said.

"Eat, in Italian," Ted said, smiling.

Liz reached out and grabbed his hand.

He'd been amazing for the past twenty-four hours. He didn't say much about what happened out at sea, except that he knew his family was in danger. Maybe he'd talk about it later, and Liz would listen.

When he was ready to talk about it.

If that time ever came.

He had dealt so well with the aftermath, with the reality . . . and the unreality.

The local police came, and Ted talked to them about the writer who snapped, who just lost it and then killed himself in the Abbadon's basement.

"Gotta be creepy writing all that horror stuff," one of the Cape May cops said.

Ted agreed.

Yeah . . . real crazy.

He didn't tell them about Daver, and Bridger's attempt to kill his son.

Later, they both spoke to the boy as best they could. But Daver's eyes showed that it would be a long time before he could talk about what happened.

He hadn't seen the gun go off, or Bridger's head exploding.

But the sound was enough.

Liz had guided the boy out, up to the lobby where the guests had already gathered, confused, asking questions.

Ted came up and told Ari to call the police, then they went upstairs.

It took only a few minutes for them to agree. "I'll start packing," she said.

And if they were running, she didn't care.

Whatever had happened in the Abbadon—and there was so much she still didn't understand—they'd leave the next morning.

She felt sorry for whoever came after them. Mrs. Plano—and who knew how much she understood?—would have to hold down the fort.

But as for the Liz and her family . . . they were gone.

Ted had stayed with Daver in his bed that night, talking to him. There would be major work to do when they got back to Brooklyn. *Major.* And how the hell were they going to explain to a shrink what had occurred?

Maybe it could all be reduced to Daver's trip downstairs, a crazy man, and then the suicide.

Not exactly neat and pat, but as clean a story they could make.

And then, when the kids were finally in bed, when Ted was sure Daver had somehow miraculously fallen asleep, she showed Ted the book.

The history of Cape May . . . and the photograph from 1929 showing one of the victims of the shark attacks of that year.

Ted had let his fingers touch the picture as if he couldn't believe that the same girl who worked in the Abbadon, who saved their son, had died more than sixty years earlier.

"Christ," Ted said. "This is crazy."

And it was. Everything they believed about life was challenged. But Liz also knew that out in the ocean Ted had saved himself, even as the other divers died. He could go back now, though she doubted he'd tell anyone about what he believed had really happened here.

He said something that actually made her laugh, a weird laugh that quickly turned into a long, quiet sob as she huddled against him.

"How I spent my summer vacation . . ." he said.

Laughing, then sobbing, until somehow they started making love, an act born of a need to get as close to one another as possible, Ted buried in her, whispering to Liz. *It's okay . . . it's okay.*

Now, he hit the turn signal on the minivan.

"Okay, we grab a quick bite, then we're almost home, back to Brooklyn."

Liz turned to see Megan, ever in the dark about things, smiling.

But then Daver turned and looked at her.

"How about it, Daver? Home sound good to you?"

He nodded. Still no smile . . . but then:

"Least I can watch some TV."

Good boy, she thought, knowing how hard it was for him to come back, even just this little bit.

Ted parked the car in the rest stop and pulled up the emergency brake.

"Ready for burgers?"

Doors popped open, the family left the minivan, and it felt good to be together, good and safe, on their way back to Brooklyn.

So good to have left the Abbadon.

She took Daver and Megan's hands, while Ted put his arm around her.

With one squeeze from him, she knew that he understood what she was feeling.

It would be a long time before they'd ever talk about it.

And perhaps, she thought, *it can't be long enough.*

Built in the 1850s by the enigmatic Nicholas Abbadon, the Abbadon Inn has a long and disturbing history. Deserted for two decades, its new owners are quickly learning that the Inn was never really as empty as it seemed.

WELCOME TO
THE ABBADON INN

The series by Chris Blaine continues:

NOW AVAILABLE

Twisted Branch
0-425-20524-X

Dark Whispers
0-425-20629-7

**So come in, relax, and enjoy your stay.
Just lock your door after dark.**

**Available wherever books are sold or at
penguin.com**

YOU ARE ENTERING

SERENITY FALLS

BY JAMES A. MOORE

"A horror story worthy of the masters."
—*Midwest Book Review*

READ ALL THE BOOKS IN THIS GRIPPING HORROR TRILOGY:

WRIT IN BLOOD
0-515-13968-8

THE PACK
0-515-13969-6

DARK CARNIVAL
0-515-13985-8

Available wherever books are sold or at
penguin.com

J844

New York Times bestselling author

MICHAEL MARSHALL

THE STRAW MEN
0-515-13427-9
Three seemingly unrelated events are the first signs of an
unimaginable network of fear that will lead one unlikely
hero to a chilling confrontation with The Straw Men.
No one knows what they want—or why they kill.
But they must be stopped.

THE UPRIGHT MAN
0-515-13638-7
Ward Hopkins is afraid. He's seen something dreadful in the
high plains of the Columbia River. It's sent him fleeing cross
country, forever running. And in his wake, one by one,
people are dying. Something's following Ward Hopkins.

BLOOD OF ANGELS
0-515-14008-2
One of the worst serial killers in history, a member of a
psychotic brotherhood, has escaped from prison. Now his
brother, Ward Hopkins must team with an FBI agent to see
how far the evil has spread—and if it can be stopped.

Available wherever books are sold or at penguin.com

J006

Penguin Group (USA) Online

What will you be reading tomorrow?

Tom Clancy, Patricia Cornwell, W.E.B. Griffin,
Nora Roberts, William Gibson, Robin Cook,
Brian Jacques, Catherine Coulter, Stephen King,
Dean Koontz, Ken Follett, Clive Cussler,
Eric Jerome Dickey, John Sandford,
Terry McMillan…

You'll find them all at
penguin.com

*Read excerpts and newsletters,
find tour schedules and reading group guides,
and enter contests.*

Subscribe to Penguin Group (USA) newsletters
and get an exclusive inside look
at exciting new titles and the authors you love
long before everyone else does.

PENGUIN GROUP (USA)
penguin.com/news